PLAINS OF SAND AND STEEL

UNCOMMON WORLD

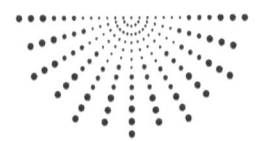

ALISHA KLAPHEKE

Library of Congress Cataloging-in-Publication Data
Klapheke, Alisha
Plains of Sand and Steel/Alisha Klapheke. —First edition.
Summary: When her new royal husband dies at the beginning of an invasion, Seren must hide his body and use the visions the Holy Fire gives her to save the Empire from itself and its enemies—though a high-ranking general is bent on charging her with murder.

ISBN 978-0-9987379-3-5 **(ebook)**
ISBN 978-0-9987379-4-2 **(print)**
[1. Fantasy. 2. Magic—Fiction.] I. Title.

Printed in the United States of America
10 9 8 7 6 5 4 3 2 1
First Edition

ISBN: 978-0-9987379-3-5

❀ Created with Vellum

For I.C., AA, & Mills

1

SEREN

A hot, desert wind swirled around the dais, tugging at Seren's beaded kaftan and combing fingers through her jet hair as she stared down at the city. Her chest ached remembering her mother, who'd died when Seren was a baby, her father and sister—gone too—lost to Invader steel. But this city, it was her new home, and it eased that ache as she gazed at its people. Her people.

Akhayma looked a lot like a hand. Fingers of water slipped from the oasis and through the many canals. Stone walls cupped everyone in a dusty palm. The scene pulled a smile out of Seren. The grin would topple soon—Meric would see to that —but for now, the turned-up edges of her mouth held.

She savored the touch of happiness like a rare fruit as the pool's mosaics scattered moonlight between conversations.

"...and your grandfather shaped the steel that fought back the Invaders..."

"Your ancestors found this oasis and built Akhayma with their own hands."

Tonight, on this most special of nights, there wasn't any talk of business. Lovers didn't argue, and co-workers kept their talk for another time. Tonight, Seren's people laughed, wove stories, passed down details about *family*. That was what this was about.

Seren's smile broadened, lifting her cheeks and helping her stand beside the man she was too young to be married to and would never, ever have chosen for herself. Her father—the former High-General—had tried to keep her from this marriage, but the former kyros had ordered it. And not even generals said *No* to a kyros.

She stepped closer to Meric, hoping it wasn't too close. Sometimes he wanted to show her affection in public, but other times, no. Only ninety odd days into a marriage at seventeen, and she had little idea how to be a wife. Her smile wavered. She forced her lips up, afraid the light, easy feeling would be impossible to find if she lost it now.

"We should do this more often," she said, keeping that smile in place and ignoring Meric's narrowing eyes.

He coughed. "The Fire Ceremony?"

"Just rolling back the tents to open the city to the sky. It makes everyone more...talkative."

The varied languages floated through the night air like music. Coming back here, to the city of her birth, hadn't taken away the pain of losing her father, mother, and little sisters of course, but it lessened the ache in her soul. Akhayma had always been home.

Meric scowled at the Holy Fire bowl. Inside the large, silver basin, Flames danced in the lahabshjara leaves.

Beside them on the dais, the head of Clan Azjorr smoothed his black-striped kaftan. "Do you need another basket, Kyros Meric?" He gestured toward a servant clutching a hefty load of the emerald leaves.

Another cough tore through Meric. "What I need is to get on with this so I can rest."

The clan leader's cheeks darkened.

Seren apologized to the nobleman, using her black eyes to show her empathy, then spun to face Meric. "Let me call the physician."

"He never heals me."

Seren nearly pulled a muscle trying not to roll her eyes. Barir did help. When Meric let him. Her husband was older than her, but he was such a child.

"None of them fix anything." Meric glared in the general direction of the physician's home. Then, taking his position over the silver basin, he raised his high-pitched voice. "We gather here to honor the Holy Fire," he called out over the crowd.

He sounded like a bleating goat. Seren would've taken a goat over him any day. Goats didn't yell at anyone or insult good people. She imagined a goat's head in Meric's finely embroidered kaftan and had to stifle a laugh with her sleeve.

Despite Meric's distinctly lackluster delivery of the ceremony's opening words, the city quieted for their kyros.

"Giver of knowledge and wisdom," Meric continued, "weapon of our people, blessed and unrelenting. Holy Fire, grant us the Flame of your strength and invention. May ideas flicker from dreams into reality."

A warrior wearing a sweat-darkened military kaftan stepped out of the line. He was a scout.

A chill slid through Seren's bones.

The scout paused at the dais steps, his helmeted head bowed reverently.

Seren hurried over. "What's wrong?" she whispered as Meric went on bleating.

Standing on Meric's other side, General Adem eyed Seren. His gaze lashed out and she flinched a little. His eyes drew a line from her to Meric, who was still praying. He wanted her to wait until Meric finished speaking to talk. But this scout wouldn't be standing out of military line if everything was fine. Something was wrong and the Holy Fire would understand if there was an emergency. Seren clutched the scrap of mountain wool she kept in her sash, a bit of the skirt she'd been wearing when Invaders cut her family down.

"What is it, scout?" Meric snapped at the younger man.

The scout hurried up the stairs and approached Meric.

The wind rose, sand giving it little teeth. Seren raised the thin scarf hanging at her neck to protect her face and to mask any response she might have to the scout's report. An old trick of her father's.

Adem removed his silver helmet, his hair a close match, and inclined his head to listen.

"We spotted Invaders on the horizon," the scout whispered between Meric's continued coughing.

Seren shook her head. Surely she'd heard wrong.

"An army of them, my kyros," he said quietly to Meric. "Some on horseback."

Adem's mouth tightened. He kept an eye on those around them. "I was afraid of this, my kyros. When we first heard of their movement, I thought they were headed another direction, to invade lower Silvania instead. But...well, they will most likely strike Kenar for supplies after their journey from the West. They could conceivably cross our borders in two days. Kyros, you must tell me what you wish to do." He stared at the Holy Fire bowl. "But please, finish the ceremony first."

Adem's face seemed to blur, his gray beard and sun-browned skin hazy. Seren blinked, the chill deepening, seeping into her blood, her heart. Meekra rushed to her side, and Seren took the handmaiden's slim fingers in her own. Despite her friend's kind touch, Seren's mind threw out memories of the Invaders' sharp eyes, their wide, steel weapons, the way they shouted when they killed like it hurt them to shed blood, but they loved it anyway. She'd known they'd return. It was why she prayed for ideas from the Fire, kept up her studies of Father's military scrolls, and trained in horse and bow daily.

"I must..." Meric's coughing doubled him over.

Chilled blood racing through her, Seren took Meric's arm and started him toward the stairs.

"But you must finish..." Adem started.

"What should we do, my kyros?" The scout twisted a hand around the hilt of his yatagan.

"He'll answer you as soon as the physician treats him," Seren said, hoping Meric *had* an answer.

General Adem addressed the city, and Seren watched over her shoulder as dark and light eyes both turned up to focus on him. "There is a military issue we must deal with immediately. Your kyros has blessed the basin, and you may come, one family at a time, to light your homefire sticks. May the Fire bless us all."

As Seren hurried Meric away, with their guards and servants around them, she said, "Call for your father, Meekra."

She didn't care that Meric thought the physician never

helped. Meric was wrong. Barir knew several ways to calm this cough he struggled with day-to-day.

The Kyros Walls rose up beside them as they entered the courtyard and headed toward the main tent. Another gust of sand grated across Seren's bare forearms and the single bell tied around her head to hang between her eyebrows.

"And Cansu," she said to the long-faced guard who'd been kind since the day he was assigned to Seren, "you will go with Meekra. I don't like this weather."

The two rushed into the night while her other two guards and a handful of Meric's fighters followed Seren and Meric inside.

In the main tent, the moon bled through the ceiling's patterned weave. Light in the shape of blurry stars dotted the room. At the door dividing the main tent from Seren and Meric's personal chambers, the guards took up positions, relieving the men that had been there during the ceremony.

"Erol," Seren said, "Protect the back entrance to my chamber along with the others serving there now. Tell them nothing. I don't want anyone worrying."

Hossam, black hair more wild than normal, pushed the door back, the woven flaps too, and helped Seren get Meric inside. Erol sped past them, heading out the rear door of the bed chamber. Hossam gave Seren a quick bow, then left to join the other armed men and women in the main tent.

Another tight cough shook Meric. Seren worked the knot in his ceremonial phoenix sash, then threw it to the ground, trying anything to make him more comfortable. White skin ringed his mouth. He dropped to sit on the bed, chin down, hands splayed and covering the bedcover's calligraphy that spelled out his name and title. *Kyros Meric, the Eternally Victorious.*

Lying back on a tasseled pillow, he shut his eyes, gasping like a fish without water.

Where was Barir?

Meric needed the physician now. Maybe Meekra and Cansu were having trouble getting to his quarters in the weather. What if a sandstorm hit right now?

Tears burned at the corners of Seren's eyes. Invaders. Sandstorms.

Meric *had* to be all right.

She didn't know how to take care of an Empire. Images of maps and lists of agreements—from Father's time as the old kyros's general—flickered through her head. Father had taught her a lot. But talking about leading was different from actually doing it. She wasn't the heir anyway. She didn't have any royal blood.

The whistling in Meric's lungs kept on, and he gasped more violently, his back arching at a painful angle. Seren couldn't stop shivering.

Barir walked into the room, tugging at his long, gray beard, his dark eyes worried. Meekra and Cansu trailed the physician like shadows.

Seren heaved a breath. "Please. Help him."

Meric's color was all wrong.

"I need to dose him with ka'ud," Barir said as he approached the bed.

Meekra tucked a curl of dark hair behind her ear, took her father's medicine satchel, and set it on the side table.

Cansu's throat moved in a swallow. His hand brushed the five high-caste bells on his sash as he joined the other guards outside the door.

Seren heard Adem's low grumble of a voice outside the door, probably asking for a report on the kyros's state.

"I'll tell him he's being treated," Meekra said.

Seren couldn't look away from Meric. The sudden hollowness to his cheeks. The hair hanging over his left eye. His kaftan rumpled under his arms and how he did nothing to fix it.

"Thank you," she said to Meekra.

Barir pulled a length of the rare, resinous wood from his bag and set a shallow dish on the bedside table. Praying quickly over the Holy Fire bowl in the corner, he lit the ka'ud with the Flames and arranged the smoking wood in the dish. Blue clouds billowed over the kyros. Barir listened to Meric's lungs, his head on his chest.

Meric's shifting legs stilled.

Something sharp and cold cut into Seren's heart and she reached for his hand. His fingers were too limp.

"Meric?" Her heart beat in her ears.

He didn't move. Didn't speak. His lips had gone blue.

Barir rose. "Pearl of the Desert, I don't want to tell you this."

She held her breath.

"Please forgive the bearer of bad news." His voice dropped to a hush. "The kyros is dead."

The buzz in her ears was deafening.

Meric, the man whose father saved her from the Invaders who'd killed her little sisters and father, the man who acted like a spoiled child one minute and a violent storm the next, Meric the Eternally Victorious, was dead.

Shaking so badly she could hardly stand, Seren positioned Meric's hands on his chest as was custom. He looked so much like his father had. Her own father's closest friend. Sweat bloomed across her forehead and chest.

No. It can't be.

Barir stared at her and moved his lips like he was about to say something.

"What should I do?" An invisible sandstorm tore at her thoughts, her heart. She gripped the edges of the bed to stay upright. In the corner, the Holy Fire's orange-blue fingers spread over emerald leaves.

"You should pray, general's daughter," Barir whispered.

"Now?"

"I've seen you pray, my lady." His mouth relaxed into a solemn line.

Seren was shaking all over. "Don't call me *my lady*. You've known me since I was a baby."

"You are the highest in the land as of now." Face grave, he nodded toward the Fire.

She went to the bowl and passed her hands over the flickering light. Bright heat tickled her palms. Her eyes fluttered shut, then open again. A familiar peace slid over her like a warm breeze on a chilly night, and her shaking eased. The small basin's copper surface reflected the orange-blue Flames. Barir stayed quiet.

Please, I need help, she prayed silently.

Holding both palms at an angle over the Fire, she took a deep breath. The skin between her eyebrows twinged and a warmth rushed through her heart, all the way to her fingertips.

A curl of Flame appeared in front of her face, hovering high over the bowl.

She gasped.

Barir said something quick and quiet under his breath.

Many prayed to the Holy Fire. Only a few in history were

blessed with the Hovering Flame, the true light of invention and purpose.

The flesh in Seren's hands glowed with the intense shine of the Holy Fire. Illuminated from within, bones showed under red skin as a vision burned into her mind.

The corners of the Empire shimmered into view. Places she'd traveled to with Father when he was still the High General. Far off towns and seas. Markets and boats. Laughing children. Men and women talking, some singing, some arguing. Light skin, darker skin, people from every clan in the plains and the border towns in the mountains where Father had taken the family when he retired.

Then Akhayma came into view.

A shadowy cloud churned in the sky beyond the walls. Above it all, a length of pure white linen wrapped itself around Meric's body. The storm near the walls shimmered, became men with wide weapons of steel, screaming and weeping as they swamped the city, more deadly than any storm. In the vision, Seren waved a hand and hid Meric's corpse in the night clouds. She took up his best kaftan—a kyros's kaftan, hemmed in silver phoenixes—and raised it above her head. The invading men blew into dust. *Kyros Seren!* the people shouted, suddenly smiling and holding their homefire branches. Their lights became the stars above the desert, and a calm covered Seren's panicking heart like a great, invisible hand.

The vision faded.

The thread of Holy Fire in front of her face unspooled and fell into its brother and sister Flames.

She faced Barir. The real world—along with its very real trouble—intruded as suddenly as an arrow from the darkness, piercing Seren's calm and bleeding it dry until she trembled again. All in the time it took to breathe in.

The things she'd seen…it had only been her imagination. She hadn't seen a vision. It was impossible. Wasn't it? The Fire had given her ideas before, but they'd been simple words and thoughts in her head, small things like the idea to free that kind-eyed young man from Old Farm and to hire the famed mercenaries of Silvania. It was odd enough to gain those ideas without royal blood, but actual visions? It just could not be. But…

"I saw something." It was like a stranger said the words. She felt detached from her own body.

Barir took a shuddering breath, the ka'ud smoke clouded around his black hair. "A vision. You had a vision." His hand went to his mouth.

She swallowed. "Maybe. I…" She was coming apart, her ears buzzing, the world spinning.

Suddenly she was in Barir's wiry arms, his graying beard brushing against her head and his shushing sounds in her ears like she was still a child.

"Do you want to tell me what you saw? It may help us all in this terrible moment. No one has seen a vision in the Fire in, one, maybe two, centuries." He held her away from him enough to look into her eyes. "You are blessed. Chosen."

Focusing on his face, the face she'd known as long as her own, Seren told him what she'd seen.

Barir's eyes sharpened. "The Invaders approach. Kyros Meric is dead, so General Adem will send for Varol, Meric's brother and heir of the royal blood. But you can't let that happen."

She'd only really heard one word. A name. Varol. She swallowed a bitter taste rising in her throat. "What?"

"General Adem will send the city into mourning. Invaders or not. He will. He is arrogant. That shroud you saw? That was the city mourning. The Invaders triumphed while we mourned."

The traditional mourning song slithered through Seren's head.

> *The soul is heavy,*
> *Three days, three days,*
> *Your shoulders are free,*
> *Take up the weight of Death.*
> *The soul is tired,*
> *Three days, three days,*
> *You slept through the night,*
> *Give your sleep to the Dead.*
> *The soul is starving,*
> *Three days, three days,*
> *Your table is full,*
> *Give your food to the Dead.*
> *The soul is heavy,*
> *Three days, three days,*
> *Your shoulders are free,*
> *Take up the weight of Death.*

Her people would be weakened. Her warriors weakened. Her adopted family weakened, and at the mercy of the merciless.

"But he can't force everyone to mourn," she said. "If everyone stops eating and sleeping, we'll be easy to defeat. He would know that."

"You saw yourself pushing the mourning away. Then you saw our city at peace. Seren. Pearl of the Desert." He used the title given to her when she was married to the kyros. "You must claim leadership of the Empire. You have been chosen."

"No. That's not…"

"Then how do you see it?"

"We must announce the death and tell everyone to wait until after the attack to mourn."

"And if we survive, which we won't, General Adem will call for Varol and he will become kyros."

She hugged herself. Meric's younger brother was so much worse than even Meric had been. The way he used people…

Father had saved a slave working for Varol. Because of the woman's skill with the horses, Father had paid for her apprenticeship with the stables here in Akhayma. She'd been raised to middle-caste before he retired. But she still carried Varol's scars. Thick, clawed fingers of raised skin striping her back and shoulders. Seren's stomach clenched.

General Adem's voice came through the door. "May I enter to see the kyros, Pearl of the Desert?"

"I…"

Barir whispered in Seren's ear. "I will claim the kyros has something that may be contagious. I will keep everyone away. That will give you time."

"Time for what?"

"Pearl of the Desert." Adem rapped on the door.

Barir put his hands on Seren's shoulders. "It will give you time to fight off the Invaders. Then, you can decide whether or not to embrace your fate."

"My fate? No. That can't be what I'm supposed to do."

"Why not? You are a general's daughter. You traveled with him. You learned from him."

"I'm not of royal blood. I'm not even fully desert blood. General Adem would never support me."

"He isn't fully desert either. Not many are."

"That doesn't matter," she whispered. "He's ruled by tradition. You've seen him. He worships the royal blood nearly as much as the Fire. And if he finds out I hid Meric's…condition, he'll have me beaten to death."

"The Fire showed you what to do. You know you trust in it."

"About this though…this is madness."

Adem knocked again. "I must insist to see my kyros."

Seren hugged Barir again. He kissed her forehead like she was Meekra's sister, another daughter.

"I'll keep everyone out," Barir said. "We can talk about the rest later. And my dear Seren." His eyes softened but were no less unblinking, his stare no less steady. "Fate rarely waits until we're ready. How many times would we say *No* in preparation for something great? Every time. We would never feel fully armed. You are more ready than most and you must believe you are enough."

Wisdom glinted in his eyes. But he wasn't right about this. There was no way he could be right about this. Mind humming, she followed him out of the room.

Shutting the door behind them, Barir bowed to Adem. "General, our kyros has contracted what I believe to be a contagious disease of the respiratory system. We must keep everyone out, except Pearl of the Desert, Meekra, Cansu, and myself since we have been in close contact already. We've all taken a ka'ud potion, so we may come and go without danger to others, but no one else should be risked. It could lead to an epidemic."

Seren bit her lip. They were lying to the highest ranking military man in the city. To Meric's right hand. Cansu looked confused, but he held his tongue.

"It is...for safety," Seren said. "We must be very careful. Especially now that we're under attack. I will tell the rotating guards to keep all of this to themselves, and to make certain no one, including them, may enter the chamber."

Adem looked to the door, blinked. "Can you heal him?"

"I can't say yet. It is..." Barir glanced at Seren. "Too soon to tell."

Adem's body tensed beneath his armor, and his jaw sharpened—a warrior trained to absorb a strike when he had to. Though this blow had nothing to do with fists or steel. It was Adem's loyal heart taking the news that his beloved royal was seriously ill. Seren had never been close to Adem, but sympathy flooded her nonetheless.

"Fine," Adem said. "I will pray for our kyros and lead the troops as best I can until tomorrow when, Fire make it so, I may speak with our kyros for his final decision on what action to take."

With a curt bow to Seren, he spun on his heel and headed for the Holy Fire bowl at the main tent's door.

Meekra's eyes couldn't get any wider. "Should I go in with you, my lady?"

The guards and fighters standing watch shifted their weight, looking like lost children instead of people trained to kill.

"Yes, Meekra. We'll tend to the kyros." She waved, indicating Meekra should join her inside.

"I'll announce the quarantine to the criers so everyone will know to keep their daily supplications to themselves for the time being," Barir said before they left.

Seren turned, knowing the tears at the corners of her eyes made her look too young to give orders. "Tell the scribe too. He must take hold of the business side of things while we...until the kyros is well."

"My lady." Barir bowed and held Seren's gaze for a heartbeat. "Remember, you are blessed."

Seren rushed into her personal chambers, wanting nothing more than to run away from the burden Barir's beliefs and her vision had stacked onto her shoulders.

2

ONA

The kyros's famous capitol wasn't what Ona expected. The city's name itself meant *tents*. Last she checked, tents were not made of rock. Slowing their horses, Ona and Lucca reached out—his hand rough with one broken finger; hers smaller and scarred at the knuckles—and touched the nearest section of the wall. Smoky, white stone lay in between layers of rock the color of dead leaves.

Lucca's sudden *hm* made Ona jump in her saddle. "Never seen anything like this. Even in the most decadent villas." He looked back. "Did I startle you? Excited about meeting a kyros? Nervous you'll want more than he can give?" He wiggled his thick eyebrows.

The kyros and his kin were known to be the most handsome men in the world. "The kyros and I want the same thing," Ona said. "Dead Invaders."

A memory of her aunt's eyes going glassy iced her. She remembered the palette knife, gripped in her own hand, dripping Invader blood, the blood of the man who'd slit her aunt's throat. Ona could still feel her innocence flying away like a frightened bird.

She flexed her hand around her sword's hilt. The promise of revenge warmed her belly.

Someday. Somehow.

Lucca's normally cool gaze held an edge of worry. He ran a hand over his curly, dark hair. "I wonder what they'll think of us."

Ona's saddle creaked as she leaned back. "We might have to prove ourselves." One young man and a nineteen-year-old didn't look like much.

Until they started fighting.

The city's walls went up, up, up, and the child artist hiding inside Ona wanted nothing more than to study the honeycomb design above the city's bronze doors. Shoving that part of her down, she bumped the horse's sides with her heels.

At the doors, guards stopped them with spears to the face. They wore helmets shaped like upside down acorns and vests Lucca called *jerkins*. Once Lucca and Ona explained—well, Lucca explained more because he spoke the trade tongue a lot better—that they were mercenaries here to serve Kyros Meric, the guards hurried them through, one man coming along as escort into the city proper.

And when Ona saw it, she gasped.

Now *this* was what she'd had in mind.

Impossibly high towers shaped like lotus flowers sprung up between swathes of suspended fabric that protected canals of rushing water from the sun. The tents, lightly rolling like waves, were every color in the world. Gray as a goose's feathers. Yellow like lemons. The greens of olives, spring grass, and the lakes near home at midday. Some were the bright red of an enemy's blood and others the purple of old wounds.

Black goat fur striped and framed all the tents, even the ones inside another ring of walls. The tents reached higher than any in the rest of the city. The colors used in the dye looked darker too. Richer. Ona bet the kyros lived there somewhere.

"When it rains, that fur swells and seals the stitching," Lucca said, switching back to their own tongue. "Everyone stays nice and dry, and the rainwater drains into rigged barrels. Ingenious. I assume you need to *soak* this in."

"Ha. Ha." Ona slapped her knee dramatically, ignoring the bite of how well he knew she still wished to enjoy art and be a part of that world.

The life she'd imagined—working as a fresco artist with her aunt—was barred to her now. To take pleasure in colors and lines, shapes and creation would be an insult to her aunt. Revenge had to come first. It'd always come first. Life was no longer paints and charcoal. It was blood and bone, pain to answer the pain.

"Please tell me you're not comparing all this fine color to something violent." Lucca loved to fight, but he appreciated the technique, not the blood. He justified every battle, whispering their enemy's crimes under his breath before every battle.

"Only the red and purple," Ona said, shaking off her stillness to joke.

"You mean the pretty rose and the nice eggplant?" Lucca said in a nasal voice.

She gave him a look.

As they trotted along behind the guard, Lucca pulled out a skin of watered wine to drink. "It wouldn't ruin everything to ease off the killing mindset a hair. We are more than mercenaries." He patted his saddlebag where he kept two small books of history and numbers. "You should look to the peaceful side of yourself once in a while." He handed Ona the drink.

The wine tingled over her dry mouth. "You should stop being such a dainty little mushroom."

"Mushrooms can kill."

"Only the poisonous ones."

"And they do it so well, residing peacefully in the forest until someone bothers them. Then," he snapped his fingers, "death as needed."

Ona pretended to shiver. "Is that your plan for a new chant? *We will ruin you! But only as needed!*" She punched a fist into the air.

Lucca laughed then, loudly. She grinned, proud to pull it out of him. "Yes, I suppose that could be my motto."

Ona snorted. Grinning, Lucca slapped his gathered reins lightly against his gray-spotted gelding, and the horse trotted on. Ona's chestnut mare hurried to catch up.

Blacksmith forges lined the road, emitting sparks and blistering heat. Ona and Lucca leaned from side to side, surveying the making of the finest swords in the world.

"I have to get my hands on one of their swords."

"*Yatagans.*" Lucca nodded at two of the skinny, slightly curved versions of a sword sitting on a table at the back of the forge.

"Right."

"They mine the iron ore over that way." He pointed to another walled area attached to the southwest side of the capitol.

A group of men and women walked by, laughing and talking really fast in the desert tongue. Some were light-skinned like

Lucca and Ona; others had darker skin. Most had black hair and eyes, but some had brown braids and green or blue eyes. A blend of the people originally from this desert, fighters from border towns brought in young to defend the Empire, and others from the borders whose families had served as slaves before rising through the castes. They all wore sweeping kaftans or military leather vests. Jeweled daggers hung from their sashes, fighter or not.

Two in the approaching group had bells jingling at their sashes, but the rest appeared to be purely of the desert blood and not required to wear the caste bells. Bells or no bells, there were some seriously beautiful people in this varied city.

At an open market, the canals' gurgling and the bang of blacksmiths' hammers competed with camel grunts, tea hawkers shouting, and the tempting call of the baker with his mound of cookies topped with pistachios. Ona bought one with a silver piece that had to be foreign to the seller, but didn't make the man blink an eye. Seemed Akhayma had plenty of visitors from far away.

Ona waved her cookie at all the gorgeous tents, the food, the children playing in well-stitched clothing. "See all this? They have wealth. Power. Smarts. With the kyros and his army, the Invaders will be crushed into nothing. Now, if we can just get them to attack."

"Your wishes are my wishes, Onaratta Paints with Blood," Lucca said wryly, prompting their old joke and using their mercenary titles.

Ona bit into her treat. The pistachios' salt argued happily with the dough's sweetness. "As long as yours don't war with mine, Lucca Hand of Ruination."

The two canals bordering the marketplace flowed into a

huge pool lined in yellow and blue mosaics. A silver gilt bowl that could easily hold three fat men stood on a pedestal above the water. The kyros's graceful language poured over the sides. Ona wished she could read it.

She touched the guard on the shoulder. "What's the bowl for?"

"The Fire Ceremony. We held one last night, small girl."

Ona flexed her sword hand. "You mean *scary woman*."

Lucca urged his horse between them. "At the end of every quarter, *tiny face*," he said with a teasing smirk that she determinedly ignored. "They pull back the tents, build a bonfire in the bowl, then after the kyros blesses it, they use the branches to light the family fires in town. The Holy Fire keeps the city's inhabitants close to true wisdom."

Whatever that meant.

"This past ceremony was...difficult," the guard said as they walked into the inner ring of stone walls. Two more guards raised their palms to him as they passed. "Normally, it is the most beautiful night. Once the fires are lit, all sit quietly and pray and reflect."

They just sat? Boring. "It sounds—"

Lucca jabbed Ona's arm with a fist. "It sounds perfect," he said.

At an enormous black and blue tent, the guard stopped, his face holding some quiet sadness. "Please wait here, Silvanians," he said before disappearing inside.

Silver stars dotted the outside of the tent and a red rug ran under the entrance flap to where the horses' hooves sunk slightly into the gritty earth. Lucca and Ona dismounted and waited under the sun.

"How long will we have to wait?" Ona asked.

Before Lucca could answer, two women and a man—each with seven bells on their tunics' sashes—gave them a mint leaf, then took the horses.

"What is the story?" Ona held up the leaf, then tucked it behind her ear and did a makeshift dance, swiveling her hips and rolling a shoulder.

"Maybe it's for our breath?" Lucca shrugged and ate his.

Ona snorted and popped hers into her mouth as the guard appeared to lead them through the flap.

The tent was even more beautiful inside. It was like being inside a structure made wholly out of the colored glass Silvanian priests used in the cathedrals. The sun glowed through the blue, turning it lighter, but richer. The red of the rug sparkled with silver threads and the fabric stars twinkled in the muted light.

Their guard-guide fellow gestured to a copper bowl of green leaves that burned a deep orange.

Lucca spoke in Ona's ear. "Fire is their way to connect with a higher power, remember?"

"And?"

Slinging his most withering look, Lucca stepped toward the fire bowl and passed a hand over the flame. "Do what I do, Ona."

She tried to appear serious as she did the same movements, but the heat did nothing to inspire her to prayer.

At the end of the room, a tall, weathered soldier, five bells on his sash, stood at attention, holding his helmet. Beside the soldier, a woman with black eyes ringed in green cosmetics wore one bell tied to a ribbon across her forehead. As she tilted her chin, studying Ona and Lucca, it rolled along her smooth skin. She worried a little scrap of wool at her sash like she was nervous. But she shouldn't have been. This had to be Seren, Pearl of the Desert, wife to Kyros Meric.

The guard introducing the mercenaries bowed deeply and held up a palm, calling himself Erol. A thick, blue smoke that smelled like night flowers streamed out of a heavily guarded back room as he spoke in the desert language, adding in Ona's name and Lucca's.

Ona mimicked the guard's respectful movements, with a side-glance at Lucca. He wasn't bowing. Or raising his hand. He stood there with his mouth hanging open.

"Lucca," she hissed.

He swallowed and dropped to one knee. "Pearl of the Desert."

Ona muffled a laugh against her arm. Even the impossible was possible. The infamously unshakeable Lucca, finally flustered by a pretty lady. He'd better watch himself. Surely, they wouldn't be too keen on a foreign mercenary making eyes at the kyros's lady.

Ona cleared her throat, running a translation through her mind. "Akhayma is so beautiful, we have trouble...telling a story...no...speaking. Yes, speaking!"

Everyone grinned.

Lucca shook his head once and seemed to come back to his senses.

The kyros's wife stepped forward and gestured to a bronze and blue enameled tray of small, cylindrical glasses. "Of course. You must be very weary after your long trip. Please sit and have some tea. Please forgive the ka'ud smoke. Kyros Meric is very ill." Her gaze fell on Ona—her eyes were so sad—before falling away to focus on the servant pouring the tea. "The smoke helps his lungs."

~

AFTER A PAINFULLY LONG stream of pleasantries—during which Ona thought Seren was going to either nibble her lip off or tear that odd piece of cloth she kept—Ona pushed her untouched tea to the side.

She looked at the man they called General Adem, an old fellow whose glare she admired. "Your kyros told one of the Silvanian kings that you all were willing to pay good silver if we train your warriors, right?"

General Adem leaned forward, focusing the blaze in his eyes on her. "We don't need training, Silvanian. We are the best fighters in the world."

Ona had to smile. "I have heard you're the best with the steel. Making it *and* wielding it. But we have something you don't. A way to improve the amazing skills you already have."

"So we can help one another," Adem said. "We teach you our fighting techniques, bow and yatagan, and you teach us yours. We've heard stories about your successes. I've read the reports. I'd like to know specifics from your own mouths. Tell us about your abilities."

"Tell us more about yours first," she said.

Lucca kicked her under the table. She ignored it. The Empire had some way they used fire, some sort of blessing Lucca had mentioned. Refusing to blink, she held herself calm as the general weighed the force of her stare. He wouldn't be finding her will lacking.

Seren opened her mouth, probably to break the stand-off, but Adem's lips slanted into a clever grin. "All right then, Onaratta Paints with Blood. If we summon Holy Fire, some of us receive ideas, strategies. Those with royal blood have been known to hear ideas from the Fire."

Seren looked at her hands, turning them over and running a finger over the veins. Why did she look guilty?

Ona focused on the topic at hand. Getting ideas from fire, that was pretty impressive. "And your people still nearly lost all to the Invaders last generation?"

Adem went very still. Seren paled, her mouth a line above her pointed chin, as Lucca's eyes closed and he breathed out through his nose.

"The Holy Fire gave...Kyros Meric the idea to hire you," Seren said.

Ona grinned. "Then it can be useful."

"Yes. Very." The general looked ready to relieve Ona of her tongue. He took a breath, then sipped some tea. "When my kyros is well again, he will decide for certain whether or not to use your services."

Anger bubbled in Ona's middle. The leader of their mercenary band would definitely do his best to kill her and Lucca if they failed to bring back a load of silver. She didn't think she could give up Silvania's forests for good and hide away. Her fist landed hard on the table. "Dom said it was all set!"

Seren's mouth fell open. Adem tensed like he wanted to strike Ona.

Lucca smiled too wide at Adem and Seren. "How about I explain a little about our abilities, the power that seems to run in some Silvanians' blood."

Adem's gaze was flat. "That would be good."

"Our people pass down the talent of warrior chants," Lucca said.

"Like the magical symbols of the northern witches?" Seren asked.

Ona grinned. "It's slightly different. We don't use *lykill*—symbols—in our work. Just the words. We, as you may know, have a fighting blood. There isn't a day goes by that we don't argue."

Seren's smile lit her face like the sun had walked into the room to shine on her pretty features. "You are a passionate people. Much like us. We come from many places, but here, we come together with a love for family, honor, fine weapons we make with our iron, and...food." She laughed, a quiet and unpracticed sound, like she hadn't relaxed in a long while. "I've read about your struggles to hold the various sections of your lands, the fights between cousins, and your love of fine fabrics."

"Not that you can tell from *our* sad clothing." Ona nodded at her plain long shirt, ripped short pants, and dust-covered tall boots.

Lucca grimaced at his own outfit. Though he topped the ensemble off with that oddly attractive face of his, Lucca's clothing was no better than Ona's.

"Mercenaries don't dress as typical Silvanians," Ona said. "We favor the freedom of living in the wild." At least she thought she said that. She really needed to work on her foreign languages.

"You still manage to look striking." Seren's curious gaze slid over Lucca's mouth, then to the white streak in Ona's reddish mess of hair.

The slaves' bells clanged as they dished out what smelled like lemon and cardamom meatballs, lamb-stuffed and roasted onions, and an eggplant and pine nut salad of some sort. Ona's mouth watered like she hadn't had a meal in days. She'd eaten a lot of Empire foods—sold at markets in each Silvanian town—lured by their spices. The dishes were as gorgeous as they tasted. Green and white nuts, red sauces, browned meats, and glistening honey. She licked her lips as the servants scooped a tiny amount of each dish onto her plate.

The contrast between the large slave bell and the tiny, high-caste bell Seren wore wasn't lost on Ona.

There were slaves in Silvania too. Also in the northern isles —Ona had seen plenty of sad folks go to that snowy place where they'd probably never escape a life of hard, unrewarding work. She'd seen them on trading days at the ports. There wasn't any caste system in Silvania or in the northern isles, so the poor souls couldn't move out of their low position. At least here they had a chance to move up.

The guard, Erol, who'd led Lucca and Ona into this tent hadn't worn any bells. So, slavery and caste definition were for those with mixed heritage, like Seren and Adem, who didn't look like they were only of the desert blood, their noses were a little different, less pronounced.

"How do you use these chants you speak of?" Adem asked, plucking an eggplant from his platter. "My kyros will need to know the details."

Lucca took over and Ona let him. He spoke more clearly. "We say the words we've learned from those before us. The chant...its intent bleeds into us." He curled his fingers into a fist and held it to his chest. "If it is a chant about strength and speed, we hit harder with our swords and fists and run faster. When we chant of agility, we can leap over opponents or twist in ways that wouldn't normally be possible."

Seren pulled her hands together and edged forward. "To have a voice that holds so much power..."

Adem glanced at her, but spoke to Lucca. "The kyros will be very interested to watch your training."

Seren put her hands in her lap, the light in her face going dull.

Ona made a mental note to go ahead and hate this Adem fellow.

"Yes, Pearl of the Desert," Ona said. "Our throats hold more power than any sword or bow. Our words are our strongest weapon. We'll be happy to give you a nice taste of it on your training fields later if you like."

Seren smiled. "I'd like that, Onaratta Paints with Blood." She looked about ready to burst into tears suddenly. What was going on here?

Adem stood and took up his helmet, bowing to Seren, then to Lucca and Ona. "I hope the chants serve as well as one thousand weapons. If the Invader wolves do come, we could be but dust on the plains by next moon. Now, if you'll excuse me, Pearl of the Desert?"

Lucca's face clouded as he studied Adem.

Ona knew that look. Lucca was guessing the general had a secret.

"Do you know if there are any Invaders in the area?" Lucca asked, dangerously quiet.

His own brother had run away at thirteen and had been taken by Invaders. She didn't know the details. Lucca refused to talk about it and she didn't want to push him.

"You'll receive military reports as we see fit, mercenary," Adem said.

Lucca pushed away from the table and bowed to the general even though Ona was fairly sure he wanted to make an obscene gesture instead.

With Adem gone, Seren cleared her throat. "I...you're welcome to rest in a guest tent closer to the rear gates, near the entrance to the training areas. I hope you'll be comfortable there. If you're not too tired, I'd love to see your techniques later this morning. At the hour of ten?"

Lucca smiled. "That'll be fine. Should we tell the general?"

"Nah," Ona said. "She's the kyros's wife. Right, Pearl of the Desert?"

Seren frowned and her eyes filled again. "You're right, Onaratta."

"Call me Ona, please, Pearl of the Desert."

"Only if you call me Seren." She glanced at Lucca. "And you as well. But only in private, please."

Lucca put a fist to his chest and bowed deeply before the mercenaries turned to go.

Back in the sunlight, Ona smacked Lucca's shoulder with the back of her fist. "You and I need to chat," she said in Silvanian.

He stared straight ahead as Erol led them to the guest tent. "I don't know what you're talking about."

"Oh yes, you do," Ona said.

"Fine. The lamb was a little dry," he said. "But I still think this job is going to be fun."

Ona crossed her arms. "I'm not talking about the lamb."

"The tea wasn't my favorite." He pretended to study a merchant's table of crockery as they passed through the last of the market.

"Not discussing tea either, Master Lusty Eyes," Ona said.

"That is not my name and you know this."

"It is now."

Erol scowled and waved a hand to hurry them along.

"No," Lucca spat.

Ona nodded. "Yep."

He glanced at Erol, the usual wariness wrinkling his fore-head. "Seriously, Ona. Stop."

The man couldn't understand Silvanian. "Fine, Master L.E. But don't think I didn't see how...*that situation*—" Ona fluttered her lashes "—affected you."

"Noted," Lucca said quietly.

"Good."

"Good."

3

SEREN

houghts and emotions tumbled through Seren,
pricking and striking, as she stared at Meric's body.
With Meekra's help, Seren had rolled him up in bed
linens and she knew very well she was some kind of terrible
soul to be able to do that without sobbing or passing out cold.
She relit the ka'ud wood. The clouds' resinous scent covered
the odor she didn't want to think about—the smell of Meric's
body longing to return to the air and earth. It was a small mercy
that no one was permitted to enter the kyros's personal quarters because of Barir's quarantine. Not that Adem wouldn't
necessarily barge in anyway. And if he did, well, Seren wasn't
sure what would happen. She could picture him dragging her
into the courtyard and...

"I am ready with your clothing, Pearl of the Desert."
Meekra's voice was light and steady through the thick, woven
doorflaps that led to Meekra's smaller chamber. Seren had slept

in the smaller bed in that separate chamber last night with Meekra at her feet on a cot.

Pulling her shoulders back, Seren went to her and let Meekra dress her in a pair of sky blue pantaloons since she was headed to the training fields to see Ona and Lucca in action. Over the pantaloons, Seren slipped on a thin, dark blue kaftan with a bright orange hem and sash. Meekra held up several silver bangles that clinked lightly.

"You'll have to unclasp your fist, my lady."

"Oh." Seren placed the tiny slip of parchment Adem had sent after the early morning meeting on her cosmetics table. The words glared at her in black ink. He'd thought Meric would read them.

I will view the Silvanian mercenaries at their work, my kyros. No need to send Pearl of the Desert, my kyros.

Seren set her jaw. He'd never liked her. Not since Father argued with the old kyros about her someday marriage to Meric. Father had seen the cruel streak in Meric. But Adem had called her and her family unfit.

"Not respectful of the royal blood," he'd said. "They have a burden to bear. The Fire sometimes speaks to them, tells them things... It is a burden of that blood, to know what will happen, to know what you must do despite your own fears and limitations."

He'd been so rude to Father. She'd been surprised Father stood there and took the verbal abuse. Now she understood. Father had retired at that point and Adem had taken his place beside the kyros. Adem held the power and Father had held none.

But despite her non-royal blood, she'd seen a vision. She hadn't

33

simply heard something—that in itself hardly ever happened for a non-royal—but images of possibilities and ideas had poured through her mind almost as real as the world around her.

If only Adem would believe her, that she was what Barir thought she was…blessed. But what if it was a one-time thing and she wasn't truly blessed and would lead the Empire into ruin? Why would Adem ever believe she was blessed when she didn't believe it herself? She knew the answer already. Adem never would.

Well, she was going to the training fields to see the mercenaries. No matter what Adem thought about it. And she would ask him what he would do if Meric died. Maybe Barir was wrong. Adem might choose to wait to mourn and properly protect the city.

That would mean your vision was false, a voice inside Seren whispered.

As Meekra applied sparkling green cosmetics to Seren's eyelids, Seren pushed the worry away. She'd question Adem. Carefully. One thing at a time.

"Do you want to talk about all of this, my lady?" With a click of metal on lacquered wood, Meekra slid the cosmetics box closed and looked at Seren with patient eyes.

"Can we think about something else? Is that horrible? It's horrible. I know it. But I have so many things to figure out. And I have to watch the mercenaries' demonstration to see if their efforts are worth our warriors' time right now."

Meekra ran a hand gently over Seren's hair and Seren couldn't help but let out a sigh.

"You're human," Meekra said. "It's all right to need a change in focus for a breath or two." She brushed Seren's hair as she talked, her words and movements soothing. Seren was so lucky to have such a devoted friend. "My sister's coming-of-age ritual is today."

Seren took a deep breath and let her mind wander from Meric and the Empire. "The blanket looked beautiful after Izzet and Najwa added that ring of bright green for fertility."

Meekra smiled sadly. "She loves it. If I may say so, my lady, you're a rare rose among the flowers of the royal household."

"I don't know about that. I do have fewer thorns than Qadira though." Qadira never failed to mention her clan's bloodlines in every conversation. She was a relentless snob, but her father, chieftain of their powerful clan, helped Akhayma's economy stay strong with his keen business sense. Needless to say, Qadira soundly refused to join in on the inter-caste weaving.

Meekra's hands went to her hips. "A *shawakk* plant has less spikes than that girl."

Seren almost grinned, then reality tore at her chest. She fought a sob. Meekra rested a hand on her shoulder.

"Did your father tell you anything else about last night?" Seren asked.

Meekra chewed the inside of her cheek. "No. Just…about the kyros. And how we must keep it a secret."

"Not why?" Seren asked, standing and going to the back door to check that the rotating guards were in place. "No one is to enter. No matter what happens. Do you understand?"

The guards nodded and bowed quickly. "Yes, Pearl of the Desert," they said in unison, worry tightening their eyes.

"Even if there is an emergency. I will handle that. As will my personal guards. One of you go now to the men and women positioned at the front of my chamber and at the main tent's entrance. Give them my instructions."

"Yes, Pearl of the Desert."

Seren ducked back inside and looked at Meekra. "So your father didn't say why we must keep this tragedy a secret?"

Meekra's gaze drifted to the wrapped body. "No, my lady. If you want me to know, I'm here to listen. But I trust you. As does my father."

Meekra's loyalty glowed inside Seren, warm and steady. "Thank you."

Seren would've asked her to stop with the *my lady*, but she'd given that up the first week. Meekra said General Adem would have her head if he heard her using anything less. He might not have been Seren's ally, but tradition ruled all for that unbendable man.

⌁

When Seren arrived at the training field with her guards, three military units were practicing with yatagans, steel flashing in the red, morning sun.

"Do you see General Adem?" she asked Cansu.

The guard ran a hand down his long face as he studied the men dodging and swinging among plumes of dust and the servants coming in and out of the stables to the far right near the entrance to the archery course. "I don't, Pearl of the Desert."

A gust of wind lifted his hair off his forehead, and she felt a little lighter seeing the calm obedience in his face. She wondered if maybe her father had looked like Cansu when he was a young man before age tinged his hair with white and silver.

Erol scowled like he always scowled and squinted his brown eyes, pointing at the sun dial. A sliver of shadow approached the hour mark as a young hawk screeched overhead. "Perhaps he will be here at the hour, my lady."

Heat pricked at Seren's cheeks. She'd forgotten that she'd set the tenth hour of the morning as the time for Ona and Lucca's demonstration. "Of course."

"Did the kyros not receive my message, Pearl of the Desert?" Adem said behind her.

Jumping, Seren turned to see him bow and hold his palm up. His tone of voice didn't match his respectful movements.

"He-he did, General," Seren said, hating herself for stuttering.

Adem made a noise under his breath. "It's quite warm, my lady. Wouldn't you be more comfortable in the shade of your tent? Or perhaps you haven't had the chance to practice your archery in a while, what with the ceremony preparations. I can easily oversee the demonstration and organize the strategy if you wish to leave."

"I don't wish to leave." Her legs were shaking again. She rolled the end of the wool piece tucked into her sash and tried to steady her voice. "Two ideas came to me concerning the Invaders," she said quietly. They hadn't announced the scouts' report yet so not even her guard knew the danger riding toward them.

"Surely your ideas can wait until later, Pearl of the Desert."

She took a breath. "We don't need to wait until some later meeting time. It's only us here, with my men and yours. A perfect moment for discussing strategy." She spoke as quickly as she could. If she stopped, her voice might refuse to work altogether. Adem was just so intimidating. "The sun dial says we have ten minutes before the mercenaries arrive. Firstly, I'll ride into Kenar with the force you select for the attack. We will—"

"You must not, Pearl of the Desert. The kyros would never want you in that kind of danger."

"I rode with him when we faced the Invaders at the last clan Gathering."

"That was a small contingent of brigands, broken from their brethren. Not an organized force like this will be, my lady."

"Nonetheless, I killed a man," Seren said.

"With an arrow. From a distance," Adem argued. "We will be head on this time with the clash coming on in a small area. It will be very different, my lady."

"Yes. It will. And I have another idea concerning that."

"Leave the strategy to me and my kaptans, Pearl of the Desert."

Her body tensed. He'd given her an order. Without Meric at her side, he would run right over her.

Hossam must've noticed her sudden stillness, her uncomfortable stance, because he put a hand on the hilt of his yatagan. She shook her head slightly. What if he'd pulled his weapon? Adem would've killed him or maimed him at least. Seren swallowed. It was nerve-wrecking to be in charge of so many lives.

Adem bowed shallowly. "If it pleases you, Pearl of the Desert," he said, correcting his tone.

Heat burning her cheeks, she glanced at the gate leading to the city. Her feet tingled, wanting to hurry away to safety. But there wasn't any safety. Not anywhere. But before she talked strategy, she needed to at least give this boar of a man a chance to prove Barir wrong. Surely he would agree the mourning must wait until after they'd dealt with the Invaders.

Clearing her throat, she tried to meet Adem's eyes. She settled for his forehead. "Kyros Meric is no better this morning."

Adem's head dropped and he rubbed his chin.

"What if," she whispered, "he doesn't pull through this?"

Adem's head snapped up. He stared into the distance. "It would be a horrible tragedy. We would of course mourn." He looked at her, eyes narrowing. "You know the custom…"

"But we're about to be attacked. Wouldn't mourning put us at further risk? No eating or sleeping? Doesn't seem like the way to prepare for an enemy."

"We won't allow them to frighten us into giving up the very traditions that have given us this life. Do you think you know better than centuries of leaders? Than those with the oasis blood, the Fire-blessed, royal blood?"

A drop of spittle marred his tidy beard. He looked over her face and took a breath.

"My lady. I apologize. But surely you must see you are in the wrong."

She definitely saw something. But it wasn't that she was wrong. It was that Barir was right. Adem would never hold up the mourning ritual. Unless…

"Have you ever had a vision in the Fire, General?"

"Of course not. I have no royal blood. Or not enough anyway. None but the kyros's direct line does. The sun is too much for you, Pearl of the Desert. Your mind is suffering."

She pushed the insult aside. "I'm fine. So no one outside the royal blood has ever had a vision?"

"Of course not." He paused. "I would like to see the kyros today. Regardless of what the physician says."

Seren's heart knocked around inside her chest. What could she say? "If you contract the illness, we could lose both of you and then where would the Empire be against the Invaders?"

Adem crossed his arms and watched a woman and a man

spar with their bows, fine quivers set to the side. "True. I'll give it another day and we will see what the physician says, my lady."

Seren did her best not to pass out with relief as she nodded. The feeling was brief though. She was still in the same awful place. Meric was dead. She'd seen the horror Akhayma would experience if Adem was allowed to lead the city in mourning. Adem would never believe she'd had a vision.

For now, she would keep Meric's death a secret. As for taking control, no. She couldn't. She wasn't of the royal blood. No one would support her. It'd never been done. At least to her knowledge. All she could do right now was give her ideas to Adem and hope she was doing what was best for Akhayma, the Empire, and the people she loved more than anything.

She'd start with an idea she'd had over the Fire after reading a scroll about a battle in the mountain region eighty-five years ago.

"I-I think we should evacuate Kenar," she whispered.

"We've already done that, my lady."

Oh. She locked her knees to stop their trembling. This whole situation was a nightmare. What would Father have done? *Keep on. Push through your obstacles. Eyes open. Heart ready.* She could almost hear his voice soaking through the hot air.

"We can hide in the buildings before moonrise tomorrow night," she said. "In the homes and shops. When the Invaders arrive, we'll surprise them."

"Your timing is spot on," Adem said quietly, "but with that strategy, we'll be separated from one another, my lady. Our archers won't be able to see their flag go up. They won't know when to attack. The foot soldiers won't be united when it comes time for a shield wall, Pearl of the Desert."

"The surprise will be worth it, General. I think." She rubbed sweating palms on her kaftan. "Especially if our warriors do benefit from the mercenaries' training," she said, trying to turn the conversation and avoid his arguments. The sun glared down on them as she tried to imagine what Ona and Lucca's chanting would look like.

They walked closer to see the fighters and the guards came up beside them.

"You truly believe they'll learn anything in such a short time, my lady?" Adem's tone mocked her.

"What good is it to believe they won't?" Seren said.

Hossam snorted a laugh and quickly covered his mouth. Adem whipped around. Hossam stilled, looking as though he'd never moved in his life. It should've been entertaining, but everything was too much, too heavy, too hot for Seren and the air filled with black spots.

Her head swam in the heat waves.

Hossam shouted for Meekra, who was several steps back, talking to the stable keep about Seren's horse, Fig.

Meekra appeared at Seren's side and held out her arm. "Are you all right, Pearl of the Desert?"

Seren leaned against her until the spots faded and she could breathe again.

"It's very hot," Meekra said. "Hossam, would you mind getting a damp cloth for our lady?"

"Of course not," he said, his eyes sincere.

"You locked your knees, didn't you, Pearl of the Desert?" Adem's tone reminded Seren of her old history tutor.

She wanted to argue, but he was right. Her cheeks grew warm again. "Yes, I think so, General."

Hossam handed Meekra the damp cloth, and she arranged it

at the back of Seren's neck. The cool wet fabric on her skin cleared her vision, and she straightened up.

Ona and Lucca broke from the wall's shade and marched into the growing sunlight. Though they were far away, it was easy to tell them apart from anyone else. Ona's walk was springy, but also predatory, like a falcon on the ground, like she hunted an animal no one else could see. Lucca loped like a desert lion, his head shifting this way and that, always on the watch.

Adem took off and Seren hurried to follow, their path colliding with the mercenaries. Lucca and Ona stopped and bowed.

"Good day, Pearl of the Desert, General Adem," Lucca said. Ona just grinned.

The sun shone off Lucca's high cheekbones. He looked different from anyone she'd ever seen.

"We're ready to see what you can do," Seren said.

Ona rubbed her hands together. "And we're ready to show you."

Adem's hands fisted. He started toward the units, motioning to a warrior carrying something in his hand. The man strode over to a stand holding six small flags. He withdrew one and replaced it with the one he'd been carrying. Seren was fairly sure each unit and training activity had their own color. The units on the far left, nearest the slope that led to the prisons, sheathed their swords and gathered in front of them like rows of silver coins. The men stood straight and still, their helmets blinding in the sun.

The sound of the iron ore mines floated over the walls. Donkeys' brays, picks' cracking, and machinery's squeaks trickled into the air.

Adem introduced Lucca and Ona to the other soldiers, using their vicious mercenary titles.

To Seren's side, Ona and Lucca whispered in Silvanian. Ona pointed at Erol's yatagan and raised her eyebrows hopefully.

"You want a yatagan?" Seren asked.

"Um, yes. Yes, I do," Ona said.

Seren nodded. "We can arrange that. If you are all you say you are."

Lucca's gaze snapped to Seren's face. Dark hair swept over his forehead and his eyes burned with truth. He looked completely different. So foreign. Why did she feel like she could trust him already? Like that mouth could never lie? That was a foolish thought. All people lied. The real question, Father would've said, was whether or not he would lie for her or against her. Wait. That wasn't right. That sounded…suddenly Seren imagined this Silvanian mercenary pressing her against a lotus tower, his lips on her jawline. *Lie against her.* She was an idiot! She wiped the fantasy away with a quick swipe of the wet cloth across her neck. Father would've said the real question was *would he lie to bring her goal to light or to drag it into the sand?*

"We are exactly what we say we are, Pearl of the Desert," he said. "I'll show you."

Her heart bumped oddly in her chest. "I hope so."

The general stepped back and held a hand toward Lucca as an invitation to begin.

Ona stepped forward instead. A smile pulled at Seren's mouth and almost turned the corners of her lips up. The mercenary pulled her wide yatagan—her *sword*—from her belt, along with a stone. A flint, maybe? Lucca said something to her. She looked to the skies in irritation but stepped back, allowing him to take the warriors' attention.

Spreading his arms wide, Lucca addressed the units. He obviously thought the troops could do with an explanation before Ona's demonstration. Lucca's features were dark slants of purpose and drive as he paced the dirt in his tall boots.

"We're so pleased you're open to learning what we have to teach." Under the rims of helmets, eyes narrowed. Meric had ordered it; being open had nothing to do with it. "And we look forward to learning from you as well. That overhand sweep to a two-step strike especially." He wiggled his eyebrows. "Plus, we'd love to work on your style of using the bow on horseback. I've heard you can shoot at the wildest angles."

The fighters grinned and murmured, elbowing one another.

"We may be from vastly different places, but we have one thing in common. We all want to be prepared when the Invaders strike. The small bands of them never stay away for long and all of us have lost someone we know. Who knows when they might come in full force." He paused, his face darkening like a coming storm.

Seren's chest tightened. The Invaders' land was ravaged by drought off and on, so they kept coming. Why didn't they try to negotiate? Why didn't anyone try to negotiate with them? And the way they killed...that haunting shriek. It was almost like they'd been possessed by some evil spirit. Like they were tortured and had to take their pain out on the world.

A hidden memory suddenly surfaced in Seren's mind.

She was closing the shutters of the house in the mountains, right before the attack. An Invader at the front of a group had spotted Cyren, a neighbor boy, and pushed him into a haystack before the rest of the unit made it to the top of the rise. To hide him. To keep him alive.

So the Invaders did have hearts. They'd spared Cyren.

Why then did they kill when they could simply injure? Why did they annihilate when they could negotiate? Seren pushed the puzzle out of her mind and focused on Lucca's words.

"As Silvanian fighters," Lucca said, "we learn to chant." His voice was deep, strong, as he walked a line in front of the warriors, not a drop of sweat on him. "Not all can do it. Seems it's like most skills—some are born to it, others can pick it up with practice, others never do learn. A chant is a phrase spoken loudly. While said chant is being shouted, the fighter strikes their steel with a flint to make a spark."

There was a flash of movement, then Ona was dragging a flint over her weapon. Sparks danced away from her hands.

"Desperta Ferro!"

Her voice echoed across the plain, against the stables, along the city walls. She drew a spark again and yelled foreign words into the air. Her arms moved like lightning, blurred in their speed. The steel she wielded was an arc of silver, a spray of shining power in her hands. No one would be able to touch her.

Seren's throat knotted. Seren had trouble speaking up to her own general, but this woman, this Onaratta Paints with Blood, had Seren's father's confidence, Mother's too.

"Pearl of the Desert, are you all right?" Meekra asked.

Below, Ona called out, "Nuh! Haris!" She held her sword poised and ready.

Two warriors sprang past the rest, Adem urging them on.

"Draw your steel and face me!" Ona said in heavily accented trade tongue.

The warriors stalked, then struck, one high, one low. She slipped three steps back, her boots a blur of darkness, until she had them stacked. They swung at her, but Ona's sword flipped and cut the air twice as quickly as the men's. Nuh almost sliced through her thigh, but she spun, flicked the tip of her steel toward their hands, and had them unarmed and on their knees before Seren's heart beat ten times.

The unit remained silent as they stared at Ona and their fellows on their knees, defeated. The only sounds came from the iron mines, everyone's breathing, and the grit under Lucca's boots as he faced Seren, watching for a response.

Seren's breath rushed out like she'd been hit in the stomach. "Amazing. It's…amazing."

Adem began stomping his feet in praise.

The unit joined in, raising shouts of "Victory! Victory!" It was Meric's war cry.

Erol took two steps forward. "I can't believe what I just saw." He turned, remembered Seren was there, and added, "Pearl of the Desert. I'm sorry. It's…"

"It's something we need to learn," Hossam said to Seren and Erol, "that's what it is, Pearl of the Desert, war brother." He nodded politely to each in turn.

Ona sheathed her sword and spoke to the units, including the two warriors it seemed she'd already befriended. "You have to feel the words inside you."

Lucca interrupted, "Most chants begin with *Wake iron, wake!*" The men nodded at the translation of what Ona had shouted.

Nodding, Ona continued, "You must believe the words. Know they work to make you faster, stronger, and they turn your weapon into another limb. Everything gets…the world falls behind and away from you when a chant is working. You move like, like the lightning before the thunder."

"It's a miracle." Adem studied her and Lucca. "We may actually benefit from this."

Seren wanted to praise them, but a hand had closed around her stomach. She wasn't sure what she felt. Having these mercenaries on their side, training her warriors, was a true blessing. But something scratched at her, under her skin.

She wanted their power.

Not necessarily the physical ability, but the raw confidence they oozed. The people fed on it, drawn to these two, already their disciples. To help her people defeat the Invaders, she needed that confidence. Confidence that her own father and mother had possessed, but she failed to exhibit.

Seren swallowed, her throat still tight. Barir was mad. There was no way Seren was chosen. She had none of Ona's type of leadership skills or power.

Lucca and Ona divided the unit into two groups and they separated on the field, the mercenaries explaining and laughing and looking generally very hopeful.

"We should return to the city," Seren said to Meekra.

Meekra took the damp cloth from Seren's neck as they made their way toward the back gate. "The Silvanian woman is a force, that is for sure, my lady."

Seren pressed a hand to her chest, wishing, wishing, wishing. "A force. Yes. Exactly that."

She'd never been so jealous in all her life. She wanted so badly to be as confident as Ona and Lucca were, to have the power Ona displayed with such ease.

They passed under the arch of the back gate and headed toward the Kyros Walls. Seren's ears buzzed with the sound of Ona's voice and the power that had flamed through her words.

"Will we get to see the other mercenary chant, Pearl of the Desert?" Meekra asked as they passed through a clutch of nobles dressed in black, yellow, and red.

Qadira raised a palm to Seren, her kaftan's wide sleeves fluttering like a nightwinger. Najwa grinned as she bowed, the three high-caste bells on her black sash catching the sunlight. Seren gave the group a nod, her thoughts pushing her toward her tent, toward an empty place to think.

What would Lucca look like chanting and fighting like Ona? Inside the main tent, Seren removed her outer kaftan, suddenly too hot. Cansu, Erol, and Hossam stayed by the main tent's entrance, giving Seren and Meekra some space and privacy.

The door to Seren and Meric's personal chamber hung still and dead between the rotating guards on duty. The ka'ud wood smoked lightly, the blue puffs ghosting through the tent's seams. Seren inhaled. Under the heavy, nectar-like scent of the wood, the odor of death stirred.

He had to be buried. Now.

Meekra took Seren's kaftan and opened the chamber's thick, inner flap. Seren flexed her hands which were lightly calloused from archery, but smooth and lacking the muscle in Meekra's. Meekra, with her strong hands, could help her dig, but then Meekra would be that much more involved in this dangerous scheme. She studied her friend's face, the small scar beside her chin. Meekra had told Seren about that scar, about her younger sister accidentally kicking her during one of their friendly wrestling matches when they were little. Their family was intact and Seren wouldn't do anything to threaten that. Seren couldn't ask Meekra to help bury Meric. She had to keep her safe. Well, safe as possible.

She could bury him herself. Maybe.

Following Meekra—neither looked toward Meric's body on the bed—through the room and into the side chamber, Seren wondered how long it would take to dig an almost six foot long hole, at least two feet deep. She honestly didn't know. What if Adem came to the door and Meekra had to cover for her? If Adem pushed his way in and saw everything, Meekra's deceit would mean death.

While Meekra prepared a bowl of clean water, Seren, stomach in knots, went back to the door and peered through the flaps at her guards. The men talked quietly with the others stationed at the main tent's door. The sun cut through the pinned flaps and illuminated one side of Cansu's, Erol's, and Hossam's faces, leaving the other side dark. If she trusted them with her secret, they'd help her with this terrible task. They probably already knew Meric was dead. Cansu had seen him right before Barir confirmed it.

Erol muttered a word to Cansu and Cansu's face broke into a boyish grin. The old kyros—Meric's father and Seren's father's closest friend—had chosen him because he noticed details most did not. The way one warrior frowned when a certain kaptan entered the room. How a foreign emissary failed to bow properly or how many times the ore masters visited the training fields to watch their steel used. He never drew conclusions, but he grabbed all the elements so she could. But his face was as easy to read as a scroll written yesterday. He'd never keep a secret with that face. And it wasn't as if she could trust Hossam and Erol with this and not expect Cansu to find out.

No, her guards were good men, but they weren't the people she needed right now. If they knew, fine. But she wouldn't confirm their suspicions. That way, if anyone questioned them, they'd be safe. They wouldn't be held accountable for what she was doing.

What would Father have done?

Not wanting to lean on loyalty and endanger those closest,

he'd have picked out two strong workers and paid them to keep quiet. Workers or soldiers with nerves of steel and no allegiance to Adem or any of the kaptans or ore masters. No secret agendas like so many warriors had.

And then it came to her.

There were two people in Akhayma with no allegiances past silver—which she could provide. Two people with nerves of steel. Yes, if she paid them enough and convinced them of the secret's necessity, they might just be the two people she desperately needed.

"Meekra?"

"Yes, my lady?" Meekra's head poked out of the side chamber's door flap.

"I'll take care of myself. Will you please tell the mercenaries to meet me at their tent at sunset tonight, after the day's training is complete. I need to see them before tomorrow."

Because tomorrow she'd have even more weighing on her. Tonight, she had to face the death sitting in her very chambers.

4

ONA

"No, no. Not like that. What did you chant? *Like the power of my grandmother's little finger?*" Ona grabbed Haris's shoulder and stopped him hacking at the wooden target. "Try this. Let me see if I can translate right...um..." Pushing the sleek man away—he reminded her of a cat—she faced the target herself and pulled out her sword and flint.

She struck it and watched the spark leap and fly. "*Wake iron, wake!*"

Her sword grew lighter, moved easily through the air as she sliced across the target's battered wood. As she drew the weapon back, she struck the flint again. She felt the sparks in her blood, fire singeing veins.

"*Strike like a storm, fast and faster.*
Like the water, unrelenting.
Iron in the hand. Iron in the heart.
A blade unstoppable!"

She leaped into the air, sword in both hands, and slashed down on the target's peak, a blow that would've blasted through any fighter's skull.

Haris hurried to the opposite side of the target, his eyes like slits and his mouth smiling cruelly. "*Wake iron, wake!*"

His flint scraped his yatagan and fire jumped from the contact. Slipping the flint in his sash, he shouted in accented trade tongue,

"*Be the instrument of my passion,*
My drive, my life.
I am a storm they don't see coming.
I am the heat inside a fatal wound.
Wake iron, wake!"

Ona sheathed her own sword, her cheeks hurting from smiling. "You basically just called yourself an infection, but all right. It worked." She stomped her feet in praise. "Much better."

A couple of other warriors came over, patted Haris on the back, began talking in their own desert tongue.

Across from a set of archery targets, Lucca's unit lined up, nearer to the stables. The sun bleached the stable roof, a lone tree's waxy leaves, and the warriors' dark heads. Holding a bow, Lucca sat on his gray-dappled horse in front of the fighters, several arrows tucked between his fingers. His other hand gripped the flint and struck it against the arrowhead. Like he'd stolen and thrown a piece of the powerful sun, a spark jumped from the flint.

"*Wake iron, wake!*
My body spins with the swiftness of the falcon."

He dropped his flint into his pocket, a movement smooth from loads and loads of practice, and let an arrow fly. It thunked into the center of the first target as his mount jolted toward the second target.

"*I dive and my enemy sees my talon, my sword, flashing!*"

His chant, one of Ona's favorites, boomed across the field and echoed along the training area's walls. He fired another arrow and hit the second target. And one more arrow, nearly splitting the first.

"*My iron consumes his soul!*" he shouted.

Lucca drove his horse past the third target, then pushed the animal back in a half turn. He loosed three arrows and each of them found the middle of the last target. His unit erupted in cheers as the first of them stepped forward, black hair waving in the wind.

The warrior repeated what Lucca had done, but at the end instead of turning his own mount around, he arched his back and shot upside down, hitting the target one time more than Lucca. Lucca shouted in smiling surprise and ran to the man, already asking how, his hands lifted in question.

Adem's raspy voice droned through a speaking cone. "Attention."

Ona whipped around to see the old man on the rise where Seren had stood earlier. The soldiers scrambled into lines and faced their general. Adem kept looking over his shoulder like Seren might return, like he was a boy afraid of getting in trouble.

Ona glanced at Lucca. He shrugged. So he didn't know what this was about either. Strange that Adem would interrupt them right after training had started.

Adem spoke too quickly and his voice echoed oddly through the cone. Ona couldn't catch what he was saying. Something about scouts. Then one word rang clearly across the field.

Saldirgan. Invader.

Ona's blood took the sparks from earlier and ran with the feeling. She could leap over a mountain, slay one thousand without sweating a drop, push the sun back to savor the day.

They were coming. The Invaders from the West, the warriors who had ruined her life, were coming to Akhayma. Her heart soared. She would finally get her revenge.

She grabbed Haris's bony arm. "I can't hear him well enough. What is he saying? When will they arrive? How long do we have to prepare?"

Haris blinked. "Um, he said tomorrow, tomorrow evening. And the kaptans are to meet with him immediately at the weapons tent. Just there." He pointed to a large, oblong shelter beside the stables. The kyros's flag, blue with black calligraphy, snapped over its peak.

The crowd was already moving back into training with Lucca lost in the mass of men and women.

"I'll walk with you, if you like," Haris said.

Ona barely heard him. In her mind, her enemy stomped toward them, their weapons stained with her aunt's blood, their hands—too pale, too cold—ready to rip someone else's innocence away like they had Ona's. Their shriek, pained and howling, echoed in her ears.

Clouds like fists gathered around the afternoon sun, squeezed the orb's pale light, then let it go in watery lines that made Ona squint. Movements smooth, Haris led her past the busy training field and toward the weapons tents. Everything had a sharp edge to it. The ends of Haris's black hair, the white stripes of the tent, the curve of her boot's toe in the gritty earth.

Inside the weapons tent's dim light, Haris said goodbye and slipped out the door. The room was filled with men and a few women talking with one another, serious looks on serious faces. A man in front of Ona straightened his dark blue kaftan and adjusted the black sash at his waist. His yatagan hung from a shiny, silver chain.

"Have you seen Lucca Hand of Ruination, the other mercenary?" Ona asked, trying to smooth her trade tongue.

He inclined his head politely. Stars, he was pretty. War and want both sent that rush through Ona's blood. The more, the better.

"No, Kaptan Onaratta Paints with Blood," he said. "I have not, but may I say I am particularly impressed by your abilities and those of your associate."

"Oh. Thank you. Kaptan…"

"Rashiel Ozan."

"Thank you, Kaptan Rashiel Ozan. Will I see you at the evening meal?" He'd be great to question for military details and also great for some after dinner activities.

"Yes," Rashiel said. "I'll look for you and perhaps we can talk more about your skills."

"I'd like that very much." Ona angled herself toward him, wondering if he was as good at kissing as he was at good manners. "Maybe I could even show you a thing or two."

She could take over the world. Her enemies were coming and they would be destroyed. The world was new, and she was ready to celebrate it already.

One side of his mouth quirked into a grin. "You are very young."

"I'm a kaptan."

"And so you are. I'll see you at the evening meal then." He smiled and lightning zipped down her spine.

Lucca's mouth was suddenly at her ear. "You're flirting and

death is riding at us." He nodded politely at Rashiel as the man turned. Adem entered the tent from a side door.

"This surprises you?" Ona said.

"Not really." The muscles around his jaw tensed and he stared ahead. "If the Invaders are coming, we should leave immediately."

Ona's stomach twisted, but hope surged over the sick feeling and drowned it. "I want my chance at them."

Lucca's eyes pressed shut for a beat. Then his shoulders straightened and he opened them, protectiveness practically shooting out of them like arrows. "What will happen if you do kill a bunch of Invaders? What then?"

"Then I'll live out my life as a mercenary, content in knowing the ones who murdered my aunt and made me become a killer are dead."

"What good will that do?"

"It's called vengeance, Lucca. Look it up in one of your books."

"If *you* looked it up, you'd find out vengeance has a pretty bitter aftertaste."

Ona felt like someone had tightened a horse's girth around her middle. Why didn't he understand?

She grabbed Lucca's sleeve and jerked him closer. "They ruined my world. They took my aunt's life like it was their right to do it." Her fingers shook. Heat seared the corners of her eyes. "I won't let them get away with it. I want to shove them into the ground and drive my sword into their hearts. All their hearts. I want to—"

Lucca put his hand over her shaking one and began plucking at her grip on his shirt. "All right. All right. But listen to this argument."

Adem was talking to a group of other kaptans and two of those ore masters, the men and women in the long, sweeping, black cloaks who ran the iron mine operations, Akhayma's main source of wealth.

"I don't want to risk my life for someone else's war," Lucca said. His breath smelled like mint. "If someone attacks Silvania, I'm all in. But this?"

"Someone else's war?" Ona's hand curled around the hilt of her sword. "It's not someone else's. It's yours! It's mine!"

A few heads turned their way, but they didn't speak Silvanian, so they couldn't know what Lucca and Ona were arguing about.

Lucca's pinched mouth fell and his eyes went shiny. She knew he wasn't going to argue anymore. Not today anyhow. She could almost see their friendship in his look. The rawness of the violence they'd committed together in the shadows under his lower lashes. The way no one else's life mattered as much as one another's during battles between the people who paid them hiding in an early wrinkle between his eyebrows. She knew he saw a lot in her eyes too. Her desperate hope flickered back at her, a gut-wrenching plea for him to understand her need to kill every Invader she could get her hands on.

Her hope won out and the heat of her anger cooled. She wanted him to want this revenge too, to really want it, not go along with her because he loved her and their friendship. This could mean his life, and she didn't want him to stay and fight if he didn't truly feel it.

"It's...ours," she said. "They hurt Silvania too. Not recently. But in the past. They ravaged my village and a dozen more past that. They tried to take yours too." She wouldn't mention his brother's abduction. Not until it was really necessary. "Don't act like that was a once in history occurrence. They could strike Silvania again if they take this territory. It would be even easier."

Twisting away, he raked hands through his hair. "I don't know how we'd leave anyway. One does not break a deal with a kyros if one wishes to keep one's head." His voice went quiet. "So I guess we're staying."

"We can do it, Lucca. We could lead our units against the Invaders." She could almost feel her sword driving into an Invader's throat.

"I seriously do not like that look in your eye." Lucca moved to get closer to Adem and his cohorts.

"You're not even looking at me," Ona said to his broad back.

"Oh I can see it. I can see it better than you."

"That doesn't make sense."

"Just...keep your head, Ona. That's all I ask. This isn't a mercenary fight, a battle for silver or respect. This will be true war. Mind your tongue, keep your options open, and stay close to me."

"You're awfully bossy, you know," she said.

"Just now noticing that?"

"Guess when we don't have the rest of the crew around, there's no buffer," she said as Adem's associates stepped back and let the older man take control of the room.

Meekra appeared at Lucca's side, dipping a small bow. She looked very out of place in here. "Pearl of the Desert requests you two receive her at your guest tent at sundown."

Lucca's mouth popped open. He shut it firmly and swallowed. "Of course." He lowered his chin and watched Meekra leave.

"What is that about?" Ona asked. She took Lucca's dimpled

chin in her fingers and turned his head toward her face. "Hey. Pearl of the Desert isn't going to suddenly show up here so you can stop staring at the door."

"What?" He looked so shocked that she'd noticed his painfully obvious longing. "No."

"Hm."

Adem clapped once to gain everyone's attention. "A middle-sized unit, some 8,000 fighters will pass our borders by tomorrow afternoon. We ride to Kenar to meet them, to surprise them tomorrow night." He detailed a plan.

"If I may, sir," a warrior said, "where is our kyros?"

Adem stilled. "Unfortunately, our kyros is unwell."

"Shouldn't Pearl of the Desert be here? Her father taught her well." A few of the other fighters murmured assent.

Adem's voice was calm. Too calm. "I assure you, I know Kyros Meric's will in military matters and have hopes that his condition will improve when we crush the Invaders before they have time to take a full breath of our air!"

The warriors around Ona and Lucca raised their fists and shouted as one. A smile cracked Ona's dry lips as Lucca sighed resignedly and nodded. They were staying. And Ona was finally going to get the revenge she'd always wanted.

"WHAT DO you think about how it went?" Lucca asked Ona as they cleaned the day of training off their necks and faces. The fires in the copper bowl by the door, and the ones hanging from chains, scattered rays of orange over the purple, black, and white weave of the guest tent.

"They're no mercenaries, but they'll do." Ona gave up on

simply washing her face and dumped her entire bowl of clean water over her head.

"They're better than mercenaries," Lucca said. "More talented with bow and sword. And they'd fall on a sword for the kyros."

"Or for Seren."

Lucca nodded. "I think so."

"And so would you."

"Ona."

"You wish she'd fall on your *sword*." She winked.

Lucca's eyes flashed toward the door. "Be careful."

"No one around here knows Silvanian."

"Willing to risk my life on that?" He gave her such an older brother look before leaning over his washbowl to finish scrubbing.

"Oh, don't get your trousers in a bunch." Ona passed him on her way to the door and kicked the back of a knee, almost making him fall.

He growled. "So our long journey didn't change you much."

"You worried it would?"

"Hopeful," Lucca said.

"That stings."

He laughed.

"Wait." Ona turned from her view of the city. Night was already growing into corners between tents and along the lotus towers' eastern sides as the sun's light shimmered pink and readied for its exit. "Are you serious?"

That Lucca shrug said so much.

Something like a dagger's prick hurt her heart. "What exactly are you hoping I'll change?"

"Uncross your arms, Ona. I adore you. I want you to be happy."

"I am happy."

Lucca rubbed his bottom lip with a knuckle. "So I'm pretty certain the kyros's wife coming to call isn't normal behavior," he said, abruptly changing the subject.

"Since when has our life ever been filled with *normal behavior?*"

Maybe if Ona killed every Invader she could get her hands on, life would have the chance to become normal. Maybe she could even think about art again. Ona stared into the night, the comforting dark spreading like the hope inside her.

5

SEREN

"**G**eneral Adem did what?" Seren stared at Hossam, who stammered and ran a hand over his hair outside the main tent's door.

"He announced the invasion and held a meeting with the kaptans after you left the training field, Pearl of the Desert."

Adem had told the troops about the Invaders! He never would've done that to Meric. She didn't know whether to storm into his tent and demand an apology in Meric's name or pretend she was fine with it and had possibly even planned it herself.

"My lady," Cansu started, "didn't the kyros order the announcement and the meeting? I would've thought..."

So they really didn't know he was dead. She'd thought maybe they'd figured it out. She'd almost hoped they had. Almost. But it was best they didn't.

"Yes. Yes, of course the kyros ordered the meeting. I was... confused about the timing."

"Ah," Hossam said. Cansu and Erol nodded, looking relieved.

Seren breathed out in a rush. One problem down, another very terrible and very big one to go. "I need to see the mercenaries."

～

THATCHED mats crunched under Seren's slippered feet as she followed Hossam, Cansu, and Erol toward a discreet, mostly unknown exit from the Kyros Walls. Her mind whirled around the day's events. She hated leaving Meric's body under the rotating guards' watch. Would they adhere to her instructions and stay out of the chamber? What if Adem came and ordered them away? She should've left one of her own men there.

A simple door was hidden by a false waterworker's station that passed through the stone barrier and posed as an outbuilding with all the usual calligraphy. *Danger. Waterworker managerial staff only.* Erol creaked the door open quickly, entered the dark, empty room inside the walls, and they all passed through, into the streets.

The city was quiet during the hour before sunset. Most were inside, preparing to eat with their families and talk about their days. Street sweepers made use of the empty pathways. They worked their wide, fan-like brooms, pushing waste into neat piles for proper distribution. Canal purifiers cleaned the water with sieves and powders that disappeared when diluted. Rock doves cooed from the few places on the tops of the stone walls that weren't spiked with iron.

But even in the quiet, the city wasn't peaceful. News of the approaching Invaders had spread. The voices past the walls were tense, snipping. A child was shushed harshly. Fear shook the air like the tremble of a bowstring before the arrow flies.

Seren gripped the piece of her old skirt and said a silent prayer for the family she still had—the people of Akhayma. Her hands shook, barely capable of tucking the green wool back into her sash let alone raising a bow or sword to defend her people. Her body longed to curl up on itself, to give in, but Seren forced her bones into a proud, confident posture. A lie she didn't think she could morph into truth.

A baby cried far off, near the outer walls. Water trickled and jumped down the canals, a splash cooling Seren's foot as she maneuvered around the tents, her guards around her like older brothers. A woman started down the street beside them, then entered a shop with a wooden sign showing a painted shoe. Seren's own slippers were green, white, and red, but not from any paints. Emeralds, pearls, and rare rosestones adorned her feet. Further blessed, her shoes had more heat protection in the sole than most in the Empire. Somehow, she had earned these luxuries simply by being the general's daughter. How could she ever be enough? Barir was wrong. She wasn't chosen or blessed any more than they were. If she was, she'd be confident, wouldn't she? She wouldn't feel like she didn't deserve any of this.

The guest tent, not too far off, where Lucca and Onaratta stayed, glowed amethyst in the twilight. Seren's stomach jumped.

Lucca's voice rumbled under Ona's beyond the woven fabric.

"Goat milk," he said to her in the trade tongue. "Remember, trade is a blend of Luk and the desert tongue."

"Since I know neither, that's completely helpful," Ona shot

back, her words correct, but her inflection off. The sarcasm was very clear though.

Erol's face bunched in confusion as Ona mimicked Lucca's earlier words. "Goat milk."

A smile touched Seren's lips. "They're having a lesson." The simplicity of it, the humility and humor, gave her the push to go on inside.

Ona dropped a wooden bowl to the carpeted floor. She muttered something about goats, dancing, and death that was maybe an attempt at a curse.

Lucca bowed, then offered his low, pillowed stool.

Light flickered in the Holy Fire bowl near the door. Seren added three lahabshjara leaves from the bowl's supporting dish to boost the flame, passed hands over the heat, and whispered a prayer. Her muscles relaxed around her neck and shoulders. She was calm, but no visions shimmered into her mind.

Facing Lucca and Ona, she took a breath. "I need you to promise you won't tell anyone what I'm about to tell you. I'll give you another payment of silver equal to the amount given for the training."

Ona's eyes widened with greed, but there was a cinder of anger in them too. Now that she thought about it, that cinder had been there all the time.

"What's bothering you, Pearl of the Desert?" Lucca said in absolutely flawless trade tongue. "If I may ask? Please remember, we're yours to command."

Ona rolled her big eyes and tucked a lock of red hair back into one of the two knots of thick waves on her head. "Quit showing off, Lucca. If you'll forgive me for saying it, Seren, your language cuts the ear like a bad piercing."

Seren had to smile. "Many foreigners say so."

A large, metal oil lamp hanging from the highest point in the tent cast star patterns on the aubergine walls, red and blue carpets, and Ona's back as she bent to clean up her spilled food.

A spicy scent tweaked Seren's nose and her stomach growled. "That's Kurakian chicken."

Ona wiggled orange-stained fingers. "It is." She handed Seren a morsel.

The chicken's flavor roared across Seren's tongue, and before she could ask for another bite, Lucca handed her a bowl.

His hand nearly brushed hers. A pleasant rush sped up her arm. A slow smile spread over Lucca's mouth, but he looked down, not meeting her eyes.

Ona cleared her throat. "You do remember I'm sitting right here."

The room was suddenly far too small for all three of them.

Lucca's gaze snapped to his friend. "Ona."

Seren hadn't intended to flirt with the man. Her husband was dead and the enemy was coming and she...

Ona broke through her panic. "Do you like a lot of spicy foods?"

"I do," Seren said. "I request the hottest dishes from around the world. It drives our cooks mad, but the people love it when I offered samples at the seeding festival. But Meric never wants me to mingle with them and I wish he'd—"

Her stomach dropped. Just like that, she'd forgotten he was dead. She'd been annoyed by him again, frustrated again.

Lucca sat back against a metal-tooled trunk and looked up at her through his thick, black eyelashes. "Why are you really here?"

Veins and tendons stuck out over the back of his hand. He had a warrior's fingers, scarred and rough. His face showed none of the ever-brewing anger of his friend's. His eyes were soft. He'd removed the green-blue brigantine from earlier. An ivory shirt stretched across his broad chest and well-muscled arms. Fine leather pants covered his shapely legs and a sword rested beside his feet, where he sat cross-legged on the floor. He was so foreign, so strange. Unlike Meric or his brother Varol. They never would've sat on the floor or comforted anyone with the idea of simply listening.

"I need to know how deep your loyalty goes," she said.

"We signed our agreement," Ona said. "You were there. Plus, if you're offering more silver, that much more, you can bet we'll do pretty much whatever you want. Especially if it has to do with smashing Invader skulls into the earth."

Seren's heart raced like Fig on the track. "I have a problem. Something terrible. But I have an idea to fix it."

Ona's grin sharpened. "It was your idea to hire us, not Kyros Meric's, wasn't it?"

Seren nodded.

Lucca smiled wryly. "I would've said *thank you* before the Invaders were spotted heading this way."

A fist squeezed Seren's heart. "I'm sorry you'll be tangled up in another person's war."

"There's that phrase again!" Ona punched her thigh. "It's not *someone else's war*. It's our war. The Invaders are our enemies too. Believe me. Whatever it is you want us to help you with, know that we are yours to command."

She seemed passionate enough. There was truth in her voice. If Seren could convince her this plan was the best move in the situation, maybe she could be a strong ally. Well, there was only one way to know...

"Kyros Meric is dead." The words fell from Seren's mouth

like a curse. "If I don't hide that fact, General Adem will send the city into mourning. Three days of fasting. Three days when no one, except the very young and very old, will be permitted to sleep."

Ona held up her hands. "Right when you have a bunch of bloodthirsty maniacs driving toward your door?"

"It won't matter to Adem. He's overconfident. And he strictly adheres to all traditions. It was torture getting him to agree to hire you two. That he accepts you and your training speaks highly of his fear."

"Then why wouldn't this same fear lead him to forgo the mourning?" Lucca asked.

"He won't. That's different. There's nothing in our books about not receiving foreign aid in military training. There is, however, plenty about proper mourning. Especially for those of the royal line. He'd say Meric's soul won't reach the Heavens without his people taking up the weight of his death. It's about balance. It's...difficult to explain to foreigners."

"You don't believe it?" Ona asked.

"Whether I do or don't, it doesn't matter. If we all starve and refuse the rest we need, we'll fall under the Invaders' steel. I won't allow my people to be taken as slaves or cut down. Somehow, after the battle, after we've survived, I'll tell Adem...I'll pretend Meric has just died."

Lucca pushed a curl of his black hair out of his eyes. "That sounds difficult. At best. What if the fighting takes longer than a day or two? Adem will be able to tell the kyros has been dead for a while."

"Not if I have Barir—he's a physician and father to my handmaiden—coat Meric's skin in ka'ud oil. The smell will overpower anything else. And it's colored. It should..." A shiver raked fingers down her back. "...mask the look of his flesh."

They all stared at the ground for a breath.

"Have you told your guards?" Lucca eyed the door.

"No."

"Why not?" Ona frowned.

"I don't want Meric's death to show on their faces." Such a frightening half-truth. "In front of Adem and the other fighters. They know them all too well. I don't think it would remain secret."

"Plus, it's dangerous for them to know. If the general finds out they helped you cover this up, they'll die, yes?" Lucca asked.

Seren had been stupid to think she'd keep the true nature of her choosing them over her guards. Lucca and Ona were anything but stupid. "Yes."

Ona stopped pacing and crossed her arms. "Oh. So the real reason you're asking us is because we're expendable."

Seren winced. "It's because you'll be able to hide the truth. No one knows you or your mannerisms. They won't spot your deceit." She was spinning around the truth, her words slicing and cutting like an Old Farm blade in the dagger dance. They *were* expendable. But there was no way she was going to say that aloud. Even if they already knew it.

Ona and Lucca traded a look, then both nodded as one.

"Fine," Lucca said. "We'll help you hide the body."

"Wait." Ona held up a hand. "Why don't you take control of the Empire since Meric is gone?"

Barir's very similar advice floated through Seren's mind. She rubbed her eyes and her fingers came away green and sparkling. "Because I'm not the royal heir. Meric's brother, Varol, is. Adem wouldn't support me. No one would."

"I doubt that," Lucca said. "I've seen how the fighters respect you. And your own guards, too. They said your father was a high ranking general before he retired?"

"Yes."

"Did he teach you?" Ona leaned closer, eyes bright.

"Yes, but—"

"Then what's the problem? You can become kyros," Ona said.

"No. That's not how it's done."

"This isn't a normal day in the Empire. The kyros is dead and you have a giant army headed right for you. Take the reins, Seren." Ona smiled.

Another shiver cut Seren through the middle. "General Adem would never allow it. He'd have me put to death as a traitor to the royal bloodline."

"What's so important about having royal blood?" Ona asked.

"Supposedly, the Fire only truly communicates wisdom to those with a lot of royal blood."

"Supposedly?" Lucca rubbed his lower lip.

Seren swallowed, both cold and hot spinning through her chest. Emotions, good and bad and in between, buzzed inside her head. She couldn't tell them about the vision. Then they'd keep on about her taking over. They didn't understand. Adem would never let it happen. And she was just...Seren. Not a kyros.

"If you are still willing to help me, we should go. Now."

Lucca stared for a minute longer like he could see inside her mind. Then he gathered up his weapons and he and Ona followed Seren to the door.

∼

THE STREETS WERE STILL quiet when they all reached the secret door into the Kyros Walls. Inside the courtyard, it was a quick walk to the back entrance of the tent.

Meekra appeared at the door. "May I help you, Pearl of the Desert?"

"Can you keep a look out for General Adem or any others who may wish to...see the kyros?" Seren whispered, glancing at Cansu, who stood closest, then at the rotating guards who stared straight ahead. "He wants to have a private discussion with the mercenaries."

A knowing look crossed Meekra's face. "Whatever you need, my lady."

Cansu and Hossam took positions outside the back door. Erol went around the front to take a place beside the rotating guards there.

Seren led Lucca and Ona past the bed and lit the lantern. It flickered like it didn't truly want to give light to the blue-black weave of the tent's walls. The ka'ud wood smoked strongly, but as Seren said a prayer over the Holy Fire bowl, a hint of death greeted them, a quiet, sneaking sweetness.

Ona stood beside Meric's wrapped body on the bed. Her lips parted to speak, but Seren pressed a finger to her own lips and pointed toward the door.

Lucca's hand covered his mouth as he looked at the kyros's corpse. "Sun and stars," he whispered.

Folding her hands in front of her, Seren stared instead at the gold phoenixes on the carpet under her slippers, wishing none of this was happening.

Normally, Meekra and Seren would be writing a letter to Meekra's cousin who lived in Jakobden, near the eastern coast. Normally, they'd giggle over the drawings Seren added to the bottom, sadly untalented sketches of the city's tents and ridiculous recreations of Qadira's latest dramatic fit about her royal bloodline. Seren had thought marriage would end the youth that she should've had for at least three or more years, but Meekra had helped her retain some lighthearted bits of it.

Now, *now* her youth was truly finished. Gone.

As Ona and Lucca whispered about what to do, Seren fought a heaviness that wanted to press her into the ground. She and Ona looked about the same age. They should've been planning betrothals and learning trades or raising nieces and nephews, not orchestrating the hiding of a body. Not holding an entire empire's fate in their hands.

But then, Seren's little sisters were dead. They'd had no chance at anything. She had to make her life worth something.

She wound Meric's music box. Tinny minor notes crept from the ornate box delivered as a gift from the powerful Clan Azjorr their wedding day. Meric played the music when he couldn't sleep, so the guards wouldn't think anything of the sounds.

Seren coated Meric's cheeks, neck, and every other exposed area of skin with fragrant oil.

Lucca crossed his arms over his wide chest. He tapped a slow rhythm on his shoulder, thinking. "Please don't think I'm being disrespectful but…"

"Considering what we're about to do, I won't ever label you anything but most loyal associate. Or even dear friend."

"We need something for the digging."

"How about this?" Ona held up a water bowl and touched the black calligraphy along the lip. "Its edge is pretty sharp."

Seren grabbed her recently cleaned chamber pot that sat by

the door to the smaller chamber. Her stomach turned and sweat rose along her back and forehead.

"This could work too. And let's use that yatagan to loosen the dirt," she said, pointing to one of Meric's many weapons. "Then we can dig out the soil with the two containers and hide the dirt under my bed."

Ona and Seren took turns listening for anyone approaching and helping Lucca dig a shallow grave. Sweat poured off Seren's chin and down her back as they finished. Ona artfully arranged a few pillow seats so nothing was obvious. For one so martially inclined, she had an eye for appearances.

"My kyros," Erol said through the door.

Seren's pulse drummed. "He is resting. He is unwell still." Earth and sand blackened her nails and she tried to dig it out, making her nail beds burn. "What is it?"

"General Adem wishes an audience," one of the other guards said.

Lucca's mouth opened and Seren's head went light.

"Is he here now?" she asked.

"I am," Adem said. That unmovable attitude of his painted his words. If she demanded he leave, it'd grow into an argument and only draw attention to her lies.

Seren closed her eyes and thought of the Holy Fire.

6

SEREN

The imagined Flame shook, then Seren saw an image of Ona on the bed, swathed in coverings with the oil lamps doused. Seren opened her eyes.

It might work.

"Good," she shot back through the thick weave of the door. She raised her voice so he could hear her clearly over the music box. "Your visit will surely help Kyros Meric. Give us ten minutes to ready ourselves, please, General Adem."

"Of course, Pearl of the Desert. I'll wait in the main room with my kaptans."

Ona came close. "We're his kaptans now too. Should we say we're meeting with the kyros? Maybe then he'd go away?"

"That won't make him leave. Those kaptans he favors, they're snakes slithering after power. Too smart, all of them." A thought hit Seren's head. "Surely they won't all demand entrance to my chambers?"

Lucca hefted Meric's body onto his shoulder, then maneuvered him into the hole. "What are we going to do?" he whispered, sweat glistening along his brow and sticking his hair to his forehead.

"Ona. I have an idea." Seren touched the wool at her sash, mind whirring.

Ona crossed her arms. "I don't like the sound of this."

"You don't even know what it is yet," Lucca said.

"Still don't like the sound of it."

"Let's finish this…then I'll explain."

They covered Meric with earth, leaving a good bit still under Seren's bed, before spreading both of the carpets out over the makeshift grave.

"I must insist," Adem said, startling them, "that I see you *now*, my kyros. I apologize for disturbing you, but I need to know if you approve of the plan Pearl of the Desert wishes to enact."

Lucca and Ona gathered around Seren. "Ona, you are going to pose as Meric," she said.

Ona tilted her head. "You aren't serious."

"I am. Trust me. Lie on the bed. We'll wrap you up so Adem can't see any of you. You're smaller than Meric, but I certainly can't play the role and Lucca is too big. Turn onto your side and let Adem speak to you. You don't need to answer."

"And if he finds her out?" Lucca's lips became a tight line.

Seren clasped her shaking hands. "She dies. I die. You die."

"An average evening," Lucca said, his tone cutting.

Ona chewed her lip and put a hand on the hilt of her sword. "I really don't like it."

Lucca's eyebrow lifted. "If it doesn't involve her sword, she doesn't like it."

"I don't either, but there is no other way. He," Seren jabbed a finger toward the door where Adem waited, "won't leave. That's why I didn't argue with him. Believe me. When he has that tightness to his voice, he'll dig his heels in. There will be no moving him on the issue."

Seren locked eyes with Ona. "I will destroy the Invaders. I will help you gain the revenge I see in your eyes. I will even take their king if I can, and spill his blood and end the suffering he causes with every new attack. Are you with me?"

Ona's shoulders moved with a deep breath. She nodded.

ON THE BED, Ona looked like a cocooned moth. Nothing of her showed.

With Lucca at Seren's back, Seren leaned close to Ona. "Remember my promise. You will have your revenge. And I will have mine."

Seren turned to Lucca. "You should go. If you're found here, Adem will wonder why Meric would be trying to hide a meeting with you."

"Agreed," he said in his oddly beautiful accent. "I'll stay nearby."

If she wasn't so shaken up, his words would've been comforting. He seemed so sincere. *Fire, please let him be. And Ona too.* She sent him out the back where Meekra stood talking quietly with Hossam and Cansu.

The wooden door opened and General Adem's hand appeared at the woven flap, the second part of the entrance. "Pearl of the Desert, may I enter?"

"Yes, but I'll go to my small chamber and give you both a moment. Know that the kyros is not awake and seems unwilling to talk."

Through a crack in the door between Seren's room and the

small chamber she now shared with Meekra, she watched Adem walk slowly to where Ona lay. As she picked dirt from her nails nervously, Ona shifted in the bed.

Adem stopped. "My kyros. My deepest apologies for disturbing you, but we launch what I can only assume is *your* plan at Kenar tomorrow night. I wondered if you had any last minute tweaks for our strategy."

Ona made a small noise and rolled over.

Seren stepped closer but didn't show herself. "General Adem," she said, "I'll notify you if the kyros makes any changes to the plan."

He scratched his beard and kept looking at Ona's wrapped form. "How long has he been like this, Pearl of the Desert? How long has he been...unresponsive?"

She swallowed. "I told you he was very sick."

"If he is not alert to give the order to move at sunset—"

"We'll move anyway." She tried to sound confident. She definitely didn't feel that way. "He ordered it when he was alert. With me."

Adem breathed in through his nose and ran a hand over his beard. "With you alone."

"Yes."

His gaze slid under her skin like a newly sharpened yatagan. She waited for the pain, her mouth working. She needed to say something to get him out of here.

"This isn't going to work," he said quietly.

Did he mean he knew what was really happening here? Or something else?

"I..." Sweat rolled down her back.

"You cannot simply pass orders on to me, Pearl of the Desert. You have no experience. If you were older, wiser...if you had royal blood perhaps, but..." He tugged at his short beard. "I will send two more physicians to see to our kyros in an hour, after he's had some rest. If they deem him unfit to rule, if his body is determined too weak to carry out his duties, we will proceed from there."

"What does that mean?" Seren whispered.

"We will see." He wasn't even really talking to her. Deep in thought, he stared at the kyros—at Ona.

"Barir is his physician," she said. "I'll call for him. Meekra!"

Meekra slipped inside, her gaze going immediately to Ona.

"Get your father," Seren said. "The general wants another examination."

Adem shook his head. "No. I will send the two that help me and my kaptans. It's wise to get more than one opinion on something so important. No offense to your father, Meekra, or to you, Pearl of the Desert."

Meekra paled and bowed under Adem's heavy gaze.

Seren forced her eyes to stay fixed on Adem. She demanded that her body stop shaking.

Adem turned to Seren. She didn't even want to blink, to give him any indication that she was at all nervous or that anything was wrong. Her eyes dried and burned. Adem stared, distrust coating every feature, every movement.

"Any-anything else?" Seren asked, willing her voice not to shake.

The general tapped his yatagan's hilt. Once, twice, very slowly. "I think we are finished here, Pearl of the Desert."

He swept out of the room.

Seren could barely hear over her own heartbeat. "I need the Fire," she whispered to Meekra.

Seren held her hands over the flickering Light as Lucca's

low voice mixed with Ona and Meekra's whispering. They were telling him what had happened. She'd made such a mess of everything. Adem's physicians would of course realize Meric was dead. Adem would know she lied. The best case scenario was that Ona, Lucca, Meekra, and Seren's guards would escape punishment and only Seren would die a brutal death for the deceit. Her stomach rolled.

The Fire touched her palms lightly as she whispered her fears. The others came closer, watching a glow blossom inside her flesh, between her fingers, turning her skin the color of the dying sun.

Ona swore and Meekra sucked a breath.

The Hovering Flame appeared in front of Seren's face, blocking everything else from view. The striped weave of the tent walls faded away. The ka'ud smoke dissolved. She closed her eyes and let a vision take her.

Akhayma's outer walls stretched toward the afternoon sun where it held court in its blue empire. But a dark substance stuck to the tops of the walls, to the parapet. The substance moved like shadows. Her heart shuddered.

Invaders.

There was no dark substance. They were men.

They crawled over the walls with ropes and slid into the city, steel drawn. The people screamed and fled. Blood ran over the jeweled tips of Seren's shoes.

The vision dissipated and Seren's eyes flew open.

She faced Ona, Lucca, and Meekra, who was on her knees.

"They're already here. The Invaders."

Ona unsheathed her sword.

"You're blessed, my lady," Meekra whispered. "Chosen. Father was right."

"What?" Lucca looked from Meekra to Seren.

Seren flew out the back. "Hossam. Cansu. Come with me. We're going to gather the army. We are being attacked."

"We are?" Hossam's eyes were big as moons.

The vision flashed through Seren's head. "They're climbing the walls. You and you," she said to the rotating guards, "stay here and do not, for any reason, leave this spot. You are not to enter my chamber. You are not to allow any others—besides myself, Meekra, Barir, or my personal guards—into the room. Do you understand? This is a matter of life and death."

The tallest man of the two swallowed loudly. "Of course, Pearl of the Desert."

She turned to Cansu. "Tell Erol to keep a watch on that front entrance. To stay there with the other guards. They must keep order here and protect the kyros and keep everyone out of my chamber."

Cansu ran into the night.

Seren twisted the wool at her sash. Just sending the army into that space wouldn't be enough. The people wouldn't have time to flee. They needed a way to defend themselves. This was all going to happen too quickly. She remembered a military scroll her father had shown her. Of a war against a larger force. The queen of this foreign country had armed the people.

"Let's go to the training field. Gather a force to meet them."

The others nodded and they took off. Not caring even a little how non-high-caste she looked, Seren ran with Hossam, Meekra, Ona, and Lucca through the streets until the back gates gave way to the torch-lit training field.

At the faintly lit training field, Hossam waved to a boy with a trumpeting horn. At the boy's expert blare, all eyes were on Seren, who stood beside him on the hill.

"Assemble. Now!" Hossam bellowed.

Lucca and Ona rounded up a few more fighters from the stables, then ran back up to join Seren on the hill.

Would the warriors listen? Akhayma had no time to waste.

As Cansu joined Seren, the fighters traded glances, but then the men and women, some armed, some coming from their rest time, lined up.

Seren didn't know where Adem was. She was just glad he didn't seem to be around here.

The units assembled in the near dark. Light blinked off armor and yatagans. Mouths whispered and eyes widened at the unusual command. These fighters needed Seren to be strong and confident.

She swallowed, then raised her voice, hoping with everything that she hadn't misunderstood the Fire's information. "The Invaders are attacking now. Arm yourselves. Take an extra weapon or two. Head to the front gates. Hand out the extra weapons to anyone who will take them. We will need all the hands we can get."

The lines of fighters shifted their weight, their faces puzzled. Two actually laughed and elbowed one another. A nearby unit hissed insults at the ones laughing.

Meekra stepped forward, gaze on Seren, asking for permission. Seren nodded. If Meekra had an idea what to say, Seren would take it.

"Our Seren, Pearl of the Desert," Meekra said, "saw a vision. I witnessed the Hovering Flame myself."

The fighters began murmuring excitedly. No one was laughing now.

Lucca shouted, "I too saw the Flame!"

"And I!" Ona said as she ran toward the stables. "Now get your tails on it, warriors!"

The two men that had fought Ona during her demonstration held up their hands. The rounder one pounded his shield with his yatagan's hilt.

"She is chosen! Blessed!"

Seren didn't know what to feel. There was no time to feel. So she just gave her people what they probably needed. An inspiring leader.

Cansu had Fig and was handing Seren a bow and quiver. Slinging her quiver over her shoulder, she pressed a hand against Fig's warm body, then let the horse nuzzle her hand with a petal-soft nose. Seren mounted and raised her bow over her head.

"We won't let them take our home. We will never stop fighting."

Both foot soldiers gathered around Fig's stomping hooves. Mounted fighters rallied, faces turned to Seren. Her warriors were a river of metal and leather, gaining momentum, and she longed to unleash their power on the enemy.

Gripping her bow, feeling familiar carvings against her skin, she raised her voice and tried so, so hard to sound confident, to feel the Fire's faith inside her. "They will regret this day until their last breath!"

With a great shout, the troops rode with her, galloping into the city, their voices giving the command to all: Fight.

7
ONA

The world was a blur of movement.

Ona's horse snorted as they dodged tables of spices and fruit in the market, women and men with scrolls tucked under their arms or children on their hips. The people stopped to stare as the Empire's army flooded the streets and raged toward the front gates. Dust coated Ona's tongue, sweat poured down her face, but she smiled. This was the day. She'd waited years for this day.

Her mount's hoof slid on the dirt and cut into a canal, jarring her. Muscles clenching, she adjusted her weight and kept her seat. Lucca looked over his shoulder to see if she was keeping up. She was.

At the tall, bronze gates, the crowd was quiet.

A chill rippled Ona's flesh.

Haris handed a blade and a shield to a man in a ragged kaftan and a sash weighed down with loads of shoddy, little bells. The man nodded, then turned to what Ona assumed was his eight or nine-year-old son.

"Hide in the agriculture district. Stay until all is quiet."

"All is quiet now." Tears pooled under his big eyes and anger like a coal burned in Ona's chest. The little fellow didn't deserve this. She hadn't either.

Lucca was talking to the barrel-chested Nuh. "Anyone up top spot anything yet?" He jerked his chin toward the archers on the parapet.

The fighters and the people who probably never thought they'd need to fight lined up to form a wall of shields, steel, and nocked arrows.

Nuh nodded. "The earth has been moved around the base of the walls but I haven't heard why they think—"

A howl tore the quiet. Ona shuddered, nearly losing her sword. Ropes soared over the walls. A flash of metal. The five, blood-red lines down the surcoats.

Invaders.

She knew them well. After all, they'd been in every nightmare since the day they killed her aunt.

They oozed over the walls, jumping from the ropes amid Empire arrows.

"Stay by me, please, Ona!" Lucca loosed three arrows of his own.

Ona fumbled for her flint and struck it across her sword. *"Wake iron!"*

Lucca threw a spark from an arrow's head with his own flint, chanting at the top of his lungs as they split the crowd of unhorsed people and came up side-by-side with mounted Empire fighters.

"Wake, iron! Wake!

Rise for me in battle!
Let your unshakable strength
Bleed power into my limbs!"

Little spears of orange and red shot from Ona's blade as she chanted too.

"Wake, iron! Wake!
Rise for me in battle!
It is the dawn of their destruction,
And the first fruits of our day!"

Ona's blood was filled with horses chomping at the bit and ready to charge. She felt her lip curling. She was ready to rip sword, tooth, and shield into the enemy. Ona could smell her own fear and rage like vinegar and blood. Her hands had never vibrated with this kind of power.

She was going to kill so many people today.

As Invaders flowed around Ona and Lucca, clashing with other warriors' yatagans, Ona blocked a downward strike with her shield, her movements foggy to even her own eyes, her body rushing like a storm-tortured river. She pushed the attacker's sword-hand back, and sliced low, taking out his leg before he could even think about defending himself.

"My iron is the end of my enemy
The beginning of his next life," she chanted.
"A last cold kiss before the soul break
His sword is a branch against my blade
A weak will and his blood is mine
I am the power he cannot fight,
The force he cannot halt,
The strike they do not see."

Out of the corner of her eye, she saw Lucca raise his sword, circling his left shoulder at a dizzying speed. His blade opened the Invader where neck met body. A spray of blood marked Lucca's brigandine, a visible shout. The scent of war swirled through the air: iron, blood, sweat, spark, and foreign oils.

The Invaders' skin smelled like disaster. Ona pushed and fought a memory of men in the doorway of her aunt's villa. *Not now.* They wore the same five slashed sigil on their surcoats, the identical faces of want and desperation and that sick mixture of loving and hating the horrors they committed. She couldn't weaken now.

Use it, she told herself. *Use the fear, the anger, the need.*

Two hulking men bore down on her. Her horse was actually slowing her, trapping her in the thick of things. Slipping off, the men blinked at her speed. The chants were working. She scooted left and right, stacking the Invaders, so only one could come at her in turns. The first hesitated, shieldless, but with sword ready. She raised her shield to distract him, lifted her knee, jumped, then kicked him in the chest with her other foot, knocking him into the next man. She soared high and drove her steel into the man's throat. Pulling her weapon free before the other man realized what was happening, she drew the blade across his cheeks.

A foul way to die for a foul way to live. The blood was black and beautiful in this light, and if there hadn't been a crowd of Invaders fighting four paces away, she'd have been tempted to use it to paint the walls.

Laughing like a demon, she hurdled the bodies, pushing back into the fray. Five men surrounded Lucca, who'd jumped onto an overturned ox cart.

She began shouting.

"*My body spins with the swiftness of the falcon,*
I dive and my enemy sees my talon, my sword, flashing

My iron consumes his soul."

Lucca echoed the chant and leaped into the air like a stag, making soldiers stop and gawk. He flashed down in a quick twist and drove an Invader's sword to the army's feet. Then Ona had no more time to watch her friend spread ruination, because a woman like a tower swung a sword at her face.

"Wake iron!" she spat.

Her sword sparked, raining orange and white and green, and began moving with her thoughts, asking only for a fraction of the power of Ona's muscles. Ona had the woman at her feet, bleeding from three wounds before she could squeal like the Invader pig she was.

A sun-colored head appeared beyond a knot of Invaders. Though he didn't have a crown or even a fine helmet, Ona knew who he was. Her heart knew who he was. Its shivering rage told her.

The king.

Sweat ran down his bearded cheeks. The moisture darkened his ugly surcoat as he lifted a large sword with both hands. It banged onto an Empire fighter's shield.

Ona turned to find Seren in the chaos.

She rode into the fight, firing arrow after arrow and taking Invaders' lives like she was Death itself—relentless, shocking, and cold.

"For our city!" Seren shouted, her earlier fear washed away.

The people echoed her and surged toward the gates.

Seren could certainly keep that title of hers if she wanted to. This was proof enough.

Ona struck another man at the neck, two more at the thigh, crushed one's nose with the edge of her shield, and spun to find Adem.

Blood covered half his face and dripped from his beard. He fought well, no wasted flourishes, no fancy moves. Just clean cuts and practiced precision. No surprise there.

She and Lucca cut through the enemies until Ona dropped her shield, reached out a hand, and grabbed the king by the hair. The strands of his sunny mane cut off the circulation in her fingers as she put her sword to his throat. Victory surged through her heart, beating like drums in her chest. This was the best day of her life.

"Back off!" she shouted to the other Invaders, knowing the steel at the king's neck would make her meaning plenty clear.

"Ona!" Lucca's face was pale. His lips made a line and he gave her a nod.

The rest of the Invaders did indeed back away, fear glazing their eyes. Those strong enough retreated to their ropes, climbing away. The injured leaned against the walls, sadness making their eyes large and hatred twisting their mouths. They were so much larger than any Empire fighter or Silvanian. But their cheeks were hollow and their skin parched as they watched her drag their king to his knees.

She held the ruler tight. He laughed under his breath and she let the sword nip him, loving the red trickling from his neck. This man was like the sun to them. She wanted to end him. Now. Now. Now. She could taste his death on her tongue like wine.

Adem found Ona's side. "Congratulations, Onaratta Paints with Blood." Though his words were pretty, he didn't seem so pleased in saying them. He had to be jealous.

Adem addressed the retreating Invaders in their own tongue. "We will send word for a ransom and terms."

Ona looked to Lucca, who seemed as surprised as her that Adem knew the language.

"Ransom, hm?" the king said in perfect trade tongue.

She nearly dropped her hold on him. "Shut it." She leaned her sword into his neck again.

Surely Adem was only talking ransom to ward them off. Ona met Seren's gaze. Seren's eyes were on fire. They shared a vicious smile and Ona knew they were of the same mind.

This king was going to die, hopefully by Seren's own blessed hands.

8

SEREN

Barir and the other physicians had settled the injured on cots near the back gates, to the Northeast, and as the sun rose over the day Seren had feared would never come, she walked among them. Even beside her loyal Meekra, the steadfast Cansu and Hossam, her insides felt cold, so cold. A part of her had truly believed Akhayma would fall under Invader swords last night. Thankfully, her body had been so tired that despite the nightmares clawing at her on the bed in Meekra's chamber, she'd slept a good handful of hours.

A fighter on a cot near a table covered in clean cloth and shining surgery instruments bit a strip of leather to keep from crying out. A physician with small, steady hands tugged a thread and needle through his wound. Seren set a hand on the man's forehead. Sand and sweat lay on his skin. She dipped a cloth in the clean water, drops falling quietly into the bowl amidst the fighter's muffled grunts of pain. He squeezed his eyes shut. Singing a mountain song, Seren wiped his brow and cheeks like her mother had when she was little and sick.

As the physician tied up the stitches with precise movement, the warrior's eyes flicked open. Seren took the leather from between his teeth.

"Our Blessed Pearl." His thick fingers curled around her hand gently. "Thank you for warning us."

The physician glanced up, gaze watchful, careful. Unlike the warrior, this physician wasn't in a haze of pain. He could see the danger in the situation. If Adem spoke out against Seren, all who supported her would be imprisoned. And that was a best case scenario. She hadn't seen the general since the battle.

"Shh. Rest now, warrior. Thank you for your courage." She offered a smile that wasn't easy to give and walked on.

Fighters lifted their palms when they could. They called out thanks and blessings, telling her she'd saved them all with her vision, that she was their leader now, deserving and righteous. The formality of chewing mint and bowing was absent and Seren wished it could always be like that. Battle stripped life to what was truly important.

But she didn't like them calling her righteous. She had a body buried under her bed. The body of their kyros, the body of her husband. She was far, far from righteous. Meric had to be properly cared for. Today. She put aside her planning to pay attention to another fighter.

An angry gash marred the woman's muscular throat and the blood flow had slowed to a trickle. Her eyes stilled. Seren's chest ached. The familiar feeling was a lot like hunger, a gnawing want, but one that would never be satisfied. She closed the fighter's lids with her fingertips and whispered a prayer.

Feeling the dead woman's sweat on her own skin helped her take some of the weight of the warrior's death.

"Thank you. You've done what I haven't yet been able to. You gave *all* for those you love. Drift to that next place, fighter, and know you died with the ultimate honor."

Meekra appeared with a bowl of water and Seren washed her face and hands.

With one last prayer said above the wounded, she and her retinue walked along the smooth city walls, toward the back gates and the training area.

On the hill above the archery range, slaves—hoping to earn their way into the caste system—rubbed yatagans with cloths, scrubbed bloodied shields, and sewed new fletching onto new arrows, ignoring purpling bruises and blood-soaked wraps on their arms and legs. The large bells over their heads rang lightly.

A group of warriors brought another load of arrowheads. The differences between the men and women were suddenly shocking. Seren had never really noticed the lack of muscle in the slaves and their hollowed cheeks. The thin hair and downcast eyes. She hated herself.

Her own ancestors had been slaves. Being partially mountain blood, they'd had to serve until someone apprenticed them. Then, the next generation had worked their short, rough lives trying to earn enough silver to remove caste bells and move up to middle. They'd failed. She remembered what Father had told her long, long ago. It'd taken her family four generations to become high caste and that was partially luck. Father had impressed the kyros during a feigned training battle during his time as a base-level fighter and he'd been moved up quickly. Father had always claimed it had less to do with himself than the fact that the kyros had been in a good mood that day because he had just learned his wife was pregnant with Meric's younger brother, Varol.

Some of these slaves and low-castes had fought for Akhayma when she'd ordered the warriors to give out weapons to anyone who would fight. And now, here they were, in the same poor position as before. Given little to no respect. The cost to remove a bell didn't seem high to her, but she'd always been high-caste, through her father's work as a high ranking general. Maybe the cost was more significant than she'd thought. And if it was, that wasn't right. If a person was willing to fight, willing to work, they should be treated the same as anyone else.

Anger surged through Seren, hot and unforgiving. Anger at herself and everyone else who'd participated in this for so long. She knew the Empire treated people better than the Northern Isle folk, but it still wasn't right.

Tonight, she'd demand the removal of every slave's metal belt-and-bell contraption.

She'd heard that Jakobden's new amir had done the same, with Meric's reluctant permission, made only because Jakobden was an odd, but highly profitable little corner of the Empire.

And war or no war, Adem or no Adem, she couldn't stomach that part of the Empire's traditions any longer. The metal bell belts were leaving. Tonight. And the cost of removing a caste bell, the price of moving up in the Empire would be lowered. She could call up the scribe. Have it announced at the feast. Maybe it would go over since everyone was simply relieved at having lived through the attack.

9

ONA

"Not so kingly now, are you?"

Ona sneered through the bars at the Invaders' king as Lucca walked down the slope separating the training field from the line of cells to join them. Mud caked the king's once shining hair and the new day's heat pulled his stink into the air.

"Muddy as the pig you are." Maybe he wouldn't understand what with her Silvanian accent and all. She gave him a very specific gesture to ensure he picked up her meaning.

Lucca knocked a knuckle against the king's bars. "Ona. That isn't polite."

"I didn't intend politeness," she said, switching to their own language.

"I suppose as long as you don't run him through before Seren and Adem do what they want, you can have your fun." He looked at Ona. "He'll probably need to keep most of his limbs for now."

She plucked her knife from her sash and reached an arm through the bars. The king's dark eyes moved, but aside from that he remained utterly still, sitting in the mud with his hands and feet bound like a Silvanian slave. She'd done the binding herself after the battle late last night. She ran the tip of the blade up his cheek and pressed lightly into the soft flesh beneath his eye.

"Eyes aren't limbs. He doesn't really need two of these, does he, Lucca?"

"I'd say one works well enough for the dirty work his kind do. But Seren might not like you damaging the hard-earned loot."

Ona's knife bit into him and a speck of blood appeared. He didn't flinch. She pressed a little harder. "They're ugly eyes anyway."

"You think so?" Lucca crossed his arms. "I think he's rather good looking. Different from us. Different from the many kinds of people here. But yes. Definitely a fine looking man."

"Are you going to fall for every foreigner you meet now?"

Lucca's eyes widened and his nostrils flared.

Ona shrugged. "He doesn't know what we're saying."

Lucca's jaw tensed. He spun and walked away. Ona sighed and returned her dagger to her belt.

"A Silvanian, hm?" The king said perfectly. In Silvanian.

Her heart tripled its pace. Maybe he hadn't fully understood her comment about Lucca and loving foreigners. And even if he did, he could never guess it was Seren Lucca seemed to be interested in.

The king closed his eyes. "I appreciate your people's talent with paint."

Everything in Ona's view, except the man's face, went white.

"I saw a young man who could craft a fresco so true to life that I would've sworn the birds he made could take flight right off the wall," he said.

Ona threw herself against the bars, sword out. Hands pulled her back. Shaking, she turned to see two of Seren's guards—Erol and his never-ending scowl and Hossam with that mop of hair. Cansu must've been injured or somewhere resting.

Seren adjusted the tie at her forehead and the bell there shot the sun back at Ona.

"Come, friend," Seren said quietly, gaze flashing to the king and back. "We should celebrate our success."

"But he—"

She looked directly into Ona's eyes. "I know. Believe me. I know. But we can't do anything about it yet. We have to be wise." One of her hands went to the wool on her sash. "Let's go to the feast."

The king laughed and they both turned.

Seren frowned. "What is so amusing? I don't think, in your position, you'd have much to laugh about."

He shook his head, looking down at his bound feet, and said something in his own language.

Seren stiffened. She turned and started off, her feet moving fast. Erol and Hossam trailed her.

"What did he say?" Ona said as she caught up.

"Merely a slur. I won't repeat it. It's some sort of cultural insult."

Ona gave her a look.

"Fine. He spoke metaphorically, but I think the intent had to do with a squirrel instigating the act of love with a lion," she whispered, making sure the guards couldn't hear.

Ona snorted. "That sounds difficult."

The wrinkles between Seren's eyes smoothed. "It would have to be. At least for the squirrel."

"She'd end up as dinner rather than lover."

"But now that I think on it, he used the female term for lion. He said *lioness*."

"She won't be bothered much then. Doubt she'd even notice his tiny intentions."

Seren pressed a hand over her eyes.

"Are you really going to ask for a ransom? Or was that only a ploy to get his men to back down? Or was that just Sweet Bean having some fun with the pigs?"

"Sweet Bean?"

"That's what I call General Adem."

Seren's face was priceless. "No, you don't."

"I do. Just in private."

Behind us, Erol and Hossam laughed quietly.

Seren cleared her throat. "General Adem already sent a message concerning the ransom. It includes a demand for silver and that all Invaders return to their own borders."

"I suppose it makes sense. Might as well get the silver coin to go with all the trouble." The Empire wouldn't have to actually release him. They could just get the silver and then kill everyone in sight, including the king. It was a smart plan.

"These raiders have sent us so many refugees," Seren said. "We need to build onto the city."

"You shouldn't have to. The bastards should leave people to their homes."

Ona's jaw pinched as she ground her teeth together. Her bones pressed against the leather and metal of her sword as she gripped it tight, wishing that foul king's warm blood covered her hand. Like a Northern witch's healing symbol, it'd dull the pain in her body and heart, she was sure of it.

"But they haven't," Seren said. "So we have to move forward."

"I'll move forward when every last one of them is bleeding at our feet."

"Even their children?" Seren's pretty, green-dusted eyes grew sad.

"They didn't spare me any horror and I was still hanging on to childhood when they came."

"And they didn't spare my two sisters."

"Is that why you keep that piece of wool? To remember them?"

Seren's eyes filled, but she fought off the tears. "This is from the skirt I wore when the...attack happened. It's the last thing my little sisters touched."

Ona let her feet lead her toward the guest tent. She felt detached. "I'm sorry for what you lost, Seren." But she wasn't sorry about young Invaders. They'd only grow up to be the same kind who'd killed Ona's aunt.

Maybe Seren needed to hear another story about the Invaders. Taking a breath, she began.

"My parents died when I was a baby. I lived with my aunt. She was a fresco artist." Ona's gaze softened. "Her fingers were always so cold...but her heart... Her villa was filled with the goats no one wanted. And the runts from every dog's litter in town. The place reeked of piss, but it was home."

Seren grew very quiet. Ona's cheeks burned and her words came fast and quiet.

"I was working with her when they came," Ona said, almost whispering. "The warning—the town bell—it wasn't nearly

early enough to do anything. I still had my palette knife in my hand when they burst through the door. They bashed the animals' heads. They cut my aunt down like a beast at market."

Seren glanced at her, face quiet. Ona searched for pity. There was only a shared sadness and anger. Ona swallowed and continued.

"My cousin had taught me about knife-fighting. The back streets of our town were not as nice as yours here. Without a thought, without even knowing what I was doing, I rammed my painting knife up and under one of the Invader's ribs when his back was turned."

Her weapon hand coiled up, ready to strike.

"Before the other man could kill me, their leader called them back. I watched the man I'd stabbed bleed to death from his mouth. His foul blood mixed with my aunt's on the stone floor. I swore that day I'd see them all dead. All of them."

Seren stopped. She touched Ona's elbow. "We will end this. Together."

"You have to tell everyone about the Fire. About how you saw them coming. Adem needs to do what you say." It was amazing what she could do. She needed to be in charge here. Not Sweet Bean and his moods and dangerous traditions.

Hossam and Erol didn't say a word, but they had to have heard Ona. If Seren wouldn't accept her role, her very obvious calling to rise up and use the special talents she had to fight the Invaders, maybe their gossip could force her into it. It couldn't hurt. It could only help. If she was considered blessed or what- ever, Adem wouldn't be able to get mad at her for hiding Meric's death either, would he? Ona doubted it.

They walked in silence, the city's colors blending into the blue and red of early evening. Men in blue-striped kaftans led a line of camels. Three boys pulled a cartload of newly forged swords, their iron black and silver and promising. This city controlled the best iron ore in the world. Under the sands and arid plains, the makings of so many weapons waited to be molded. Ona took a deep, cleansing breath. It was good to stand atop such a place of power with the woman who would soon be in control of it all.

Seren wasn't really going to give the king back. She wouldn't. Not after the talk they'd just had. That was key. She was only faking to get the silver to build up the city for all the refugees. That was fine. It was smart.

The main tent, where every noble and their brother seemed to be laughing away, rose up in front of Ona and Seren, blacking most of the sunset sky.

Ona smiled as Seren took a breath.

It was time for her to claim her place. *Only hope Sweet Bean won't get in the way,* Ona thought as they pushed into the tent to join the celebration.

10

SEREN

eren's breath stuck in her throat. A double line of nobles, ore masters, advisors, and fighters created a corridor inside the main tent, under the flickering oil lamps and moonlit star shapes fitted into the ceiling. Seeing her, they stomped their feet on the thick rugs and shouted for her.

Her heart stood still.

"Blessed!"

"Pearl of the Desert has saved us!"

"Chosen! The Fire has chosen you!"

"Kyros Seren!"

The tent glowed all the more. The woven walls Seren knew so well were both brighter and darker—the black, white, red, and blue contrasting brilliantly. The patchouli and ginger Meekra had added to Seren's hair wash rose into the air. She smelled like a kyros. Her kaftan was the darkest black and embroidered with silver phoenixes, a kyros's kaftan. But though the cheers and beauty of it all warmed Seren, she still didn't feel like a kyros. She was an imposter, like a girl wearing her mother's shoes and trying not to trip.

"I'm not k—" she started, but Ona grabbed her arm gently.

"Take the title, my lady." Ona's grin sharpened. "You can do so much more with it and Sweet Bean won't be able to touch you. No matter what he finds out."

Seren's face grew too hot then. "He could still do much," she whispered before raising her hands to the gathering. Barir was there, next to Meekra. His face was bright as a star as he nodded.

"Thank you," Seren said, trying to sound calm and sure.

She did want to be who she was supposed to be. But this wasn't going to be simple. It was dangerous. She was breaking all sorts of traditions. According to her sources, Adem was finishing up injured warrior counts with the kaptan charged with overseeing the medical procedures. He would be here soon if he wasn't already. She craned her neck, trying to see further into the crowd.

"Thank you all," she said, pushing her worry away for the moment. At the Holy Fire bowl, she said a quick, but fervent prayer, then turned to face her people. "You saved us. All of Akhayma joined together to save ourselves. I'm just blessed to be a part of it."

Like her thoughts had called him up, Adem stepped out of gathering, face grim. Seren swallowed.

"So. You saw a vision in the Fire."

It didn't sound like a question. It was an accusation. He thought she was lying. No surprise there.

"I-I did."

"Even though you have no royal blood. You are the first to see a vision in centuries."

Seren swallowed.

"And you believe you should hold the title of *kyros* in Kyros Meric's absence?"

"I think I have to." She clasped her shaking hands. "The Fire showed me taking up his royal kaftan."

Qadira and a few other nobles murmured things like "See?" and "It's a miracle."

Adem's left eyebrow twitched. His lips parted, but he didn't say a word. With a bow, he disappeared into the crowd.

Seren stared at the spot where he'd been as the tent filled with conversation.

Lucca appeared, smiling at Ona and Seren. His face still glowed from battle. He seemed more alive. "May I escort you to your table, Kyros Seren?"

"I will never get used to that title."

She looked into Lucca's face, glad that the person who had her arm was someone who knew all her secrets and still respected her. His hair was wild and his eyes, too. It was like she was really seeing him for the first time. He was different from other men. Rough-edged but lovely. Strong, patient, humble—thrown together in a wonderful mix. All his movements spoke of strength and grace and a restrained wildness. There was a flutter in her stomach and it was a wonderful departure from what she'd been feeling lately.

"Thank you for everything you've done for me so far and I truly hope this horrible set of events have ended and we will be at peace and you and Ona can finish training with our fighters because the way you moved today in battle was breath-taking and you practically glowed. Did you know you lit up like that?

Can you feel that?" She sucked a breath, face flaming. She was a babbling idiot.

But Lucca simply smiled. A dimple appeared in his cheek. "You impressed me today too, Kyros Seren. Congratulations on the triumph." He kissed her hand and his hair brushed her wrist.

Her skin tingled. Heat spread down her arm and into her body.

Adem walked up to the high table and took his seat like he hadn't challenged her in front of everyone.

Seren gave him a tight smile as the musicians took up their instruments.

Lucca gave Seren a look that said *Do you want me to stay?* and Seren shook her head.

"Go enjoy some time with Ona and the other kaptans," she said.

With a low bow, Lucca walked away. At the other table, he said something to Ona and she threw her head back to laugh, the oil lamps lighting her cheeks.

They'd made this horror less of one. Seren didn't know what she would've done without Meekra, her guards, and them. She was grateful for their courage, loyalty, their ability to shift and move with what had to be done. She could never be Chosen without them, she thought, smiling sadly to herself.

Barir waved to Meekra and slipped away, probably going back to his patients. He was a good, good man.

Seren relaxed into her chair, determined to ignore Adem— Sweet Bean, she thought, grinning—and his scowling. This was where she belonged, in the middle of her friends and those she considered family. At last, Seren felt...complete.

The white-haired *riqq* player stood and held the goat-skin

drum with both hands, his fingers starting a rolling rhythm like a fast heartbeat. The metal discs along the riqq's sides clinked together like dropped coins. A man with a large nose lifted a polished oud to his chest and plucked the strings as only an expert could. All around, feet tapped under kaftans and tunics.

Soon as the music lessened, Seren would thank everyone for their courage today, and she'd make the announcement about the slaves and the caste bells.

A raucous group of warriors beside Lucca burst into a traditional song, drumming their fists against the wood in a double and triple sort of beat.

"The water rose and called them,
To the plains they came,
For yellow fruits and sun-warmed skin
Days without war and wanting."

Their voices, male and female, twisted together in a clashing set of notes that painted the scene inside Seren's mind. A mountain accent and several Akhayma natives' lilts blended beautifully.

"So spin your wife and daughter,
Twirl your husband and your son,
Bring your spark and feel your heart
Beat and sing for the promise of the plains!"

Loving the chaos of the instruments and the professional musicians mixed with the impromptu singing, Seren closed her eyes. The happy sounds spilled over her and cleaned out the thoughts of battle, of blood, and the horrible things she'd done, at least for a moment.

A soft voice startled her. "Sorry," Lucca said. "If you want me to leave you alone, I will." She opened her eyes to see him bent at the waist, mouth quirked into a smile that made her heart tumble.

She straightened, hands suddenly sweaty on the chair's arms. "Of course not. What is it?"

"I know it's risky. I know we're in the middle of a war. But I wondered if you'd like to participate in the musical mess happening there?" He shrugged toward the tent's center where nobles and merchants, advisors and kaptans, lifted hands and feet to the beat of the music.

On the outskirts of the jumble, Ona twisted like a column of smoke, her hips drawing a good bit of attention from the fighters nearby.

"I can't dance with you." Everyone would see and as far as they knew, she was still married.

"No, I'm a terrible dancer. I do however play the ocarina." He produced an odd, almost oval-shaped...thing with holes. A green glaze shone along its sloped edges. "It's a folk flute from Silvania. And I could teach you how to play."

Dancing wouldn't work, but learning an instrument? Surely none would take offense to that. Not in the middle of this wild feast.

Smiling, she moved away from the table, checking quickly to see that Adem was busy talking to an ore master. The master's black hood was pulled away from his face. Both men wore serious faces, but they weren't looking at her.

She trailed Lucca to his table, stopping here and there to greet people.

Izzet came up to her, big eyes glistening. "I want to thank you again, Kyros Seren." She grinned wide at the new title. "For everything."

"Did you finish weaving that green fertility ring for the blanket?" Seren asked.

Meekra's sister was about to come of age and Seren had pulled together a group of girls—all around the same age as Seren—to weave the ritual blanket. It'd been difficult to say the least, convincing the high and middle castes to work with the low. The low-castes, like Izzet, had been scared as kittens at first, jumping at every one of Qadira's snooty commands. But with a little coaxing from Seren, a few jokes from Meekra, and some well-placed comments from high-caste Najwa, the group had settled into a rhythm.

"We did!" Izzet's smile was contagious. "It looks beautiful. I hope she likes it, my kyros."

"She will. You're truly skilled at weaving. If I can talk the Azjorr's weaver into taking you on as an apprentice, would you like that?"

Izzet clapped her hands, then looked nervously at Erol, who'd come closer to make sure all was well with Seren. "That would be perfect," Izzet said, reining her excitement in.

Lucca turned to see what had kept Seren. She waved to Izzet, then hurried to catch up with him.

Greeting Ona with a nod, Lucca sat on a high stool and cupped the ocarina between his large hands. The instrument was a bright green, a lot like the weaving Izzet had worked on. It caught the light and shone like Lucca held an emerald. He blew softly. Mellow, low notes floated from the instrument and turned a few heads nearby. Lucca's eyes shuttered as his song spun toward the draped ceiling, high and straining and lovely. The notes plunged into something deep and dangerous and quite fast. Seren's heart matched the rhythm and she allowed herself to imagine dancing with Lucca.

He'd give the ocarina to Ona and begin circling Seren with slow steps like a hunter. Seren would lift her hands and bend them at the wrists, back and forth and back again, sharp and quick, as she looked Lucca in the eye. She would be the symbol of Fire. As the music grew more complicated, he would move his arms down and out in smooth motions, simulating the rhythm of a hunter's horse galloping. Normally, one would need to be solemn, but Lucca would definitely grin slyly as his circle around her tightened. Soon, he'd be so close that she'd have to raise her arms over her head to keep her movements correct. His hand would brush her side and she'd shiver. Her arm would graze his shoulder and they'd bump together a little, laughing.

Seren put a hand to her cheek, feeling warm.

Ona leaned in, whispering. "Seren, Seren, Seren. If you ogle him like that, don't expect him not to come after you when everyone's gone to bed."

Heart pounding, Seren's mouth popped open. Lucca lingered on a discordant sound that was oddly pleasant and goosebumps flickered over Seren's arms.

Lowering the ocarina, Lucca looked up, eyes warm. "Want to give it a try, Kyros Seren?"

"She definitely does," Ona said quietly, smirking.

Seren reached out a hand. She copied the way he'd held it, positioning the first four fingers of each hand over the larger holes on the top.

He hissed a little and grimaced. "Not so rough, my lady. It's an instrument, not a weapon."

Ona laughed and elbowed Seren. "That's my girl." She laughed again.

Seren grinned, not entirely sure what Ona meant but glad to

make her smile.

"Like this." Lucca was suddenly very close, his mouth mere inches from Seren's and his breath sweet from the mint he'd chewed. Black stubble lined his strong chin and darkened the dip below his nose. His lips looked soft and she wondered how they would—

He took her fingers in his and goosebumps rose, tingling and warm, along her arms again. His gaze wandered from their hands to her arms, then back again, some emotion she couldn't name moving his mouth into a half-grin. Gently, he posed her fingertips on the ocarina.

"Keep your fingers curled," he said, his dark amber eyes glowing, "sitting just heavy enough to close the opening." Seren couldn't stop looking at Lucca's mouth. Her whole face went hot. He smelled so good. "Keep them ready to leap away to form new notes." Thankfully, he didn't seem to notice how bizarre she felt around him.

Seren nodded at his directions, not trusting herself to talk. She felt like a young girl around a first crush instead of a widow and a kyros. Another miracle.

When her hands were in place, Lucca continued. "Now blow out with a sound like *too*. And lift a finger one by one, starting from here, on your right."

Her notes were nothing like his, but they were simple and pretty and she found herself pulling the instrument away and smiling like a fool.

"You did well!" Lucca nudged Ona with his foot and set her to stomping in praise, an indulgent look on Ona's heart-shaped face. "You can be more gentle with the mouthpiece too. You don't need to bite it."

Ona erupted into laughter, and Seren had the distinct

feeling she was missing something. Lucca glared, and Ona threw an arm over her mouth. Once again, Seren was a little lost, but it wasn't so bad. Being lost with Lucca was actually very pleasant.

Meekra appeared at Seren's shoulder.

"Kyros Seren," Meekra whispered, her pensive gaze on Ona. "General Adem left the tent."

"Did he tell anyone where he was going?"

"He headed toward his tent. With those two ore masters that hang on his every word."

Ona had taken the ocarina from Lucca and had it on her head and was swiveling her hips. "Queen of the Squawking Horn Pipe," she sang.

"You look seriously intelligent right now, Ona," Lucca said dryly. "Gentle folk," he held out a hand, "look upon my proud war sister, Onaratta Sings like Dying Dog."

Seren almost laughed, but Meekra was wringing her hands and was right to worry. "If you see him, tell me. If you hear anything, let me know right away. Please double check the guards are in place at the back entrance to my chamber."

Meekra nodded and slipped back into the dancing and joking, disappearing into colored kaftans, flushed faces, and the smoke billowing from Seren's chambers.

Lucca grabbed the ocarina from Ona, an indulgent look on his face, then began to play. Ona grinned at Seren—Seren had never known smiles could be aggressive but Ona managed it— and linked their arms, pulling Seren into a dance.

Ona sang in Silvanian, something about daggers and eyes, and Seren lifted her hem and moved her feet in time, trying to keep up until Erol walked up with Seren's bow in hand.

"I think we should have a contest, my lady." Erol scowled,

but it was his happy scowl. Seren was fairly certain his face didn't really know how to not scowl.

"Archery here? In the tent?"

Erol nodded and gestured toward a barca set up in the corner beside Hossam and Cansu. The leather target's decorative bells twinkled in the lamps' light.

Ona rubbed her hands together. "This'll be fun. Eh, Lucca, you need to be a part of this."

Lucca lowered the ocarina and eyed the target. "If you insist, Onaratta. And if it pleases you, Kyros Seren."

He dipped his head at Seren and her body felt lighter, like she was made of light and shadow instead of flesh, like a breeze might lift her and take her away. Her worries and fears couldn't settle on her shoulders. They slipped right through her and she let herself enjoy the feel of it.

"Definitely. Just know that I'm going to beat you, Lucca Hand of Ruination."

"He is pretty good, Kyros," Ona muttered.

"And so am I." Seren took her bow from Erol as he raised his voice.

"Nobles, war brothers and sisters, friends and respected guests, please clear the aisle. Kyros Seren, the Blessed, the Chosen One, is about to start an archery contest!"

"What is the prize, Blessed One?" Qadira called out, her perfect eyebrows lifting. She smirked at Seren, most likely hoping she'd make a fool of herself.

Seren spotted Kaptan Rashiel in the audience. He'd helped Meric with the contest on her wedding day and was the type that got along with everyone.

"Kaptan Rashiel!" The man turned his head, then quickly put his cup down and stood, smoothing his military kaftan. "What should be the prize for this impromptu archery contest? I'm entering so it's not right that I choose the winner's gift."

Ona whispered to Lucca and wiggled her hips as she eyed Rashiel. Lucca's fingers drifted over his sly smile and Seren had to drag her attention back to Rashiel.

Rashiel cocked his head, thinking. "Noshu's colt?"

Seren smiled at the mention of Fig's mother, Noshu. She'd given birth to a lovely ebony colt with a fine head just eight days ago. "Perfect, Kaptan Rashiel. But whoever earns this prize must promise never to sell him. Fig will want her half-brother nearby."

Lucca grinned as servants brought in several bows and a lashed bundle of arrows. Blue and black fletching brightened the ends of each one and new steel heads gleamed from the tips.

Ona's eyes shone and she mumbled something about the horse and Seren's demand. "You are kind, Chosen One," she said, louder now. "Too kind."

"Why don't you go first, Erol?" Seren lifted a hand toward him.

With what passed as a pleased look for Erol, he took three arrows from a servant's hand, raised a bow to aim and spread his feet. One, two, and three flashed across the tent. Two near the bull's eye and one a little right. The room stomped feet in praise.

Erol nodded his head and stepped aside. Three more fighters and a scribe lined up to give the contest a try.

Lucca handed Seren a stick of minted lamb, which she took and gobbled up quickly, happy to have her appetite back.

"The scribe's not bad." Lucca's eyebrows lifted.

"But not as good as you."

The corner of his mouth moved. He shrugged in what Seren

was learning was a very Lucca-like movement. It meant *yes, but I'd rather not say it aloud and seem prideful.* He held his three arrows, his thumb smoothing the first one's fletching as he leaned against the lotus pillar. She pressed her back against the pillar too, her arm brushing his. Warmth from his olive-toned skin rushed through the point of contact and suddenly her heart was beating too quickly.

"Think you can beat me?" Seren swallowed and stared at the phoenix on the tip of her shoe. Its rosestone eyes seemed to blink in the flickering light. Lucca wasn't answering, so she raised her head.

He'd turned to face her, his deep, reddish-brown eyes hot. "I won't insult you by not trying my best, my kyros."

Shivers rode down her back though she wasn't sure why. She wanted to say thank you or make some clever quip, but her mouth didn't want to work.

He leaned closer. The collar of his green brigantine vest rucked up a little. It rubbed the side of his neck and trapped a strand of his thick, shoulder-length hair. Without thinking, she reached toward him, slipped her thumb under his collar and straightened it. His nostrils flared in surprise, his lips just inches away and his gaze burning into her eyes as she pulled away. She could still feel the softness of his brigantine, the heat in his skin, the strength simmering under his restraint.

"If you want…" she said, his breath mingling with hers. "We could maybe…"

His fingers danced over her closest hand, glancing to see if anyone was watching, then moved back the slightest step. His throat bobbed once, from the hollow at the base all the way to the slope under his jawline. Chest moving up and down, he whispered, "If this is your strategy to make me lose the contest, it's a good one."

"I wouldn't—"

He interrupted with a teasing smile. "I know. I was joking. But we should laugh. I should walk away. This archery contest is about to turn into a display of my longing for you, and I don't think that would be beneficial to either of us—past the point of pleasure, anyway."

Joy spread arms wide inside Seren and she felt like she was falling, but in a good way. Breathless. Free. Untethered.

She was about to argue for him to stay, but Meekra appeared beside Rashiel, her face drawn and pale as she approached, a warning in the coiled tension of her clasped hands and tight jaw.

"Kyros Seren," she started.

Adem walked up behind Seren and Lucca made a noise like a growl.

"Pearl of the Desert," Adem said quietly, the fires' light cutting across his eyes.

Seren nearly dropped her bow.

Turning, she saw Adem had brought two men, black bags in hand. Not ore masters this time. These were physicians.

Seren's heart clenched and stopped. This was the end.

11

SEREN

A dem had brought physicians to evaluate Meric's condition. Seren was going to be sick.

Extending a palm to the physicians, Adem addressed the room, "In my great concern for Kyros Meric, I've brought two physicians, fresh from a long rest. Thank you for the opportunity, Pearl of the Desert. Welcome, good men. This way, please."

Completely ignoring Seren's open mouth and the permission she definitely, absolutely had not given him, he led the physicians toward Seren's chamber. Hossam and Cansu stood guard. They seemed petrified, completely unable to move, their gazes cutting to Seren. The brightly painted archery target beside them looked completely cheerful and completely out of place.

Seren's hands shook. "What is this?" Heading toward Adem, she bumped a table sharply with her knee. Pain leeched up her

ALISHA KLAPHEKE

leg and she wished for what felt like the thousandth time that she was graceful and confident like Ona, like Lucca, like Meekra, like Barir, like everyone around her but herself. She fisted her hands around her scrap of green wool, frustrated that she couldn't seem to raise her voice and take hold of the situation. She would die. Meekra would be implicated. Barir would definitely die. They would be beaten to death. Probably tonight. And left in a ditch outside the city walls, rubbish to fall under Invader boots.

"Go on in, physicians." Adem wasn't even paying attention to her. Like he hadn't heard her.

"No." Her voice wasn't nearly loud enough.

The first physician stepped away from the door, but the second put a hand to the wood. They hadn't heard her. Lucca was at her elbow, Ona too. She could feel their hot rage on her behalf. Meekra joined them and whispered a prayer under her breath.

They gave Seren the strength to speak up.

"I said *stop!*"

The second physician shoved the door open.

Hossam drew his dagger. He thrust the weapon into the man's side.

Adem had his own blade to Hossam's throat before Seren could say a word.

She grabbed Ona to keep from falling.

"Stop," Seren whispered, everything moving too quickly. "All of you. Stop!"

Adem's physician dropped to his knees and clutched at his side. Blood pooled around his slim fingers.

Hossam looked from Adem to Seren, panic stinting his

116

words. "The physician disobeyed you, Kyros Seren. It isn't a fatal wound. At least...I didn't intend to kill him. I—he disobeyed, my kyros."

The injured physician slumped all the way to the carpets where he lay with arms outstretched and face white, his bag by his side. His associate, lips pulled back in a grimace, kneeled beside his limp body.

The physician was dead.

Seren's order had killed an innocent man. Not an Invader. Not an enemy or a criminal. A physician who probably had a family, children, a life. Bile rose in Seren's throat and she fought to stay standing, her legs trembling.

At Hossam's throat, Adem's arm twitched.

It wouldn't take but one small move to end Hossam's life. His broad smile would be gone. His fierce loyalty.

"This is not how tradition mandates," Adem snapped. "No matter how ill the kyros is. This is not how we run the Empire."

She had to be strong. To be the kyros. If not, Hossam was going to die right now. *Holy Fire, help me.*

She drew herself up and let go of Ona, who gave her arm an encouraging squeeze.

"General Adem. My husband's health is my business first." Her voice didn't sound like her own. It wasn't nearly strong enough. Confidence didn't glow from the tone like Ona or Lucca's words always did. But maybe pretending to feel it would fix some of this horror. "This is how *I* run this Empire. You had better get used to it."

Adem stared into Hossam's chest, not meeting Seren's eyes.

He would order her arrest. There was no way this would work. He had history behind him, years and years of only strong royal blood ruling like she was trying to do. He'd never swallow her sad attempt at authority.

But slowly, slowly he lowered his weapon.

Hossam took a breath, his bushy beard moving as he worked to keep his face from showing anything. What did he feel? Anger at Seren for putting him in that position? She wouldn't blame him. This was a mess. A tragic mess.

Still not meeting her eyes, Adem barked commands to remove the poor man's body, bowed to Seren, then left the feast with two ore masters whose draping cloaks followed them like spilled ink.

It had worked. She'd done it. She'd taken command over Adem. She was kyros. A shiver rocked her, but she held her chin high. Now if she could just feel right about it. If she could be confident in this…

Ona's grin could've swallowed a world. Lucca relaxed against a pillar, arms crossed, nodding like he'd expected her to succeed all along. Meekra's eyes shone with tears and she touched her family ring, probably thinking of her father, Barir, and how he was the first to tell Seren she was blessed.

"Meekra," Seren whispered. "Please quietly let Lucca and Ona know that I need them to come to my personal chambers after the feast. If they're willing."

"What about the quarantine? Won't someone question them coming in?"

"I'll simply bring them in and do what must be done. We don't have time to worry about someone reporting it to Adem. I've jumped past the line of what is dangerous anyway. I have to smooth out the mess I've made. We'll keep Erol, Cansu, and Hossam only at the doors. I'll send the rest of the guards on errands. Oh, please get more ka'ud ointment from your father.

We'll need a lot of cloths that we can burn…after we finish what we need to do. And a burial shroud. Can you get your sisters to help you gather everything? Am I asking too much?"

"I know what we must do. You don't have to explain anything. And no, you could never ask too much of me, Blessed Pearl, my kyros. I would give my life for you. For Akhayma. For the Empire."

Meekra bent her head and looked up at Seren through thick, black lashes. Seren knew very well she'd be lost without her.

Seren rubbed a palm over her friend's silver rings. No words would be enough, but she needed to say them anyway. "Thank you for your courage. I'd be lost without you." She squeezed Meekra's hand and Meekra squeezed back. The corner of Meekra's lips lifted despite the fear flickering through her eyes. "If at any point, you can't do this," Seren said, "you don't want to be a part of this, you go. Go back to your family's tent."

"I will never, ever leave you, my lady." Meekra's voice was almost a growl. Seren imagined her as a mother desert lion, watching over her cubs. "Never."

Seren hugged her, breathing in her comforting scent of olive oil and soaps, and went back to the high table.

The table of district heads turned, faces lined with worry. Clan Azjorr's chieftain sat very still beside the waterworks district's head. They had paused their seemingly deep conversation. The man she was looking for huddled with the records keepers, every one of them squinting to see, their eyes weak from years spent pouring over scrolls.

"Scribe?"

The man scurried over, back hunched a little, but face bright and intelligent. "My lady? I, I mean, my kyros?"

"As of this day, the Empire will no longer enslave those

captured in battle or foreigners who wish to live in the Empire. The Empire will no longer take a *volunteer*," Seren sneered at the word because they were no such thing, "from every border town so said town may rule with their own local customs. We will take true volunteers into our army and reward them so that they will come of their own free will. Foreigners will be low-caste, but the cost of bell removal will be halved."

The district heads erupted into questions, polite but demanding. No one dared disagree openly but their unhappiness with her decree showed in their faces. Seren held up her palms and they quieted.

"The only reason we eat here today instead of bleeding to death under Invader boots, the only reason we hold the Invader king and are about to accept a sizable sum of silver and the surrender of our enemies is because every caste gave blood—slave, low-caste, all—to fight. Together, we protected our city and our Empire. And now, we will respect one another and live to fight another day."

Almost everyone in the tent stood and most stomped their feet in praise, drowning the district heads' questions. Meekra ordered household staff around the tent to help slaves remove bells outside and called in the criers to spread the word to the city. The scribe went to his pedestal in the corner to record her pronouncement.

There were pockets of those who narrowed their eyes at Seren and whispered behind heavily ringed hands. The head of the waterworks district raised his voice, but Clan Azjorr's chieftain shoved him back into his chair, shutting the man up.

"She saw a vision, fool. She is blessed!" The chieftain turned and bowed deeply. "May we all learn to be as merciful as you, Blessed Pearl."

Seren's hand went to her chest, swallowing. She felt like she was at the edge of a cliff, toes barely hanging on. The music started up again, and she slipped into her smoke-filled chambers to wait for the others to arrive so they could take Meric from his temporary resting place under the ground beneath the rugs, and pretend that he had just died. Ka'ud had thoroughly soaked the air and every fabric in the chamber. Hopefully, it would hold when the body was unburied.

At the archery target, bows, and arrows were swept out of the tent by those wise enough to know the contest wasn't going to happen now. Seren leaned against the lotus tower's cool stone and sighed. Her bones were too tired for somebody so young.

AFTER THE FEAST, when the main tent emptied, Seren sent all the guards except her own to see to the release of the slaves and be sure their names were recorded in the books and their new low-caste bells attached to their sashes.

Meekra still hadn't returned with the ka'ud ointment when Lucca appeared at the back door, his slightly curly, black hair shining in the sunlight and his dark eyes serious. He put his hands on his wide, leather belt, then crossed them, then clasped them.

"I'm here to help. In any way you need, Kyros Seren."

Despite his obvious worry and nervousness—which was completely understandable—something about his presence made her feel like she'd taken a step back from that imagined cliff's edge.

"Thank you. You...know what we have to do?"

"Yes." His voice was dark.

"Then let's do it quickly and never talk about it again." Her stomach knotted as she removed her outer kaftan, rolling her shirt sleeves up. "Is Ona coming?"

Ona herself answered as she slipped in. "Yes, she is." She smiled sadly and patted Seren on the back roughly. Seren didn't think she meant to be rough. It was just Ona's way.

They used the same two bowls as before to dig up Meric's body.

Death's scent ghosted from the wrappings as they brought him up. The subtle odor clung to their damp skin as they brushed the dirt away from the fabric. With the ka'ud smoking, they peeled back the wrappings, and with wet cloths, cleaned Seren's former husband's face, hands, and feet. Not too much of the sandy earth dirtied his clothing, but it had sneaked into his ears and around his hairline. Touching him, even through the cloth, sent shudders rippling through her. She'd never forget the feel of his dead flesh, the stillness of his chest and eyes.

Lucca helped to lift him onto the bed and clear away the last of the dirt.

"Kyros?" Meekra's voice streamed through the door.

Seren's heart jerked like an arrow had struck her back. "Come in. No one saw you? Followed you?"

"I don't think so." Meekra held a stack of cut cloth, a shroud, and a crockery tub tied with twine. "Everyone is too worried about themselves right now. And all anyone wants to talk about is you freeing the slaves. Some of the nobles are angry. They'll have to pay their workers now. All of them, Blessed Pearl."

"I'll meet with the district heads soon. We'll figure out some solutions together. Maybe by then Adem will have accepted things the way they are."

Seren took the crock from her with careful hands and a whispered prayer, like this was a part of Meric's funeral. She hadn't loved him. But he had been her husband. And everyone, no matter how they acted, deserved at least a little respect in death. She dipped fingers into the translucent mixture and smoothed it over Meric's eyelids, cheeks, hooked nose, thin lips.

With a look that asked permission, Ona reached for the crock and Seren nodded. Ona took a portion and ran it along Meric's forearms and hands.

Meekra, showing her skills as the daughter of a physician, expertly wrapped Meric from his feet to the crown of his head, securing the strips of linen with more ointment.

Seren scrubbed her hands in a bowl of cold water. Lucca stood with his arms crossed over his chest, staring at Meric's body.

"What was he like?" he asked quietly.

Goosebumps drifted over Seren's arms. "He was..." She didn't want to speak ill of the dead.

Ona laughed without any humor and put her feet on the floor. "Your face says it all."

"Meric didn't respect me. He ignored almost all of the ideas the Holy Fire gave me and he shouted often. Even though nothing he was angry about was ever my fault. He was mercurial."

"He was a horse's back end," Ona said.

Lucca made an indeterminate noise.

Erol cracked the door open, but kept his gaze on Seren. He had to know everything that was going on. All of her guards did. Thankfully, they were steady as rock, unwavering in their position. "Kyros Seren. We have news. The Invaders are here. A small party with a cart and what appears to be a trunk of silver."

Closing her eyes, Seren breathed deeply. "The ransom." Then she looked at Lucca, who held himself silent as a memory, his eyes giving her that same feeling, that illusion of safety in this dangerous, dangerous world.

Ona clapped a hand on Seren's shoulder. "We better get our units ready. Just in case." With a wink, she was out the door.

On his way out, Lucca touched Seren's arm. A tingling warmth pooled under his fingertips, heating Seren's skin like his touch was another kind of healing balm.

"I will be by your side. I will keep eyes on Adem."

"Why are you so loyal to me?" A touch of guilt twinged inside her, but she needed to understand. She knew Ona's motivation. Revenge. Ona believed Seren was the key to getting it. But what did Lucca see in Seren?

"I've followed three people in my life." His hand fell away from her arm. "One. My father." His lip twisted as some past event cut him. "Two. A Silvanian king." He looked to the tent's striped ceiling in exasperation at this king. "Three. The leader of our mercenary group, Dom. All of them are cunning as foxes. None hold others higher than themselves though. You do. You truly care. I never realized it, but I think I've been looking for a leader like you all my life."

Seren took his hands in hers, soaking in his presence as best she could before she had to leave and deal with complicated enemies she was sure were far wiser than her.

Lucca's gaze dropped, his cheeks going a little darker.

"I will do everything, everything in my power to deserve your loyalty," she whispered.

The Holy Fire in the bowl behind them flickered and snapped.

Lucca kissed Seren's hand and left.

Please, Holy Fire, she prayed, *give me the ability to live up to that man's hope.*

12

ONA

L ucca's snores woke Ona. At least he was finally asleep. Now if only she could do the same. It'd been the longest couple of days in the history of the world.

Moonlight from the edges of the door lit Lucca's upturned face. Ona pulled an overly tasseled pillow from under her head and threw it at him without any real force. He grunted and rolled onto his side, one hand resting on his shoulder, fingers twitching in a pattern she knew as well as the hilt of her sword. Ring finger, pointer, pointer, small and ring together. The first tune he played on the ocarina every time he picked the silly thing up. He had hands like her aunt's—muscled but graceful. Memories fevered Ona like a sickness. Her aunt's face floated to the surface of her mind, then shattered into sharp pieces that stung and pressed against her head. Losing someone never got easier, no matter what stupid people said.

Lucca's blanket slipped to the floor.

Ona crossed the room and put the ridiculously ornate

blanket back on him. "Filthy wild man." She smirked. "You've come a long way from the forest floor."

Shaking her head, she lay down and remembered the day they met.

She wasn't sure when she'd started running that day, the blood covered palette knife still in her hand, but she'd ended up in the forest beyond her town, across the river. A very confused group of strangers had faced her. They had weapons. Loads of them.

Lucca wasn't the first one she'd seen. It was Dom. Tall, fair, bearded, and possessing a scar the length of her favorite paint-brush. The badly stitched line ran from hairline to nose, and diagonally to his ear, where a silver bob dangled.

"You don't look like much either, if you don't mind my saying." Dom's voice was strong, but had a watery quality like thinned paint.

If she opened her mouth, she'd start screaming for her aunt again, so she settled for the most obscene gesture she knew to combat his tone and make him think twice about using the club at his belt.

"Oh!" Dom laughed and the others with him.

Their fire ring—stones hastily stacked—was cold and black. They knew better than to light a fire that might alert the still-roaming Invaders.

"I suppose you've met the nasty Western pigs, then?" He motioned to a girl about Ona's age and she brought her a cup and a cloth.

Ona didn't know what to do with that either. Horror had stuffed her head full to bursting.

"So you can abrade me with your fingers but can't seem to figure out what to do with a generous offer of wine? Hm."

And that's when Lucca appeared. He'd been stretched out by the fire ring, one knee up. A position Ona now knew he took every time he sat on the ground. He'd stood, and pushed his black curls out of his face. His eyes matched his hair and he had a mouth her cousins would've swooned over. Ona preferred boys with sharper features, like the trader's oldest son, Cesco.

Cesco was dead too. She'd seen his body on her flight out of town.

They were all dead.

Dead. Dead. Dead.

Lucca frowned at Dom and waved at Ona's hands. "After that…" She wasn't sure if he was talking about her palette knife or her obscene gesture. "…yes, I think she's a born fighter."

He looked into her face like he was reading a map of some far off place. He took the cloth from the girl and wiped her free hand clean. "I'm going to take this palette knife now."

"What? Oh. Good." Her voice was a stranger. She was so cold.

He uncurled Ona's fingers from the metal and wood. Her muscles and tendons quaked. She'd been gripping the thing like it was the key to unlocking the door holding her in this nightmare.

Dom snorted as Lucca rubbed the blood from Ona's nails. "Planning to keep her, Lucca?"

Lucca's gaze seared the other man, then he turned back to her and his eyes gentled. "You're welcome to stay with us until you feel like yourself again." He must've read the road she'd been down on her paint and blood-stained face. "Or, at least until you make a decision about who to be now."

"Wh-what are you?" A few new faces peered at her as she shivered. None of them looked like her aunt or herself or anyone in town. Their features were straight, strong, and confidence beamed from their every move. One cleaned a sword with a dirty rag. Another held up a jeweled necklace and made some joke about it with their friend. Shiny-coated horses and two ponies tore greenery from the base of a tree where another man used his hands to explain the layout of the next town down the river.

The smell of her aunt's villa burning pushed her out of the now for a beat, and the ice in her gut spread. She put her palms on her knees.

Lucca's fingers gripped her arm. "Eh, you're all right. It's over."

She opened her eyes. "You never answered my question." Her voice sounded more familiar. She willed her heart to stop quaking.

"We're mercenaries, military for hire. I am Lucca Hand of Ruination. I'm a condottieri, along with Dom. We lead this band and fight for the families that hire us."

"I know what mercenaries are. I'm seventeen, not stupid."

Lucca barked a laugh. "I think she's going to be fine, Dom. And we're going to want to train her." He looked at her palette knife where it rested beside the cup of wine. "You could wield a better weapon against those who'd like to take things from you."

A surge of some unknown emotion heated Ona's freezing insides. She felt alive again. "A better weapon." Her smile cracked the cut on her mouth. She licked the new, salty blood. "I'd like that."

A year later, Ona was the youngest ever to become a condottieri, a leader like Lucca. That cold helplessness would never hold her again. She refused to let anyone or anything make her feel like that. She would get her revenge. She would see the Invader king dead. Nothing, absolutely nothing, would stand in her way.

The now-familiar sensation of heat rolled down her body, just under her skin, starting at her head and searing its way to the tips of her toes and scarred fingers. She didn't need any Holy Fire to justify her actions or lead her into this war. She was a living, burning, scorching flame made into flesh, armed to protect the only loved one she had left and to exact justice for the loved ones brutally stolen from her.

13

SEREN

A river of calming, comforting sounds poured from the stables' open double doors and into the cool night. Seren knew she shouldn't be here. She should be planning and plotting. But she needed space and quiet. Just for a little while. Horses shuffled their heavy hooves in the dusty straw, the tips of their shoes clipping and knocking the wood floors. Fig's half door squeaked lightly on its curlicue hinges as Seren slipped inside, laying a hand on the mare's suede nose. The horse snuffled against Seren's fingers and found the sugar lump she'd brought. Fig's proud, black head rose, and twisting her swan neck, the mare nuzzled against her owner.

Seren's mind loosened as she smoothed Fig's sun-hued mane. She truly wished she could sleep here in the barn. So much had happened, but the stables remained quiet and comforting. But so much had happened. Meric's death, for one. She didn't really miss him. Not in the way she should've. He hadn't been kind. Or respectful. And they hadn't had that fever that Father used to talk about when he remembered Mother. He'd claimed he felt a rush of heat when he looked at her. Said there were moments when the fever was less, but it was always there.

But Meric and his father had saved Seren from a horrible fate and given her Akhayma again, a new family that couldn't replace hers, but that she loved nonetheless. Meekra, Barir, Cansu, Hossam, Erol—all the people of the city. She couldn't mourn Meric as a wife should, but she'd honor him by doing everything within her power to save their people from what her first family went through. She didn't want another Empire girl to lose her sisters and father right in front of her eyes. Ever.

The fever had Seren thinking too.

Really, the only instance she'd felt something like that fever Father had taught her about was when she looked at the city, the faces, and heard their voices, their varied languages. She was in love with them. Holding Fig close, she savored the feel of the mare's pulse near her own beating heart. Fig snorted lightly into Seren's hair. She smiled, tension leaking away.

Fig knocked a hoof against the door, her foreleg a bright white against the black of the rest of her. Grinning at the demand for more stroking, Seren began to fashion a tiny braid between Fig's ears. She used to braid her little sisters' hair like this. Her heart surged in her chest. She swallowed. There were days when she'd coiled her sisters' light brown locks in a way similar to Ona's. Maybe that's why she felt so close to Ona already. It wasn't just Ona's hairstyle. It was the way she plunged into life like her sisters, Beti and Cati, had. Ona definitely would've approved of how they used to sneak pastries from Mother's tin and point to Father in blame. Beti and Cati would've grown up to be a lot like Ona if Seren had to guess.

Seren smiled, sadness a familiar song in her heart. Ona was so strong. A blessing to have on her side. And Lucca. Seren's heart reared its head again, but in a completely different way. A warmth traveled up her chest and into her face. Hm. It felt much like a fever.

She shook off the feeling. "I know it's late, Fig. But are you up for a ride?"

Fig snorted approval and pushed to leave the calm of her stall.

WARRIORS ON PATROL watched Seren as she wedged arrows between her fingers. When she nudged Fig into a gallop, the mare tossed her yellow mane. Her black body shot forward past a line of flickering torches.

Despite the fact that, tomorrow, Seren would face men set on tearing her world apart, she smiled wide enough to hurt her cheeks. Maybe because of it. She wouldn't let them destroy those she loved. She'd enjoy her horse, her archery, her people, her city. Their threats wouldn't stop her from living her life. The ransom would work. Or it wouldn't. Nothing could keep Seren from feeling gratitude, such fantastic, beautiful gratitude.

The first barca's painted circles and stars dared her to hit them. She raised her arm, aimed, fired. One to the center, a second to the right. The next target proved wilier. It lay on the ground, and she had to point her elbow to the stars as Fig blasted past, hooves raising dust that clouded Seren's already dulled night vision. Her shot went right and she snarled in frustration. One more barca. She twisted in the creaking saddle to launch a last arrow behind her, at a target positioned opposite of the first. The shot thudded into the thick leather, but too far right. Again.

Finished, she tossed her bow gently on a haystack. She pressed a heel into Fig's side to turn her. "Run, girl. Run."

The horse snorted in agreement and her sides heaved as her hooves pounded the earth. Fig wasn't the most expensive mount in the stables, but she was fast and she was Seren's friend.

Cool wind rushed over Seren's head, unspooling the ribbons of her hair, and she urged Fig to go even faster. They tore around the training field. The stables, the watching soldiers, and the surrounding walls blurred, leaving only sound. The tightness in Seren's shoulders fell off her and she wasn't the Pearl of the Desert or kyros. She was just Seren.

Fig threw her head and snuffled. Seren let her slow down and rubbed the dip below her left ear, her favorite spot. Her warmth was better than any blanket. Fig trotted up to a thick-framed boy recently taken on to man the horses at night.

The boy gave Fig a gentle rub. "Kyros Seren. Our Fig might be in a different stall while they put in the new feeder systems, if it pleases you, my lady."

Seren dismounted and picked up her bow. "Ah. Yes. Because she doesn't care for the hammering."

"Of course, we may not be putting the system in now that… that we are…" The boy's throat moved and he stared at the walls as if he could see the Invaders beyond them, readying for the ransom that would hopefully come tomorrow and end all of this.

Seren touched his arm. "It will be fine. Replace the feeders. Start on it tonight if you think it won't wake everyone." *Staying busy sometimes means staying sane,* Mother had always said.

"I'll be happy to fetch your arrows, my lady."

Thanking him, she headed back to where Cansu and Erol waited on the path toward the city gate. Sleep wasn't going to come tonight. She knew that. But Meekra wouldn't rest until she returned, so Seren hurried back to her quarters, praying every step along the way that the next day would go as planned.

14

SEREN

Six men worked to open the city gates. Four tugged at the wooden posts of the cranks, and the other two swept sand and rock from the doors' path with wide metal flats like fans. With a shudder, the gates thudded against the city walls and a plume of dust clouded into the air. Seren drew her shoulder blades down toward her spine and lengthened her neck, as Meekra had shown her. *A long neck can do wonders for the will,* she said. Seren had sent Meekra to stay with her family, to help her parents protect her sisters. Just in case.

Ten Invaders in red and white surcoats and metal boots surrounded a large cart that transported wooden trunks through the towering doors. Coins clinked inside the chests, and the jointed metal on the enemies' feet grated together, sounding remarkably similar to a venomous dune beetle's warning.

Seren wished she could hold a weapon at the ready. Wished she could've worn the leather, bronze-studded vest Meekra had ordered to be made for her. But she had to appear peaceful and trusting. This was a delicate thing. Her foot bounced. She flexed her hands, her palms damp and sticky. It was nearly impossible to stand there and just watch the people who'd killed Father, Cati, and Beti traipse right into her home.

One man stopped at Cansu and bent at the waist toward Seren. It was an ugly bow and his upturned face showed little respect. Meric would've said something. He would've quipped and thrown out a smirk and kicked sand in the man's eyes. Then, the warriors with the lead Invader would've traded trunks for swords, and Meric would've ruined it all only for his vanity.

Seren knew better. *One fool shouldn't ruin peace,* Father had always said.

"Good sun to you, warrior." Seren took her time with the unfamiliar language.

Her fighters on the walls tensed. Was it something she'd done or had they noticed something that she missed?

She scanned the Invaders and the trunks they set at her feet. Red, irritated skin surrounded the Invaders' eyes. Was the arid climate hampering them? Their country was in full drought, so she'd heard. But drought didn't mean they'd be accustomed to the dry wind across the flat rises of the hammadas or the acidic breeze through the lahabshjara trees clustered in areas where groundwater hid under the sandy earth.

The chests they brought were far too small to hold a warrior. So no surprise attacks there. The Invaders' weapons sat at their belts, untouched by twitching fingers or curling hands. Their gazes didn't waver from the back of their leader's dark blond head. They were focused on him, as expected. Seasoned warriors took note of exits and armed soldiers with quick side looks instead of gaping. She'd learned that much from watching Father in new situations when they'd traveled the Empire.

She turned to Erol and Hossam. "Present our prisoner."

They took up the ropes on the silver-gilt Empire cart, the one that held the king in his wooden cage, and brought him forward. The king's beard hung limply, all of its curl gone. A cut on his cheek still showed red, and one along his neck, but no blood leaked from the wound. He held his shoulders straight and nodded once to his general. A darkness flashed over the Invader general's eyes and he opened his mouth to say something.

"He has been our prisoner," Seren said. "I wouldn't present him to you in some false way, in a false show of some imagined respect. You'll receive honesty from me, if not in battle, then when we are face-to-face."

Their general gave a curt bow, but didn't look at her as Adem worked the fist-sized bronze lock on the cage. Adem swung the door open and stood at the back of the cart, offering his shoulder to the king, so the man could step to the ground with some dignity. Disgust poured off Adem, waves of fury she could almost see.

The king ignored Adem and hopped to the ground. His gaze shifted to Seren. "May I please have my sword? It's a family heirloom."

Seren waved to Cansu, who brought the shining weapon forward and presented it to the king.

An unsteady, fearful warmth traveled the length of her. This was the peace the Empire needed. The only way to keep it would be to help these terrible people. Without relief from their drought, they'd come back again and again, desperation whipping them on like a vicious master. Akhayma was just lucky they'd only brought a middle-sized force and not their entire army.

A shudder wrapped cold arms around her.

Father had told her about the Invaders' full-scale siege of the formerly rich trade city of Vadi. He'd narrowly escaped. His story painted a clear picture of the Invaders' colored tents that indicated who would live and who would die if the city surrendered. Each day they put up a new tent, a new color. Each day the threat grew worse and worse. Now, Vadi was nothing more than a wraith of a town, twisting in the sandy wind. A victim to the white tent, then the red, then at last, the black—the worst of them all. The air howled through the empty mouths of tumbled towers and moaned about the horrors seen there.

Beside Lucca, Ona's face twisted. She stood still, too still, murder in her eyes.

Seren was fairly certain Ona mouthed the words *Bad idea* as she nodded at the king's sword.

But Ona wasn't the leader here. Ona didn't know what it took to keep two peoples, so vastly different, at peace with one another.

Seren had watched Father and the old kyros sign a contract with a violent group from the North who had magic in their blood. With trade agreements, the Empire had no further trouble from them. If both sides gained what they saw as fair and good for their people, there was no need for bloodshed.

"I propose one more agreement," Seren said.

The king stood beside his general and cocked his head. His hair was nearly as bright as his weapon, despite the dust.

"What is that, Kyros Seren?" he asked in the trade tongue.

"We'll help you dig wells along our border," she said. "For your use. We know you attack out of desperation."

The king's eyes chilled. "We are to come begging at your wells to keep us alive?"

Adem stepped to Seren's side. "It's a generous offer."

"It must seem so to you," the king said. "You'd much rather separate my head from my body. But for me, one who knows what my armies can do, well, let us say it's not an offer I take with a smiling face and open heart." He looked at the single bell hanging from the tie at Seren's forehead and frowned.

Out of the corner of her eye, Seren saw Ona move. Lucca put a hand on Ona's stomach to stop her. His lips moved as he whispered to her.

"But we've made peace here," Seren said. "I don't think you understand. This is an offer made out of goodwill. No other silver need exchange hands. No further allowances made."

The king's upper lip lifted. His hands became fists. "My people were in stone castles the size of mountains before yours learned to milk goats. We will not bow to your tented *city* of puddles and ignorant fire."

He drew his sword.

A dozen Invaders dropped from the underbelly of their cart, rolled free of the wheels, and stood, armed and seething, before anyone else realized what was happening.

There was a shout. A mass of red and white poured through the gates.

Shock pulled any word Seren could've said right out of her mind. They'd tied themselves to the bottom of the cart. She'd been tricked.

The world exploded into a storm of steel, wood, and sound.

Before she could get her mouth to work, Cansu, Hossam,

and Erol were in front of her. All she could see was a wall of vest and helmet and muscle.

She shoved Hossam, but he didn't move. "I need—"

Lucca handed her a bow and quiver over the guards. "I'm into the fray!" he shouted before taking off toward the gates.

Pushing through Cansu and Erol, she climbed onto the Empire cart and crouched near the silver-painted planks of the far side for protection. She nocked an arrow and aimed at an Invader who was picking off Empire archers on the parapet like plums from a tree. She took him down with a shot above his metal plating. Seren fired again and again until she had no more arrows. She froze, lost on how to move on, the world spinning around her, attacking her with metallic smells and screams that clawed at her heart.

Her Akhayma would be lost—Meekra, Cansu, Erol, Hossam, Adem, Barir, Qadira, Najwa, Izzet, Lucca, Ona. She'd lose this family like she had Mother years ago, then Father and her sisters.

Ona shouted above the chaos, her sword in the air. She was vengeance come to life. Her words, though intelligible, were sharp as her blade. Every move was an artistic stroke, throwing death like a color onto the canvas of the city.

Onaratta Paints with Blood.

The title fit too well. As violent and horrible as she was, a fierce love showed in the way she fought. In each determined move, Ona's devotion to her aunt's memory shone.

Seren had to shake herself out of this daze. She'd only escaped the last few Invaders' swords because of the thickness of the fight. But her limbs were made of stone, her heart suspended and silent.

"Kyros! Fight! We fight with you!" Lucca began his own

chanting, his arrows hitting fast and true.

Lucca's face held none of the gentleness she'd seen before. His dark eyes were cold like he'd turned his heart off. His movements were exact as a mathematician's work. Measuring distance with a glance, he threw his bow aside and drew his sword. Fighting fit the weave of him, of who he was. This wasn't personal, or, he didn't allow it to touch him the way Ona did.

Either way, they were supporting her, risking all for her people.

A brightness poured over Seren, waking her up. She grabbed her dagger and dove into the fray, heading for Lucca and Ona.

Together, the two mercenaries burst through a handful of sword-wielding Invaders like knives of lightning. Their limbs glowed. Their speed numbed the mind.

Ona leaped over an attacker, and as she did, slit the man's throat. Chanting in Silvanian, sounding like an ancient warrior goddess, she dropped behind another. One swift strike to the side of the neck, and he was gone.

Lucca threw foreign words like daggers and spun as an Invader made to run him through. He was faster than wind, vicious as a desert lion, with bared teeth and feral eyes.

Seren grabbed a fallen quiver. She fired one, two, three more arrows into the roiling mass of men and women. She hit the first two—heavy-bodied Invaders raging toward Erol—but missed the third, who cut down one of her warriors.

Seren draped a steel plate over her heart. Battle was no place for feelings, she reminded herself as the odor of blood and sweat poured through the rising dust and swirls of sand disturbed by feet and falling bodies.

A group of Invaders broke through their contingent and ran west. They'd go after her people, the innocents, with the strategy to break the city's spirit. Seren thought about the little boy who'd offered Meric his incense stick during the Fire Ceremony, about Meekra and her sisters at their loom. An Invader's broad sword would cut clean through the boy's neck and his parents would see it all. An Invader's shield would bash Meekra and her family's heads, destroying their world in a flash.

The metal Seren had imagined over her heart shivered, tried to crack. "Stop them!" she shouted. "Cansu! Hossam! Stop those men!"

Cansu turned. His mop of hair flapped across his bleeding cheek. Hossam grabbed Cansu's jerkin and pulled him away from the fighting.

Fire, let them be fast enough.

Two more of Seren's men surrounded her as she stood to shoot from the cart. An Invader's arrow peeled past her ear and knocked into the wooden floor behind her.

"If you're going to fight, do it better!" a familiar, grainy voice said. Adem.

Seren jerked the arrow from the cart and lodged it, and two others from her quiver, between her fingers. With the first shot, she moved the next into place and let loose, and then again and again.

"Better!" Adem grunted and drew his yatagan up and at an angle to slice an Invader's thigh. The man fell. "Why did that contingent go west?"

Seren didn't know if he was truly asking her or if he was thinking out loud.

A huge Invader with silver hair and a ruddy face pushed Adem to the side with an oval shield and climbed onto the cart.

The wagon lurched forward. She almost fell, grabbing hold of the side. The Invader, weaponless, struck out with his shield. She tried to move to the side, but the heavy wood still banged her jaw.

A tiny bloom of white marred her vision. A strange tightness broke across her head and neck. But no pain. It'd come later.

She swiped her dagger at the red-faced fighter. Gasping, heart skipping, she missed. One of her own fighters came at the man from the back. She angled herself and slashed across the bridge of the Invader's nose. He growled. His hands flew to his bleeding face. Adem aimed for him and swung his yatagan. Seren ducked behind his fallen shield—which had caught on the side of the cart—to catch her breath. The man fell under Adem's blade.

With her pulse beating in her tongue and temples, Seren rose and jumped over the side. Her dagger bit into an Invader's exposed forearm. He finished off an Empire fighter and faced Seren. Blood ran into his smile. He spit out a phrase in his language. Sword poised, he lunged right, then cut left, striking toward her legs.

Spinning, she dodged behind a panicked horse and shouted, "Onaratta Paints with Blood! Lucca Hand of Ruination! Get the king!"

She stretched to see their weapons blazing through the crowd, laying enemies low. The glint of the king's hair shone just past Ona's glowing reach.

Seren's fighters moved like the point of a huge arrow and pushed the Invaders closer and closer to the gates, away from Akhayma's heart.

Ona drove her sword against the king's. His dropped to the

ground. Seren rounded the horse and ran. Ona's arm shot out—too fast to see—and wrapped around the king's shoulder and neck. Ona's sword tipped toward the tender spot below the king's chin and worked her way back to the bulk of the Empire's warriors.

Seren shouted something; she didn't even know what she'd said. They had the king in hand. All was not lost.

Then, with another swathe of men downed, the Empire had ten or so Invaders surrounded and the rest in retreat.

Akhayma's warriors shut the city gates and let up a shout of victory.

"Take the rest as prisoners." Seren climbed back onto the cart. "Give up your weapons." She made a sweeping motion to ensure they knew what she meant. "We won't harm you."

Ona's head swiveled and she glared directly at Seren. The rage of battle still heated her. Surely, that was the only plausible reason for her to look at Seren like that.

Hossam ran from behind a clutch of black tenting. Blood spatter dotted his cheeks. "Kyros! They are attacking from the West. A full scale attack!"

Adem took the king from Ona and threw the man at another Empire warrior. "Go!" he shouted at the Empire fighters.

Seren waved her dagger. "Ona, Lucca, go!"

Ona handed the king off to three other fighters, an ugly sneer marring her face. She and Lucca mounted two unmanned horses and galloped away alongside Adem and the rest of the warriors not currently holding prisoners.

Fire, help them, Seren prayed.

15

ONA

How many times would Ona have to capture the king before Seren ended him? Rage sliced at Ona as she rode beside Lucca, wind slapping her hot cheeks.

Ladders of rope hung over the walls' striped stone, lank as corpse hair and crawling with hundreds of Invaders. Ona's new mount reared. She tightened her legs around the horse's middle. The sneak attack by the front gates had been a feint. Where had they hidden from the watchers on the parapet? It was those trees. They'd hidden in those thick-trunked trees. Clever pigs.

Lucca chanted beside her, eyes wild.

"Wake iron, wake!

I am the blade and the blade is me.

I move like wind, invisible, untouchable.

Death is my storm

My enemy is grass

Bent beneath my steel!"

Shield on his forearm, he struck his flint across his weapon. Red and yellow sparks leaped joyously over the incoming army.

Ona drew her own sparks, screaming a chant, her skin feeling like it was on fire.

"Wake iron, wake!
Deliver those who've shed the blood of my kin,
Throw their bodies at my feet,
Their heads rolling at my heel,
Let the blood in me rise to avenge my loves!"

Sparks burned her hands, but no pain bit her as she swung steel and sliced through an Invader's throat. Blood painted Ona's blade, brought it to life as it lit up to match the light under her skin, the fire in her heart.

Her aunt's round face flashed through her mind, stopping her heart. In the memory, her aunt turned away. The image faded.

Ona sucked a breath of sandy, copper-and-horse-and-sweat scented air and kicked heels into her mount, driving the gelding toward Lucca. He struggled against a group of three huge men. He was keeping them at bay, his horse's hooves dancing, his blade clanging off one sword, then another, a shield, then another.

"Wake iron!
Help me leap like the sparks from your flint!
I fly like fire in the wind!"

She drew her feet under her as the horse kept on, then she jumped.

The world seemed to still as she rolled her left shoulder back and drew an invisible arch with her blade, using her legs to shift her weight, and slashed steel across the neck of one of Lucca's attackers.

The man beside him roared, leaving Lucca, and thrust his sword at Ona. He screamed and moaned in that sick combination of sound only Invaders could make, like they hated war but loved it too. Ona dodged his strike and cut his leg, her arm jarring as steel hit bone. The pale man fell, face twisted, and she thought of those addicted to the gray plant. That's what it was. Invaders were addicted to bloodshed, to killing.

Ona stepped back, pausing in the chaos.

Was she being merciful by ending their lives? She wanted nothing to do with mercy.

Shoving her battle-fevered questions away, shutting out any thought that led to not killing Invaders, she drove into the fight. But there were so many of them. As she took down three more, the wave of attackers pushed forward. More swamped the walls, falling into the battle with fresh arms and steel begging to be wetted with Empire blood.

She found Lucca and he glanced at her, his sword still working.

We're going to fall.

The Invaders would win. They'd take all. They'd live on to laugh and have families and breathe fresh air. They'd live on while Ona's aunt stayed dead. They'd live on while Ona died under their boots.

A guttural scream clawed its way out of her mouth. Lucca's lips parted. Shaking overtook her sword arm and she dropped her weapon. Her scream matched the Invaders.

No. No. No.

She couldn't *understand* them, their love-hate feeling for battle. Never. She couldn't be *like* them. Ona had thought she'd seen her worst day in this uncommon world already. But this, this was the worst.

"To me!" a bright voice called out in the desert tongue. "Rise, Akhayma, and fight!"

Ona grabbed her sword. As she fought a bear of a man, she strained to see who was shouting.

The Empire warriors called out and surged forward, renewed by whomever this was.

A tall figure in simple trader's clothing rode a stomping, black stallion and sliced his way through Invaders on the edge of the battle. That was no trader. Power practically poured out of the man's vicious gaze. Whoever it was, she wanted to meet him. If they lived through this.

Arms aching, Ona brought another enemy to his knees, then looked around. All the Invaders were either dead, scrambling back over the walls amid arrows flying, or held by Empire fighters.

The Empire, Lucca and Ona too, had won.

It was over.

The tall figure who'd rallied everyone raised his yatagan high. "I salute you, Akhayma warriors. And I, High General Varol, invite you to feast with me tonight!"

Varol. Meric's younger brother.

Lucca turned to face her, blood coloring his chin. He didn't need to look at Ona like that. She already knew this was going to make announcing Meric's death and claiming it'd just happened a lot more dangerous. But Varol had saved them. The Invaders would've won if he hadn't showed up. How had he snuck into the city?

Bumped by other injured, battered fighters, Ona found herself following Varol's steed out of the carnage and toward Seren's force at the front gates. Varol gestured widely, taking up space. He was tall, but it wasn't his height that made him *larger* than everyone else. It was the way he moved. How he commanded. Questioned. Demanded. She stared as he doled out orders about prisoners and securing the front gates and sending warriors out of the city to follow the retreat and make certain it was genuine.

Lucca trotted up. "Seren has her work cut out for her now," he whispered, keeping an eye on Varol who had maneuvered his horse back a little to speak with Adem.

Ona tried to concentrate on his words, but she was still buzzing from the battle. He'd cleaned his face. She hadn't. She wore Invader blood like a testament to how much she'd loved her aunt and how much she hated the Invaders. Part of an old Silvanian poem flitted through her mind. *With battle, with blood, she painted her love for the lost.*

"Ona? Are you listening?" Lucca leaned into her face. "You all right?"

"I'm fine. So Varol is here. That might be a problem."

Annoyance flickered over his face. "She has to announce the death before Varol even gets back to the main tent. It'll look suspicious regardless, but if he finds his brother's body, it's all over."

Seren's force streamed away from the front gates. Kaftan sleeves billowing around her, she shouted an order to give the prisoners water, then take them to the cells.

"Water," Ona scoffed. "She should kill them all." A bitter taste sat on her tongue. "Why is she keeping them? Does she enjoy torture? I could try that idea on, but she doesn't seem the type."

Lucca crouched and drew his sword across a little mound of sand gathered against a lotus tower. Some of the blood came off the glinting metal. He sheathed it and glanced behind them. "I guess she has a strategy."

"They'll turn on her the second they get the chance."

"She won't give them the chance."

"Won't she? I've seen the bleeding heart inside her. I like her —don't give me that look—but she seems the type to forgive too easily."

"You think anyone who forgives at all does it too easily," Lucca said.

"No, I don't."

"You do."

Ona gritted her teeth. "You're wrong."

"All right. Maybe, *maybe*, you'd forgive someone on your deathbed. Never a moment before."

"What's the problem with that? You can't forgive them when they still have the opportunity to hurt you again."

Lucca squeezed his eyes shut and shook his head. "We need to find you a tutor."

She nudged her horse into his, nearly bumping him from his seat and knocking him into Nuh, who walked beside them. Lucca nodded toward Ona to show Nuh who to blame. Nuh gave a tired smile.

"I don't need a tutor, idiot," Ona snapped.

"You don't understand the meanings of some words," Lucca said, using his older brother voice. "Like forgiveness."

"Do you grip the meaning of this?" She flared her fingers at her forehead, making Nuh suck a breath.

He cupped her hand, ruining her beautifully rendered obscene gesture.

"Give Seren a chance," he whispered. He said her name like a strange chant made stronger through whispering.

"She was actually going to ransom the king." Ona hadn't realized how mad she was until now. Fighting had pushed all that away for the last three hours.

"For peace. To avoid a siege. Don't pretend you knew what they were up to."

Ona's normally loud and perfectly functioning mouth jumbled into a mess of anger and tight lips.

Seren had lost her pretty head if she thought Ona would sit idly by while she actually ransomed the king. Ona had thought it was Seren's ruse to gain silver. A ruse gone bad when the Invaders showed how much they valued an agreement with the Empire. Ona bumped her fist against her thigh as she stormed away from Nuh and Lucca. Seren had tried to release the king! Seren making deals with Invaders was like watching a mouse fight a rattlesnake. Bad idea, mouse. If Seren wanted to win against snakes, she had to become a snake. Ruthless. Unforgiving. Striking first, not waiting for peace.

Ona had to talk to Seren, to make her see sense. The king had to die. He was the head of that army and the head had to be severed. There was no making peace with Invaders. How could she even think it? She'd come so far—getting over that dead husband of hers, claiming the title of *kyros*, showing Adem what she'd put up with and what she wouldn't. Why give all that up and go soft? She'd end up as a meal and the rest of Akhayma as a side dish.

16

SEREN

arol was here. Chilled to her core, Seren drove Fig back toward the Kyros Walls. She needed to meet with the kaptans, but before that, she had to do something about Meric. Varol's sharp silhouette rode ahead of her, dark and slim. With Hossam at her side, astride a black gelding, she set a hand on Fig's neck, soaking in the familiar warmth. If Varol made it back to the main tent and found Meric's body, it would be difficult indeed to explain everything —*to lie* about everything—before he ordered her death. She couldn't imagine him listening patiently. Definitely not.

Ahead, warriors on horseback and on foot, kaftans torn and voices rough, moved through the city, following Varol like he was the star in the sky that could lead them home. One man handed Varol a skin of water. Varol tipped it high, drinking all without a thought to the thirsty, dust-coated fighter he'd taken it from.

"Kyros Seren, I congratulate you on your win." Kaptan

Rashiel bowed from his saddle, his hair falling over a bruised cheek.

"Thank you, Kaptan Rashiel."

"I can't wait to hear how High-General Varol managed to sneak into the city."

"Me either." Seren tried and failed to keep the worry out of her words.

Hossam made a noise that said he felt a similar distrust of Varol.

Rashiel gently kicked his horse to get closer. "I am your ears and eyes when you need me, Kyros Seren."

Lucca's voice rode over the crowd, his accent punching through the chaos. "Kyros Seren! I will make sure no one disturbs this hard-won reprieve." Skin subtly glowing from the fight, from his chanting, he cut his eyes right, over the crowd and toward the tent where Meric lay. Reluctantly, she followed his gaze, then nodded.

"Hossam, a little help?" she said.

"Clear the way for your kyros, please!" Hossam raised his fist and urged his mount onward.

Slowly, too slowly, Seren and Rashiel took up Hossam's wake and sailed through the merchants injured in the fighting they hadn't been trained for, the mothers who'd taken the strike of an Invaders' shield to defend their families, and the exhausted warriors.

Inside the Kyros Walls, Lucca disappeared into the main tent with Nuh at his side to check on the rotating guards, to see that nothing was amiss. Lucca knew as well as she did that something must be done now. This very moment. Seren hurried to dismount, handing Fig off to a stable boy. Rashiel held the heavy doorflap open for Seren. Varol wasn't beside the high table. He wasn't standing at the Holy Fire bowl. He wasn't here at all. Good.

Seren stopped to pray at the Holy Fire bowl as Nuh spoke to Lucca at the door to Seren's chambers.

She needed help with two things.

Spinning the tale of Meric's death and thinking up a way to finally defeat the Invaders. They would set up a siege. It was only a matter of hours before that horrible white tent went up in the plains beyond the city walls. There'd been so many of them. There would be more.

The Holy Fire bowl burned bright and promising. Flames brushed Seren's palm as she prayed silently about Meric, about everything.

I need a strategy to fight the Invaders, to defeat them without losing all of my army. I can't sacrifice every warrior. Then, I'd only rule a city of the dead.

There'd be no Fire Ceremony with hope and happy faces, no Age Day rituals, no weaving in groups as people told stories and sang songs. It would be a city of mourning. A city without enough hands to keep it from disappearing into the unforgiving sands of the Emptiness.

Pale shapes flickered in Seren's mind.

Clouds?

She squeezed her eyes tight and focused on them, trying to *see* them more clearly. They disappeared into darkness. Seren stepped away from the bowl and put her head in her hands, her fingers still warm from the Fire. Why couldn't she see anything that made sense?

She'd have to come back later. Varol could arrive any second.

Leaving Rashiel to his own prayers, she hurried toward Lucca and Nuh.

The men bowed and held up their palms. Nuh hefted a spear from the corner and took up his stance on the opposite side of the doorframe. Lucca's skin was its normal olive tone again. Seren fought the urge to touch the blood on his chin, to make sure it wasn't his. She put her hand on her dagger's hilt instead.

"Is Ona all right?"

His mouth pinched a little, but he said, "She's fine. Now, what can we do?"

"Just be here."

"Always."

His dark eyes, the piney scent he carried, his devotion—Seren suddenly felt empty. The muscles in her legs, stomach, and arms tensed, like they were ready to close the distance between Lucca and her. She wanted to enjoy the fullness she knew she'd feel in his arms.

Blinking the ridiculous feeling away, she pushed into her chambers. Her mind buzzed with the horror of battle, Varol's arrival, Adem's mercurial support, the pull she'd felt toward Lucca, the pained look that crossed his face when she asked about Ona, and this—Meric's body on the bed. Ka'ud smoke swirling around her head, she turned quickly and simply stood at the closed door, staring into the stripes of wool instead of at the wrapped corpse in the room. She took a deep, slow breath, tasting sweet-dark ka'ud.

I can do this. For my people, because I've been called, I can do this.

At the back entrance, she spoke to the other guards. "I need rest. See that no one disturbs me, please."

Both men nodded. "Of course, Kyros Seren."

Varol wouldn't barge in. She had given herself a little time. Hopefully.

The door opened and Seren's heart reared. But it was only Meekra. "Let's clean you up, my lady."

Seren trailed her into the side chamber, both of them knowing they didn't want to remain in the same room as Meric's body. Meekra poured a bowl of water, dipped a cloth, and motioned for Seren to sit on her stool. Seren closed her eyes as Meekra wiped blood from her cheeks and neck. She brushed her hair out, humming a melancholy tune that made Seren want to cry. But she was too overwhelmed to cry. Worries and dark images of the long, long day flitted through her mind like bats. She lay on the bed in Meekra's chamber for a while, not sleeping, as all that had happened washed over her. Varol wouldn't stay away forever. He'd be here soon and she had to figure out how to handle it.

DRESSED in an emerald kaftan decorated with silver buttons the shape of phoenix eyes, a pair of lime green pantaloons tied tight at the ankle, and an orange sash—clothing she hardly remembered putting on—Seren pushed her chamber door open and returned to the main tent.

Lucca was there, talking quietly to Nuh. Both had cleaned themselves of blood and dirt, but dark circles under their eyes said neither had rested. Lucca's gaze found her and her heart jolted at the concern in them. He blinked and a wrinkle flashed between his thick eyebrows as he touched his full, bottom lip with a knuckle like he was thinking. Cansu and Hossam had returned, and everyone bowed to Seren. The atmosphere in the

157

tent was like the brief time between thunder and lightning as Seren stood beside the high table and tried to think of what to say, what to do, how to act like the leader the Empire needed.

The main tent's door opened. The bleeding dawn brought in Varol and Adem, who walked side-by-side toward the high table—lithe Varol, in his prime, with smooth skin and a cobra's stare, and weathered Adem with his cold, calculating gaze that measured Seren, sizing her up. Seren's bones felt brittle and weak. She had to be strong, to believe she was strong. Imagining the Holy Fire, she called up the memory of that first vision. Her mind showed her Meric in the pale ivory death shroud and the storm churning beyond the city walls. Her hands fisted, nails cutting into her sweating palms.

She had to do this. It couldn't wait any longer.

One more breath as the two men in her way stared her down, advancing, nearing, closer, closer.

"Kyros Meric is dead," she said.

Varol took three decisive steps, raised a hand like he was going to hit her, then froze. "How?"

Her guards put hands to their hilts, but she stayed them with a look.

Adem simmered behind Varol, the early sun oozing through the tent and over his studded vest and graying hair. If he didn't suspect anything, he wouldn't have looked so angry. He would've been shocked, saddened. But she had to plow through, keep to the plan.

The ka'ud burned her nose, the scent like fingers scratching at her eyes. "The cough that always bothered Kyros Meric grew worse." She focused on Varol. "He developed a fever. I'm sure you've heard this from General Adem."

Mixing truth with a lie helped it soak into its audience.

Seren hated herself for knowing that, for using what she'd learned at Father's side as he dealt with politicians and back-stabbers. Father had never been dishonest. It was one of the reasons he'd been practically forced into early retirement.

"He has been very ill since then," she said. Lucca's gaze warmed Seren like a touch. She wished Ona was there too, ferocity shining in her face. Seren needed more of that fierce demeanor to rule here. "His life flickered to dark just as we had word of the Invaders arriving. Then there was the attack...I wrapped him myself so his body would be clean for his funeral."

Hands shaking, her gaze flicked to Adem. If she could talk him into believing her version of the timing of Meric's death, he would lead Varol her way. But only anger colored Adem's features. Was he really so sure she was lying or was she misinterpreting all of this?

Varol inhaled sharply, tugging her attention to him. Rage tore at his sharp features, distorting them so she couldn't tell what made him angry. Did he know she was lying? Or was he furious that he'd been denied saying farewell to his brother? Or was he grieving?

As one, Varol and Adem practically pushed past Seren—not touching, but oh so close—beyond the rotating guards, and into the sleeping quarters. Seren began to follow, heart clicking like a beetle on its back.

Lucca caught her arm. His fingers dropped away quickly, but his gaze stayed on her. "Should we come in with you?" He glanced at her guards.

Seren had to handle this without looking guilty. "No. But thank you."

Lucca's mouth tucked into a grim half-smile as she pushed the chamber's flaps open, riding Adem's heels.

Meekra, quiet and steady, slipped in too, and stood at the back entrance of the inner chamber. The lotus pillar partially shadowed her face from the flickering oil lamps.

Ka'ud smoke billowed around Varol and Adem as they bent to examine Meric's wrapped body. Meric looked like a grotesquely large doll, nothing like a person. No humming presence came from him anymore. His spirit was tightly bound inside that shell of a man. He had to be burned soon so his essence could rise to the heavens.

Varol hovered over his brother's covered face and tensed. His hand went to the bed's edge, long fingers clutching at the silver-tasseled hem. Seren thought Varol might fall to his knees, grief shoving him down, but he straightened and turned. Chewing the inside of his cheek, he dragged his gaze over Seren's face. The unspoken accusation was there, visible as the hooked nose on his face.

Seren found she was suddenly very angry. She wanted to snap at him, to tell him that he had no right to look at her like that. She'd supported Meric. His death wasn't her fault. Sure, she'd woven lies around the tragedy, altered outcomes to suit her goal. But her goal was only to insure the safety of the Empire, to rise to the Holy Fire's call. She needed to say all of this, but the words wouldn't wake up. They slept inside her, quiet as the dead. Again, she wished for Ona's fiery determination, blazing courage, powerful voice. The same courage Seren's parents had both possessed in bulk.

As her heart hammered away, chiseling at her ability to stand there and act as the person the Fire had called her to be, Adem pressed a finger to Meric's throat, feeling for a pulse. He jerked his hand back, his fingers splayed. "He is gone, High General Varol. He has been for a long while."

Had he thought she'd wrap a sick man and bury him alive while his mind slept? Fire, no one could be that horrible. She swallowed, her stomach twisting. "Perhaps the funeral should take place—"

Varol lifted a hand and curled his fingers into a fist. "The funeral will be as I order it."

Adem stepped away from the bed and raised his fist to Varol. "May the Holy Fire welcome your brother." He turned to Seren, his eyes cold as the black ice that lined the roads to the ports of the north. "May the Holy Fire welcome your husband."

Varol was trembling. Sweat shone on his face. He picked up a glass pitcher from the side table. He threw it at Meekra. It burst against the pillar beside her. She screamed, covering her face.

Mouth dropping open, all nerves forgotten, Seren ran to Meekra.

Varol and Adem strode out of the tent, not a thought given to Varol's behavior.

A shard had stuck in Meekra's cheek and Seren gently plucked it free, fingers trembling in the hot anger running through her. Blood welled and trickled down Meekra's face.

"It'll be all right," Meekra whispered, taking a slip of dark cloth from her sash and pressing it against the cut. "I'm all right. But..." Her wise, brown eyes pleaded with Seren. "He is as awful as he's always been."

And Seren knew what Meekra meant. That Seren had to keep hold of her reign here and drive Varol out of the Empire.

"He is no good for our people," Seren hissed, ears ringing from the crash and from her own anger.

She helped Meekra gather the broken pieces, ignoring her tuts of disapproval.

Rage-filled tears leaked out of Seren's eyes. She rubbed the hot flecks of salty water away and set the last of the shattered pitcher on the table. These weren't tears for Meric, but they'd give her story the look of truth. These tears were for her people and the tangled leadership they'd have to deal with. And all of this during a siege.

Seren had no idea what to do.

17

SEREN

t the funeral on the training field, Seren's people
gathered into an enormous circle and hummed, a
pulsing noise deep in their throats. Adem, Cansu,
Erol, and Hossam lifted Meric's wrapped body up the ladder set
against the pyre's thick stilts and settled it on the lahabshjara
leaves and striped pillows. Tongues of Flame glittered like
amber in sunlight around the ivory linen encasing Meric's thin
arms and legs. Tails of silk, a different color for each of the
Empire's noble clans, flickered in the breeze beneath the pyre,
slowly beginning to smoke. Chieftains removed their yatagans
from their sashes and set them, hilt first, on the ground around
the pyre tower. Though Meric had never set foot on a battle-
ground, as kyros and leader of the army, he would receive a
warrior's funeral.

The women of the high-caste—many who'd never accepted
Seren because of how she talked to the low and middle-caste as
equals—gathered into a smaller circle within the larger one.

They took up the prepared buckets of oasis water. A few gave Seren kind, sad looks. Perhaps Seren's part in defending the city had won them over.

"May the Fire bless you, Chosen," one of snobby Qadira's friends whispered, her face clean of any judgment. She seemed sincere.

Seren dipped her head in thanks and clutched the handle of her own bucket.

The water sloshed as the women took the traditional three steps, nine, three, pausing appropriately to say a quiet prayer as they continued toward the pyre's base. They joined in on the humming with the rest of the city's inhabitants.

Seren raised the proper notes in the back of her throat, enjoying the feel of being a part of her people's ritual. The humming filled her, calmed her, and strengthened her legs so she could keep on. As one, the women stopped. They poured the clean water into the dusty ground, watering the tiny purple flowers that grew there, and protecting the city from fire.

Varol, as a blood relative, received the lit torch of lahabsh-jara branches and began his brother's ascent to the next life. More ka'ud burned around Meric's body. Only a kyros's funeral could demand such a rare sacrifice. The flames leaped and strained toward the sun, the blue smoke like a great hand raising Meric up and up and up.

Seren had never loved him, but the thought of never seeing him again strangely cut her heart. She was glad for the moment when the rest of the city came close, tucking in together.

Ona came up, her hands clasped in front of her. Seren couldn't tell whether Ona was ready to embrace her or run her through.

Meekra approached too, but she gave Seren and Ona space

to whisper, her own eyes on the pyre and a chaotic look of anger and sadness on her face.

"Death is a thief," Ona said very quietly. "It doesn't ask permission. It always makes me feel cheated." Her nostrils flared as she stared at the ground.

Seren set her bucket at her feet and linked an arm around Ona's, nervous about the gesture of closeness, but wanting it enough to risk making an idiot of herself. Seren hoped this new friend's courage would burn into her own flesh. "I hope you weren't injured badly during the battle."

"I'm fine. But...we should talk." Ona toyed with the hilt of her sword. Seren had never seen her nervous.

Varol blew the ram's horn, sounding his grief to the world and making Seren's soul shiver. With Adem at his side, Varol then tucked the horn under his arm and began to climb the earthen stairs to the hill that sat above the field, on eye-level with the pyre itself. Seren's heart stilled. His pale brown mourning kaftan, a match to everyone's clothing, whipped in the wind and made him look like a simple nomad, heading to his flock of goats.

"What's he doing?" Ona followed as Seren and Meekra walked toward the hill.

That was exactly the question battering Seren's mind. She shrugged, and Ona broke away to join Lucca at the base of the small slope.

Varol cut a proud shape on the rise as he lifted his hands. His voice carried and an ugly feeling crawled through Seren, like he was infecting her people.

"People of Akhayma," he shouted. "I feel your grief along with my own. Our dear kyros has left this world."

Smoothing her hair, Seren took a place beside Varol while

Ona and Lucca joined Rashiel, Adem, and the other kaptans to the right.

"Kyros Meric has been taken too soon." Varol turned his head slowly and looked at Seren. He wanted to see if she would fight him for a place here, for the right to speak during this holy time. And she must. She didn't necessarily need to outdo him right now, not at this solemn moment, but she did have to keep him from announcing a full mourning. She had to hold on to her title, her rank.

Shaking, she stepped forward. "We'll continue our mourning, as is tradition, for two more days. But we'll only dress in our earth-colored clothing and say our prayers over our Fires." To Varol's right, Adem stiffened. "We must be ready to fight again. Kyros Meric would've wanted us to protect ourselves, not weaken our bodies with lack of water and sustenance."

That was a lie. Meric would've wanted all to die along with him. He would've seen it as unfair that anyone live past his death.

Varol looked at the ground and nodded. Relief cooled Seren like a breeze.

Whispering and comforting one another with touches and hugs that Seren was painfully jealous of, the people went to the pyre and began their group prayers. Their voices rose with the smoke. It was sad, but also lovely.

Adem seemed to shake himself. He slipped behind Varol and ripped his helmet off, his hair rumpled. "Pearl of the Desert. We must observe the proper mourning duties or Meric won't be accepted into the Fire's afterlife." His eyes were fire, and she was very afraid of being the next to burn.

But Varol joined her as she stared Adem down. For once, she and Varol were on the same side.

Seren opened her mouth, but Varol talked over her. "My brother's soul is beyond reproach. Nothing we do could keep his soul from crossing over."

"General Adem," Seren said, "we can't let our people fast and grow weak staying up all hours to hum and mourn."

She touched the green wool, her fingers shaking as Varol's eyes pierced her resolve and left her bleeding doubt. Did he support her in this or not? The man was as unpredictable as a storm in the Emptiness.

"The general and I will handle this, Pearl of the Desert," Varol said.

They weren't calling her *kyros*. The Holy Fire's vision had shown her the city's only chance at defeating the Invaders was with her at the lead. It seemed arrogant. The role was too big. But the Fire had called and she had to answer.

Down the way, Ona argued with a man twice her size. Beside her, Lucca shook his head and his lips moved, saying something that was probably wry and wise in equal measure. Barir whispered with Meekra, their steady gaze on Seren. Meekra's cut was visible from here.

Seren straightened her back. "You mean *Kyros Seren*, don't you?"

"You should join the others." Varol smiled, sickeningly sweet. "Soon enough, you may return to the Green Mountains to retire like your father."

Her throat burned, words pushing at her tongue but too weak to rise. She couldn't leave here. The Holy Fire had blessed her with ideas. She was meant to care for the Empire, not to molder in a far-away town.

"You'll have a quiet life as a former kyros's wife should." He turned away, dismissing her, and addressed the people, breaking their mourning sounds apart.

"As next in line," he shouted, spreading his arms wide, "I humbly accept the role of kyros and will do everything in my power to protect you, to honor my brother's memory."

Meekra and Barir's mouths dropped open. Down the line of kaptans, Ona frowned at Seren. Lucca cocked his head and took a step like he wanted to join Seren. She didn't know whether to ask them to come forward or not.

Small groups, who managed to hear over the pyre and the distance, wore confused looks. Several fell to their knees to show respect. The rest realized what was happening and kneeled alongside their neighbors. Questions showed in the way they moved and leaned close to whisper. This wasn't the way things were done. None of it.

Seren's guards were still and too quiet at her sides. Cansu's eyebrows had shot together, pensive and seemingly frustrated, but not really surprised. Did they know this was going to happen? Surely not. They were loyal. She was awful for even thinking it. Cansu looked at Erol. Erol's eyes were angry. Hossam's chest rose and fell too quickly. So they hadn't known. They were still loyal.

One couple in the crowd below the rise noticed Seren and held up their palms distinctly turned toward her instead of Varol. He didn't seem to notice.

Another family held their palms toward Seren, and another, another. Their concern tugged at her heart. She grabbed the front of her mourning kaftan, a deep pain slugging through her chest. Her people were supporting her, asking for her support in return. She couldn't let Varol take them from her. They were all she had left. They were her family.

Varol and Adem started back toward the city and the crowd dispersed as she and her guards, Meekra too, left the pyre. Lucca and Ona quickly found her side.

"What are you going to do?" Lucca whispered. "Shouldn't you speak out against him?"

Ona bumped him out of the way. Her foreign eyes were wide and she almost looked fevered. "You aren't going to keep that king alive, are you?" Her sheath clicked against her belt's buckle. She was a ball of energy. Dangerous energy. "Will Varol put him to death? You know the Invaders will begin a siege any minute, right?"

Seren had to think of a smart way—not some tantrum-throwing or power-hungry way—to remind her people that she was kyros here and she cared for them first. Unlike Varol. Akhayma was tired. And hungry. Emotionally exhausted. What did she want right now? What did her body need? Food. Simple food and the knowledge that someone cared.

Seren stopped and Hossam nearly ran her over, mumbling embarrassed apologies through his beard.

"Wait," she said. "Cansu, Erol, Hossam, spread word that Kyros Seren will host a simple meal for the people inside the Kyros Walls. When the sun is high."

Lucca grinned, taking some of the chill out of Seren. "This is a great idea."

"But what about the prisoners? The king?" Ona snapped.

"I'll deal with all that later. First, I must gain control again and comfort my people."

"There's no sun for comfort, my kyros." An ugly tone tarnished Ona's pronunciation of Seren's title. She stormed away. Seren reluctantly let her go.

Lucca touched Seren's arm briefly. "I'll talk to her."

"Thank you."

A smile surprised Seren as it crossed her mouth. This was good. This might work. She gave details to Meekra and messages for Erol to deliver to the high-castes, organizing, not a feast, but a coming-together, a humble way for the people to draw together under her wings.

~

SEREN SETTLED at the head table the house servants had placed in front of the main tent. The sun glinted off platters of chicken kabobs and bowls of flatbread and nuts.

Lucca walked over and refreshed Seren's hot tea even though a gruff house servant argued against him doing that sort of work.

"May the Holy Fire continue to bless you, Chosen One," a tiny woman wearing a striped, brown mourning kaftan said.

Seren handed the woman a piece of flatbread piled with meat for the little ones jumping at her elbows. "May the Fire bless us all. We're going to need it."

The crowd split and Adem marched through, a circle of kaptans and two ore masters around him.

Father once gave Seren some advice when a group of girls were being particularly mean during their small group tutoring: Treat your enemy as your friend and watch them fall into the role. When Seren had invited the girl who told lies about her to a special Age Day party, she'd ended up telling Seren she was only jealous of her looks. They'd never become friends exactly—Seren couldn't trust her—but at least the gossip had stopped.

"Another shout for our brave General Adem, who helped

defend our city at our most desperate hour," she said over the multitude of conversations.

Everyone turned toward Adem. Watching Seren curiously, they stomped their feet and raised their fists. "Our general!"

He bowed his head respectfully to Seren, but he didn't stay. He moved quickly into the main tent, his circle trailing him. Through the open flaps of the tent's door, Seren watched him sit at his usual spot at the high table inside. A red silk scarf hanging from a lantern fluttered between them, so only half his face—furrowed brow, angry eyes—showed.

She had to get a read on the man, to manage a guess on what he and Varol were planning.

"Meekra."

Her friend came forward and offered a plate to Seren, who took it and whispered, "I want to send a bowl of clean water to the general. And another portion of this meat." Seren leaned closer. "Have you heard anything about Varol?"

"He was seen going into his tent with two women. I think he is…taking some time for himself." Meekra rolled her eyes.

"I'm thankful for it. His absence allows me to gain a hold on the city again." Seren glanced over her shoulder toward Adem. "When you take the provisions to Adem, see if you can hear anything his friends there are saying."

Nodding, Meekra hurried off and pasted a humble smile onto her pretty face. Seren had a guess that simple beauty could glean more than any unit of armed torturers, but she knew she'd have to play the latter role soon with the prisoners.

Seren would have to find out troop counts. Mounted versus on foot. Information on the Invaders' food supplies and their wounded.

Facing the crowd, Seren raised her voice. "From the Fire

that burns within my heart and around my thoughts, I thank you all for your sacrifice and dedication. We've suffered a terrible loss, losing our Kyros Meric, but at least we have a victory to temper our grief. Lucca Hand of Ruination and Onaratta Paints with Blood, we owe you a heavy debt. You fought as if your own people hung in the balance, and you spearheaded the last push that drove the Invaders from our city!"

Ona wasn't in the crowd, though Seren pretended she was. She was most likely sleeping somewhere. A well-deserved rest.

Lucca, showing nothing more than a ripped sleeve and a swollen sword hand, grinned and tilted his chin down humbly, raising one fist to his chest in acknowledgment of the cheers and well wishes.

With happy shouts ringing, she closed her eyes to think of Meric. She didn't miss him, but this should've been his moment. And that was a tragedy.

"Erol, Cansu, Hossam." The men turned to face her. "I need to go to the parapet and see what the Invaders are doing."

She should've had reports from the scouts already. Maybe they were reporting to Varol.

Would Varol openly rise up against her as she fought for her title? Or would he continue to be absent like he was now?

"Lucca, would you go with me? I'd like a mercenary's view on this. You've seen fighting styles that my father probably never experienced."

"I doubt I'll be much help, but of course, I'll go. So," he whispered, "what are you going to do about Varol?"

"Ignore him and carry on."

"You think that's safe?"

"Nothing is safe. He probably believes I had a hand in

Meric's death. He'll be furious when he hears of the food I gave out and my speech, the way I'm clinging to my role here. But he has yet to show his face, so perhaps he only wanted a title and not the trouble that goes with it."

"From your mouth to the sky's ears."

"Where is Ona?"

"I'm guessing she is in our tent, fuming."

"Fuming? What is she angry about?" Seren kept her voice down as they passed two converging canals. Water splashed under the cover of the tents, sounding like a crowd whispering.

"That you didn't kill the king. That you're keeping prisoners alive. You shouldn't trouble yourself with what one mercenary thinks but—"

"But there could be more who share her anger. And now Varol is here to happily take on disgruntled warriors to fight me."

"Exactly."

"I'll have to execute the king eventually. I can't say I'll be very mournful about it. But I have to wait and see what makes the most sense strategically. There could be uses for him that we haven't yet thought of. Kaptan Rashiel agrees."

"Maybe you could listen to what Ona has to say? Maybe it'll give you some insight on possible outcomes?"

"I agree."

Lucca watched the road, eyes wary, his body close to hers. Nothing in his face said he judged her incompetent. He simply stood by her and helped when she seemed to need it most. Her heart glowed warmer and warmer as they walked on.

"I thank the Holy Fire I met you, Lucca."

He blinked, then smiled. "I hope you don't regret that after all this is through. I should probably stay away from you completely, considering."

"Don't you dare. Anyone who tries to take you from my side will suffer severe consequences."

Lucca's eyes shone. "Your wishes are my wishes, Kyros Seren."

"Is that a Silvanian saying?"

"It's a Lucca and Ona saying. Ona always follows it with *As long as yours don't war with mine.*"

"Yes. That sounds like her."

Seren hoped she could help Ona understand the need to be careful with their prisoners and not act rashly. Ona would be the worst kind of enemy. Seren would have to make time to listen to her, to explain too. But that would have to wait until she had a firm grip on what this siege looked like. Seren wanted to see the battlefield with her own eyes.

Qadira's father, leader of Clan Azjorr stopped near Seren, bowed low, and raised a palm—more than necessary for a casual public appearance. "Kyros Seren, we support you in full."

Qadira herself, and her younger sister and mother, joined him. They bowed too, but Qadira sneered, giving Seren a pretty clear picture of what she really thought about this unplanned display of support.

"I appreciate your words, Azjorr," Seren said to the chieftain, nodding to both husband and wife.

The wife smiled sadly. "Kyros Seren, we are your people."

"Please," the chieftain said. "Please claim your place."

An ore master, possibly one Adem had been whispering with lately, came around the corner. He walked behind them, not even noticing Seren's presence.

Lucca tensed.

Seren turned to the family. "Please be careful."

Qadira twisted to see who Seren was looking at before Seren and her retinue continued on.

So Azjorr would support her against Varol. But to keep her place, she'd have to think up a way to win against the coming siege to prove she was meant to be the Empire's kyros, its protector and caretaker, its leader blessed by the Fire. If only she could figure out what the Fire had shown her. What had those cloud-like objects been? She needed to talk to some engineers or inventors. She needed fresh ideas from afar.

Something Seren couldn't name gnawed at her as they started through the market and toward the front gates. Something was wrong. Very wrong.

The merchants weren't shouting about their spices, bags, or shoes. A snaggletoothed boy and twin girls each carried a ball around the bubbling shallows of the canals that branched away from the sacred bowl and pool. Normally, they'd be kicking them, racing to see who could get their ball to the city walls first. Even with the mourning, children were children. The animals were acting strangely too. Camels, donkeys, and goats munched and shuffled too quietly, subdued.

She stopped. Turning to Erol, a cold sweat rose along her back. "The tent is raised, isn't it?"

A weathered scout coated in dirt and wrinkles ran up and bowed hurriedly. "My kyros. You must see this." Three more scouts, young like Seren, came up behind the more experienced man. They looked like they'd seen ghosts. Or thought they'd soon be ghosts themselves.

Rushing toward the front gates, Lucca nimble beside her, passing wide-eyed faces and too-quiet rows of black-striped tents, Seren said one prayer, a thousand prayers.

Two large men, steel blinking at their sashes, appeared on the path. Dust rose around them like dark wings.

Seren stopped, turned, then rounded a corner, her men with her and the scouts trailing.

"Are they following us?" she asked Hossam. Her heart stuttered, then began to beat too quickly.

Cansu looked over his shoulder as they hurried on, heading down a different route. "I think so, my lady. Do you want me to go after them?"

"No. Just...stay alert."

Hossam nodded and said something quiet to the scouts.

Those two...they had to be Varol's men. Or Adem's. Only the Fire knew what their plans were. To watch her? Or to do something more sinister? This was her life now. Dodging attacks and telling lies.

AT THE TOP of the walls, Seren stared out at the plains and the hammadas behind them. The ground spreading from the city outward weren't dusty and brown anymore. The earth was silver and white and red and gold with more Invaders than sand in the Emptiness.

She gripped the smooth stone to keep from falling. Lucca, the scouts, and her guards grew very still.

In the midst of the warriors, a white tent displayed the Invaders' silent message loud and clear.

"What does the tent mean, Kyros?" Cansu asked.

Seren was fairly certain he knew. He just didn't want to believe the tales. He was hoping she had a better answer than what he feared. What they all feared.

"If Akhayma surrenders today, all will be spared. Tomorrow, the tent will be red, and next, black. The stakes will rise with each day. They have committed to this siege. There's no scaring them off now."

Groups of Invaders pounded their shields with fists, the low thumping echoing up and over the stone barrier. The sound echoed the panicked beating of Seren's heart.

"But you won't surrender, will you, Kyros?" Erol's voice was sharp as a dagger's edge.

"No. And I'll be thrown into the vast sands of the Emptiness before I let Varol or Adem do it either." She knew what came with surrender. Father had told her those stories too. Mother had never made any songs about those terrible, serious talks. "I'd rather us all die fighting than live to become Invader playthings. Surrendering to an Invader is far, far worse than any death."

18

SEREN

After sending Erol and Cansu to look around and listen for information about Varol and Adem's movements or public statements, Seren, Lucca, and Hossam headed to the guest tent.

"It'll be quiet there," she said. "I need to pray."

Inside, Seren paused at the Fire and passed her palm over the orange and blue light, Lucca standing beside her with hands clasped in front of him and Hossam near the door. Seren tried to let go of her worry and stress, to trust in the Flame and the calm solidness of Lucca nearby. She'd hoped to have some space, away from the main tent and everyone else, and this was perfect. The Fire had shown her something earlier and she needed to know what it was and how it could help. The Flames wouldn't have bothered with a vision if it wasn't important. Besides, she didn't have any other ideas on how to deal with the siege and Varol and all.

Spreading her palms wide over the flickering tongues, she

pushed that urge to flee or scream or crumble aside firmly. She closed her eyes and eased into the feel of the Holy Fire, the heat running fingertips over her skin. A gray night washed over the darkness behind her eyelids. There were those clouds again. The odd shapes faded, then she saw tiny black puffs of smoke, then a blink of white light in the vision.

Her eyes flashed open. "Black powder?"

Lucca frowned. "Like the easterners use in their cannon?"

Seren twirled her wool scrap around her finger. "We've never used it here because the Invaders don't have access to it. I suppose Akhayma's never needed it."

"How would we use black powder anyway? You don't have any cannon, do you?"

"No. But I don't think the Fire was showing me that anyway." She pressed her fingers against her temples. "Why can't I see it clearly?"

"Would it help to tell me what you think you see?"

His kind eyes warmed her middle. "There are these ivory... clouds. But I'm not sure they're clouds. They're rounded, floating. I...I don't know. Somehow they're connected to the powder. The black puffs came from the bottoms of them, or were around them. I can't see it. I can't." She pressed the heels of her hands against her eyes, an itch building inside her chest. "I can't."

"Don't knock yourself over the head about it. You can only do what you can do. Maybe if you try not to think about it, it'll become clear. That happens with me sometimes. When I focus on something else, the problem untangles in my head. Ignore me if I sound like an idiot. I don't know anything about your Fire or running a war."

She couldn't help but smile. "I'd never ignore you. Even if

you weren't a trained mercenary who does indeed know a lot about war, about fighting."

"War isn't simply fighting and you know it."

"But some of the elements are the same."

"How did you learn so much about war, Kyros?" Lucca asked as they walked out of the guest tent and into the last of the day. The orange-red orb bled into strips of clouds like bandages.

"I read all of the military scrolls and books I could get my hands on. My father, the former High-General, encouraged it. We used to talk until late at night, boring Mother to death. When she'd had enough, she poked fun at our serious talk with little songs she made up." A smile drifted over Seren's mouth. If only they were here… "But I still have so much to learn. I don't know why the Fire has chosen me."

"Because of your humility. You're willing to learn and try new things, risking your reputation. I've seen nobles whose egos hogged all the acreage in their big heads."

"I probably need more confidence."

"You have enough to get the job done, Kyros. Listen, if it pleases you, I'll find Ona and try to talk to her again."

"That would be helpful, thank you. I need to question prisoners."

A shudder jarred her, shaking off the warm feeling of talking with Lucca. Somehow fighting in a battle was less horrible than doing damage to captured enemies.

Lucca almost took her arm to steady her, then he glanced at Hossam and stopped himself. She wished he wouldn't hold himself back. "I can come with you, my lady," he said quietly, words full of respect.

"No. I'll be…" She couldn't say fine. Killing and torture and questioning was the furthest thing from *fine*. "I can handle it."

He gave her a nod before heading away.

She started toward the back gate, under black-winged swallows that dove and spun to catch their prey. Seren's feet knew the way to go and it was a good thing because her mind was occupied with strange pale shapes and blasts of black powder. Someday, she hoped, there wouldn't be as many terrible duties and frightening visions. But today was full of them. She found that invisible armor for her heart and set out to bleed information from her enemies.

~

"THE KING—HAS he been placed in the larger cell away from his men?" Seren walked under the back gate's arch, Hossam at her right, adjusting his sash and brushing dirt from his uniform.

Erol and Cansu came out of the gate's shadow and into the moonlight. They'd been listening and learning all they could about Varol's movements, his orders, and how Adem was playing into them.

Seren paused, a hand going to her chest. When had she gone from doing everything she could to protect them and keep them out of danger to using them to spy on the men who could have them killed with a word?

"Yes, Kyros Seren," Hossam said, worry etched in the wrinkles around his big eyes.

Seren started walking again. She had to keep going. There was no way to keep these wonderful, loyal guards safe anymore. No one was safe anymore.

"What did you learn, Cansu, Erol?" she asked. "I'm fine, Hossam." She smiled at him to soften her curt words.

Erol and Cansu bowed their heads as they worked to keep up with her increasing pace moving into the training area.

"An ore master and several guildmasters met with High General Varol in his tent, my lady." Erol's jaw tensed. "Two scouts reported to him as well. Not the men who came to us. Those two are in the barracks, resting. They are loyal, it seems. Also, those loyal scouts told us High General Varol entered Akhayma through an abandoned mine. Hearing about the newly accessible mine, the scouts used it to watch the Invaders fall into their siege camp. Looking through an opening in the shaft, the scouts counted the Invader troops."

"Adem cleared the mine for Varol." Seren rubbed her lip, talking to herself.

Cansu looked at the sandy path in front of them, his voice taut. "The Invaders number at 40,000."

An invisible knife touched Seren's throat and she halted again, just for a breath, before continuing on. She'd seen them. She'd known there were a great many. But 40,000. How could they fight that many without losing every man, woman, and child in the city?

Overhead, darkening clouds hovered over the training field, the walls housing the iron ore mines beyond, and the hammadas in the far distance. 40,000 warriors. Akhayma was boxed in, trapped, surrounded and Seren couldn't see a way out.

Cells lined the slope leading away from the training fields. Torches flickered like dying stars, lighting the grounds unevenly and throwing yellow and white beams against the shadows. Seren waved the prison guard forward and the man slipped a mint leaf from his pocket into his mouth, bowing as he hurried. His plum-shaped face was familiar. Ah. Meric had used the man twice to interpret for captured Invader scouts during her first days as his wife. That felt like lifetimes ago.

Hossam took a prisoner from the crowded cells. Perspiration wet the captured man's light brown hair. It clung to his face as Hossam shoved the man's cheek against a stone block. One visible eye turned to look from Seren to Hossam to the interpreter.

"Give me your best guess on what your army will do next." Seren gave the interpreter a minute to do his job. "And we can kill you and be done with it. I've no desire to cause you additional pain."

The prisoner spat at her slippers.

Sick with this duty, Seren stepped back, holding her kaftan away, and shook her head.

"Take another finger then," she said quietly.

Erol raised his yatagan over the stone block as Hossam forced the prisoner's hand into position. Seren's stomach clenched. But this was war, and she'd cut a thousand fingers to save her people from what her family had endured.

The finger came off with a horrid thunk and a soul-ripping shriek not unlike the screams the Invaders released when they killed—full of pain and drive both. Cold sweat beaded on Seren's forehead and upper lip. She bent to look the prisoner in the face.

"Now, will you talk to me?"

He spat on her cheek.

Raising herself up and taking Cansu's offered square of linen, she pronounced the man's sentence. "Run him through, quickly for his courage, but properly for his crimes against our people."

Hossam laid the body in the growing pile they'd haul outside the walls tonight.

The guards brought a new prisoner to the block. An unseen hand pushed Seren closer. This Invader was wiry like Haris—one of the fighters who'd taken to trailing Lucca and Ona—but a much fairer version, with pale eyes and unusually short hair. His fellows called out what sounded like encouragement in their language from behind the cell bars. This one was liked. Could that be what was drawing her to him?

"Will we see the same fate come to you, soldier?" Seren asked. She quieted to let the interpreter do his job.

On his knees, the wiry Invader stared ahead at nothing.

"What job did you do for your king?" she asked and the interpreter spoke quickly.

The Invader turned to the interpreter, then to Seren, surprise and caution twisting his mouth and eyes. "Sword. Shield. Like most."

His eyes said something entirely different. "No." She pointed to his face. "I see intelligence there. A man like your king would see it too. Surely he had more use for you than merely raw fighting. Do you really want to continue supporting that dog of a king only to lose your life?"

"Could I ever have a full life here?" the Invader asked.

When the interpreter finished speaking, Hossam almost dropped his hold on the man.

"Yes...you could," Seren said.

Cansu and Erol traded a look. She gave them one that snapped them back to attention, almost confident for once.

"If you can give me a solid idea about your army's probable next move and aid me with fresh strategies to counter," she said, "you could live in the tented city as a rich man for as long as the Holy Fire wills it."

"I'm an engineer."

"One who makes gears?"

"Yes. And systems. Mechanisms. I don't know if that translates..."

"I understand. Like ways to move water or waste."

"Exactly."

Seren wound the green wool at her sash around a finger and paced. The prisoners behind the engineer had gone quiet.

"What about...black powder?" she asked quietly.

The interpreter stopped, his face wrinkled in confusion. Seren cupped her hands together, then quickly fanned her fingers and spread her arms wide. The engineer's eyes opened wider.

He nodded slowly, swallowing. "But," he said through the interpreter, "you must promise I stay here after. If we create something together."

A dark hope bloomed inside Seren. She leaned in close enough to see the dirt in the pores on his nose. "Before I promise," she whispered, the interpreter at her knee, "tell me why you're willing to do this horrible thing to your people."

"It's this or die, yes?"

"Yes. But you could die...honorably, or so your people would say."

"You know what we do. You've heard the stories?"

Seren fisted her sweating hands. Her sisters' screams seared her memory, so perfectly recalled that her eardrums burned like coals. "I've lived the stories."

The engineer's face tightened. "So you know there is no

honor for me to claim. I don't care to suffer for my people. I'm not like them."

The sadness in his voice tugged at Seren's heart. *But he could be lying.* She swallowed her fear. "It is agreed then. I swear on the Holy Fire to protect you for as long as you care to live in Akhayma if you help me win this war."

"I swear on the only one I trust. Myself," the engineer said.

Seren nodded. It was sad, but it seemed an honest oath. "Hossam, bring this prisoner to the mercenaries' tent." She didn't want this plan flashed in front of Adem or Varol. Not yet. Employing an enemy didn't seem like the best way to garner support for her position as kyros. But if this worked…

"Yes, my lady."

"And call for a kaptans' meeting right now. I'll meet with them before Adem can realize I've called them together. I'm surprised he hasn't called another of his own." Too busy meeting secretly in his own tent or Varol's. "Send out the messengers to let everyone know. Lucca too. And Ona." Her cheeks heated, realizing how casually she'd mentioned them, with no titles, in front of her fighters. But she wasn't going to take it back or correct herself. Formality wasn't important in this case. These men knew her well.

"Of course, my lady," they all replied.

Hossam helped the engineer up and started toward Lucca and Ona's lodgings, the place it seemed Seren would always come back to.

19

ONA

Grit clouded each of Ona's steps and coated her scuffed boots and threadbare leggings as she paced from the agricultural section of the city and through another merchant area where a little whip of a boy flung himself at her.

"Kaptans meeting now, Onaratta Paints with Blood!" He tugged at her sleeve and went on in heavily accented trade tongue she could hardly understand. "Kyros Seren has called you there. You must go now."

"Ergh." Ona feared she wouldn't be able to hold her tongue with Seren right now. She was too frustrated with the fact that the king was still alive.

"Now." The boy bounced on his toes, the twelve tin bells on his sash jangling. "You have to go now. Please."

"What are you, ten? Maybe nine years old? What happens if I don't go because I'm kind of irritated, and they find out you told me and failed to get me there?"

He cocked his head as he worked out what she'd said. "No food tonight. Maybe a beating."

"Skies. A beating?" Ona sighed heavily. "I'll go." She shooed him away and he left reluctantly.

She stormed past tables folded against tent posts and half-walls. Families blabbered behind the thick fabric of their homes and shops, some cried over the dead, although not so many had been cut down. Others mourned their worthless, former kyros. Why? Ona couldn't figure it out. Meric had been pretty pointless from what she'd heard.

Honestly, she couldn't figure anyone out.

Where was Varol? He was all *I'm here to take over!* then he promptly disappeared. Ona wanted to see him again, to watch the people around him react to his naturally powerful presence. It was intriguing. The man didn't need chants. Must've been that royal blood. She couldn't help but be impressed. So why wasn't he using this power to get this war over with?

And Seren, why was she not murdering the king and dancing on his disgusting body? What reason could there ever be to hold on to a monster like that? The Invaders' white tent said they would only stop their siege with full surrender. There was no turning back now.

"Why doesn't she understand? I thought she understood!" Ona shouted, shattering the night's quiet sounds.

"Kaptan Onaratta!"

The moon did its level best to cut through the suffocating clouds. Light glinted across a smooth brow. A warrior Ona didn't know waved, a helmet on her knee as she scooped a handful of water from the canal with a wooden cup and splashed her neck. "Did you hear the kyros is questioning prisoners? Someone said she is keeping one alive, maybe giving him freedom, to work on strategy. She is wise, isn't she? Is your leader as wise?"

Ona's chest caved in. First, the king. Now this? That was it. She had to talk to Seren in private. She could explain everything in terms she'd understand.

"Well, Kaptan, what do you think?" the fighter asked.

"What do *you* think I think about it? And what business is it of yours?"

"Our Kyros Seren certainly weaves a different pattern than Kyros Meric ever did. Fine work during the attack," she said, droning on and on—utterly blind to Ona's glare.

Ona started down the main roadway to the market, her ribs strangling her heart. Seren was freeing the very people who took Ona's and Seren's own loved ones. The people who destroyed both of their childhoods. And she wasn't just letting them go. That would be bad enough, but she was employing them!

Her sword was drawn before she knew what she was doing. She dashed it across a cart's wheel. That big, fancy sacred bowl at the oasis would be an even better thing to smash. Ona took a rough breath, then coughed with all the stupid sand in the air. She let out a swear. She needed a good cup of wine five minutes ago. Ten minutes ago. Yesterday. Her throat was a wasteland.

"Ona," a voice growled near the oasis' pool of gurgling water. Nuh's belly hung over his belt as he bent to fill a skin, drank a mouthful, and wiped his mouth with the back of his hand. "That's the goat farmer's cart you damaged. He's one of the middle-castes Kyros Seren asked to advise her. He'll be one of her favorites. Better watch your actions, friend."

"Better watch yourself."

"So sorry, Kaptan Ona!" He grinned. "Hey, aren't you supposed to be at a kaptans' meeting? Might be over by now."

Ona seriously considered slicing the smile off his stupid face. It took a lot for her to turn away and keep on.

In a narrow lane, a girl no bigger than a desert tree sapling offered Ona a green scarf—an imitation of the strip of wool Seren wore on her sash.

"I will give you a good price," she said in a cracked version of the trade tongue. "Maybe you can earn Holy Fire with the kyros's kind of clothings." She pushed the fabric into Ona's free hand, then saw the sword and drew back.

Ona sheathed the weapon and gave her a quick smile. It wasn't easy. "No. Thank you."

The little girl grinned back weakly, tears in her eyes. "Thank you for the fight. For helping us stay safe."

Throat even drier, Ona stared at the Invader blood under her own nails—crescent moons of black-red blood carried from the birthplace of those who stole the life from her birthplace.

"I'll always fight for you." Her aunt's nimble hands flashed through her memory. "I'll never rest until all the Invaders are dead."

The girl made a circle on her forehead with her thumb and dipped her chin.

"Learn to use this." Ona pointed at her sheathed sword. "It'll do a lot more for you than Holy Fire or those tears of yours."

The girl nodded and hurried into her family's tent, jabbering about something, Ona maybe. Ona turned a corner, and the child's finch-like voice faded beneath the night noise of the market, camels snorting, water rushing, the sounds of cooking, and the occasional groans of the injured assembled near the holy place.

Ona had to convince Seren that every single one of these Invaders was capable of making children like that little girl cry.

Seren would make a great leader. She was decisive, her looks gave her an air of power, and she had great ideas. Surely, she'd come around and see sense. Releasing an enemy into her own city was only a slip. A mistake born out of her good heart. She'd wise up. And Ona was the one to help her do it before it was too late and they had a wolf loose in their own woods.

Ona suddenly wished she wasn't spending the day alone. She wasn't going to grab another random soldier to talk to or kiss. Those moments never added up to satisfaction.

For the thousandth time, she longed for a match. A true match.

Lucca was the closest, but he was like a brother. She huffed. And other boys, well, they were too easy to figure out, and also, to intimidate. The only person who'd come close to really capturing Ona's whole self was that duke's son from the raid when she'd almost died and Lucca saved her. The lordling had been curt, cutthroat, and very close to perfect. A good challenge.

Voices sneaked from the closed flap of the guest tent. All thoughts of boys spilled away as Ona pushed in and found a challenge she wasn't expecting.

SEREN

S eren blinked as Ona walked in and froze, looking like a very surprised and very angry statue. Where had she been all this time?

"Kyros Seren," the engineer said through the interpreter, "what is the idea trying to hatch in your thoughts?"

Giving Ona a nod—if she wanted to watch this, maybe that was good as it might change her mind—Seren explained what she'd seen in her vision.

"This sounds like a balloon," the foreign man said, his angled eyes focused. "Maybe a square of fabric filled with air and set into the wind. Our people make them for Children's Day."

The celebration's name pinched Seren's heart. The enemies had families. Of course they did. But it was so much easier to fight them without being reminded of the fact that every time an arrow landed, it was taking away someone's mother or father, brother or sister. She tried hard to imagine Invader families participating in an event named for their children. All that light-colored hair waving in a breeze, smiles on their broad faces instead of grimaces, fingers wrapped around colorful crafts instead of gripping the hilt of a sword.

"But the...balloons I saw rose on their own," she said, trying to focus. "Steadily, not simply with the wind."

The engineer snapped his fingers, looking less and less like a prisoner of war as his passion overtook his fear. "I talked to a friend of mine about the possibility of this." The interpreter scrambled to keep up. "I thought maybe if we used hot air, the balloons could do just that."

"How do we make hot air?" Seren asked.

"With fire?" Cansu said, looking sheepish.

"That fire." The engineer pointed to the Holy Fire bowl near the door.

Ona unfroze slowly and looked at the Flames, her lips parted.

Seren rubbed her lip, thinking. "A bowl attached to the square of fabric, open only to catch the hot air?"

"The fabric would need to be painted with rubber. Rubberized," the engineer said.

This actually made sense. "And it floats over the enemy..."

The engineer looked at the ground. "Yes," he said mournfully. "It is filled with black powder that..." He made the explosive movements with his ivory hands.

"But how do we keep the powder from going off before it is where it needs to be?"

Drawing an invisible line in the air, the engineer said, "Long fuse."

"Your king's army will lay siege to the city if they gain reinforcements," she said.

"And they do."

Ona's face flushed, her teeth gritted and showing. "Why. Are. You. Trusting. Him."

She drew her sword.

Before Cansu, Erol, or Hossam could move, she had the blade at the engineer's neck from behind. "Let me end him for you, my lady. I'll help you with your idea and no information will be leaked to our enemies."

Hossam moved toward her, but Seren held up a hand. "Ona, I—"

"Please." Agony wrinkled Ona's brow and pulled at the corners of her mouth.

She'd been through so much. Seren knew how it felt, the need to do something about the hollowing, cutting, burning pain of not having your family any more, of someone taking them from you violently. Seren's arms ached to grab Ona, to hold her close and grieve with her. Ona needed to cry, to release that dark pain. It wouldn't stop the agony, but it'd do her so much good to allow tears to clean the vengeance from her blood.

"Ona. Listen. What if this man," she pointed at the engineer who to his credit stood erect and still, "is the key to finally defeating the rest of them?"

"Will you..." Ona glared daggers at the interpreter so he wouldn't translate, "...kill this one after we have the deed done?"

The engineer's gaze moved from Seren's face to the hand and blade at his throat. He didn't know the words, but he understood Ona's meaning well enough.

"Of course not." Seren stepped forward and touched Ona's dusty sleeve. "What if he isn't like the ones who hurt us? What if he was simply born to this violence and knows nothing different?" Seren looked into the engineer's eyes, willing him to say something that might help his case.

Ona's fingers shook against the hilt of her sword. Seren could've ordered her off the man, but Ona was lit up like a fuse, ready to spark a fight Seren didn't want to win or lose. The lantern's light touched the white streak in her red-brown hair. Seren had seen others with a streak like that. It sometimes resulted from a terrible shock. Ona had risked more pain pretending to be Meric. For Seren. For her people. After all Ona had been through, she deserved Kurakian chicken and laughs with friends, not...this. Seren's heart strained against its own beating.

"This man, he is different from the others," she said.

"No, he is not." Ona's voice was tight and low. "It's in his blood. They're all...pigs. Vermin. Filth."

A line of red leaked from the spot where her blade kissed the engineer's skin. If she killed him, the idea could be lost. This was Akhayma and the Empire's only chance against a siege. Seren felt it in her skin. This could mean Meekra's life, and her younger sisters' lives, the wise as an owl noble Najwa, her cousin Qadira, and the giggly low-caste Izzet. Lucca and his warm smile would be wiped from the earth alongside Ona, her fierce energy snuffed out like a northern candle's flame. Seren clutched at her stomach. Everyone she knew and loved would die.

"You're my friend," Seren whispered. "Don't force me to use my rank against you or—"

"Or what? Come now, Ser—Kyros Seren. I don't understand where your head is. We're on the same side. Why can't you see they *all* have to be eliminated?"

Seren closed her eyes against the raw pain in Ona's face.

"Enough." Seren gestured to her guards. Cansu and Hossam grabbed Ona.

Ona swore. "Get off me." Jerking free, she raged out of the tent, not sparing one look for Seren.

With a word, Seren held her men back from going after Ona. Meric would've had her killed for this disrespect. Seren said a prayer that her friendship with Ona would last through the fight.

Erol tended the engineer's bleeding neck with a cloth.

"My apologies, prisoner," Seren said to the engineer. "My friend has suffered a great deal at the hands of your countrymen and she...well, it won't happen again."

The engineer gave Erol a nod of thanks and held a second cloth against his wound. "Am I still 'prisoner' then?"

"I...I don't want to..." It was such a difficult situation. Seren had never faced something like this. She thought of what her mother would've done. *Honesty, that's the only way through things,* she'd always said.

"Am I?" the engineer asked again.

Seren looked the man in the eye. "You are if you know what is good for you. A free man would be dead by sunrise. Onaratta would take you, or another of my own warriors would. Probably Erol right there. Don't give me that look, Erol. I can see how you look at him. Either way, you," she said to the foreigner, "wouldn't walk on two legs for long. This venture of ours... won't be popular."

The black lacquered tray Seren had ordered Cansu to bring sat propped against a stool. She took it, sat, and emptied a pouch of sand across its surface. "This is how I'm seeing this new weapon."

The sand curled around her finger and the emptied lines

formed a rounded shape connected to a firepot instead of a bowl.

"The fire would need more cover to stay lit in the open like that. Plus, we'll need space for more ingredients below. A sealed spot underneath the flames."

The engineer leaned over to draw and Hossam moved closer, hand on his hilt. The engineer added a long fuse coming out of the side of the bowl, then a deeper well to the container. "The ingredients that explode will go here," he said through the interpreter.

"So the cloth is rubberized silk," Seren said. "The fabric will hold the hot air, the contraption will lift off and float above the enemy as they sleep."

He swallowed. "So this will fly above your enemies, then blast apart, setting fire to tents and men. Throwing shards of pottery like arrowheads."

This had to be terrible for him, betraying his people.

"It's this or you die," she said quietly. "I'm sorry you're in this situation. But you are. And don't think for a second that I'll change my mind." She spoke with far more confidence than she had. "Remember: it wasn't us who began this war. If this works and we humble them further, perhaps we can negotiate a lasting peace. I have no desire for violence, but they have to be humbled. You all displayed the fact rather plainly, don't you agree?"

He nodded. "I did not choose this war." He focused again on the sand drawing on the tray in Seren's lap.

"The problem is how to keep the fire from sparking the powder too soon," she said, trying not to think how many like him were out there, simply doing what they had to do to survive. "Also how to stop the fire at the right moment so the balloon will float down or at least explode in the air. Could we simply shoot them down with arrows?"

"Might disturb the contents before the proper moment," he said.

They both made a thinking, humming noise.

"What if we made small, clay firepots with only enough oil to take them so far. We could try different amounts and see how far they go," she said.

He hummed again. "And how high. I've never worked with the powders and explosive ingredients so there will be...tries."

The interpreter frowned, knowing the word was off.

Seren smiled. "Experiment. He means experiments."

"Yes. Experiment," the interpreter agreed.

"You might end up dead," Seren said, watching for his fear. It was there, but his eyes also showed the will to do this horrible thing and live to see another day.

"I escaped death twice this day. Why not try for three?" he said, his tone dry as the Emptiness.

"Silvanians claim third time's the charm." Seren smoothed the sand in the tray to hide the weapon from anyone who might tell Adem what she was up to. She needed the first time to be the charm, so to speak. This one and only try was stolen, snatched between the threat of damning secrets and wavering loyalties. If this went badly, not only would she be killed, but she might end up killing her own army inside their own walls.

It simply had to work.

2 1

ONA

Ona threw the tent flap out of her face, the pinch of Hossam's strong fingers lingering on her arms and shoulders as she wove through the moon-bleached city. The striped tents were skeletal beasts that murmured in jumbled languages.

Seren was a fool. Well, maybe not a fool. But too soft. Much too soft. Gah! The look on her face when that pig mentioned some special day for children. As if they truly celebrated anything but killing. No way. Ona couldn't imagine that in one million years.

And the Invaders would use Seren's weakness to find another, larger crack in the Empire's defenses. Offering the king for a ransom had been the first break. This engineer was the second. If he didn't slit her throat while they worked side-by-side, he'd find a way to get the gates open at the training field, the mines, or the main entrance to the city. Maybe he'd smuggle counts of weapons and fighters out by way of another traitor in their midst. Thousands of possibilities spread through the situation, spidering like mold from a leak in plaster.

The scent of hot iron, fire, and a banging that just about fit the force of Ona's anger poured from one of the many blacksmith forges. They were running non-stop now that war had arrived on their pretty doorstep. One of those spooky ore masters in their too-long black cloaks accepted a new yatagan from a smith in a soot-smudged apron.

The ore master turned the blade and moon and fire light washed over the man's face. He'd been beside Sweet Bean at the feast. They'd whispered like old pals.

"That's a beauty," Ona said in the trade tongue.

"It is, friend of our Pearl."

Not using her title, hm? "I need to speak with General Adem. In private. Do you know where I can find him?"

The man's gaze was as sharp as the yatagan.

Ona stared back. "Are you going to help me or stand there with your sword in your hand all night?"

He sniffed a laugh, paid the smith with a suede pouch of noisy coins, and led Ona away from the city center and to a towering blue tent where the general himself stood outside, pulling at his beard and chewing his cheek. Seemed Ona wasn't the only one plotting.

She reminded herself to be careful with this. She cared for Seren. She didn't want her punished or shamed overmuch. Just because Seren was wrong in this, didn't mean Ona wanted her dead.

Adem stopped, frowned. "To what do I owe the honor?"

"We need to talk." Ona nodded toward the tent.

His eyebrows lifted, but he pushed the flap aside and stopped to pass his hand respectfully over the bowl of Holy Fire. The inside of this tent was very different from the sunset purple light of the guest one. The deep blue gave the illusion of being underwater. Slits, cut around the tent's peaks let in moonlight and made Ona think of the sun on the tips of the ocean waves near home. She put a hand to her head, suddenly in pain about what she was doing.

But she'd be careful. Seren didn't have to suffer in this. Not if Ona handled it like Lucca would. Smooth. Calm. Level-headed.

For a second, Ona wished he was here to smooth the situation and pet Sweet Bean's ego properly. Too bad he wouldn't have helped her with this. He was all for Seren, no matter what she did. She'd claimed his heart. He'd never judge her actions objectively. No, Ona was all on her own.

She thought of her aunt. The way the side of her mouth used to tuck up when Ona spilled the vase of priceless brushes or decided she had to paint a goat's horns in green and yellow stripes. It was a smile that said No and Yes. Ona had to go behind Seren and Lucca's back this time for her aunt. The Invaders had to be stopped. Seren and Lucca would understand once this was over and they were safe.

She squeezed her hands into fists, feeling every knuckle and nail. *For you, Aunt. I won't let them live. I will see every last one of them dead.*

Adem gestured to a three-legged stool near a low table that held scrolls of parchment, ink, quills, and groups of dark stones positioned in what Ona had to guess was where he believed the Invaders had retreated to beyond the hammadas.

"I'm not sure how to start." Ona ignored the stool and kept a hand on her sword. She chanted *Wake iron! Wake.* to herself silently in case he decided what she said called for a quick death.

"With the most immediate need." His voice had fangs.

"Kyros Seren—"

"You mean Pearl of the Desert. High General Varol is kyros now."

"Whatever."

Adem's mouth twisted.

"She spared the life of an Invader prisoner and is working with him to develop a weapon she wants to use against the Invaders."

His mouth turned down, moving his trim beard. "And?"

"And? And he is with her, by her side, capable of killing her, spying on us—any number of crimes."

"It doesn't matter."

"How can you say that? You hate them as much as I do. Am I the only person who hasn't been hit on the head too hard? He is the enemy. They all must die for what they've done over and over again to your people, to mine, to the Empire. The kyros offered peace and they tried to slay us all again. Doesn't that prove the color of their souls?"

He held a hand out like Ona was a snorting horse that needed to be gentled. "You'd already know everything if you'd cease your rambling." He pointed to the stool.

Ona still didn't sit. "Fine. Spill it then. What are you up to, Sweet Bean?"

The look in his eye could've split her head in two. "First, you must swear by the Holy Fire and reaffirm your role as a warrior for the Empire. For the true heir to our lands, Kyros Varol."

She looked to the ceiling. "Oh, please. Like an unannounced meeting or chatting about politics with a Silvanian mercenary keeps with tradition. You break what traditions you choose to break. Haven't you noticed this about yourself? When are you going to ease up?"

He spun, took up his Holy Fire bowl, and held it out to her. Blue flames licked deep green leaves. "Swear. Or this meeting is adjourned."

"In the name of all the…"

"Mercenary!"

"Fine. Fine! I swear by the Holy Fire to fight on the side of the Empire, for the true heir of the power of the Empire, now and forevermore, may my soul be wiped from time if I break this hallowed oath. Will that do it for you?" It didn't mean anything so who cared who she promised to support. These were just words Adem needed to hear.

With one more steely look, he turned, set the fire on a long desk beside a chest of drawers, and said quietly, "I am going to take Pearl of the Desert…away."

Ona suddenly wished for the fire's heat. Her insides had gone cold. "Away?"

"You don't need to know the details. She will not be harmed, but she will be removed from the situation here so her ridiculous tactics and lies about being Blessed don't get in the way of Kyros Varol's strategy to win against the Invaders. Will you help me smooth the transition to a leader who won't spare a single Invader, no matter what they offer?"

Ona's heart pounded in her ears. If she said the wrong thing now, Seren could be sentenced to death. Maybe Lucca too. This felt surprisingly similar to the day she'd walked onto the iced up lake near Aunt's villa. The glassy surface knocked and echoed under her boots. A crack cut across the blue-black and she raced to the shore before she could lose her life to the cold, winter water.

Now, Ona's sweaty fingers flexed on her hilt. "I could talk to the fighters who might lean toward supporting him."

"Good."

Ona's heart gave a kick as she pictured Seren's trusting grin. "The Pearl of the Desert should be protected. In every way. No matter what Varol thinks she has done, or is doing." She sounded like a simple child. But she didn't want to say anything that could be directly related to the crimes Seren had already committed. Vague seemed the way to go.

"Of course," Adem replied, his voice slicker than Ona liked.

She could talk to Haris, maybe, then let him nurture the others' desire for a ruler of the royal blood and someone with a stronger policy against the Invaders.

Ona's first two fingers popped as she flexed her sword hand. An errant question flittered through her mind: *would my hand look different if I'd been able to wield paint brushes and charcoal instead of steel?*

She met Adem's cold gaze. "Lucca and I are with the Empire. No matter who reigns as its head."

A muscle at Adem's jaw twitched. "Lucca." He was no Lucca supporter. That was pretty obvious. "Very well," he said. "But don't think you're not being watched. I have eyes. Everywhere."

Ona shooed his warning away. "Varol has experience in battle?"

"More than the Pearl of the Desert."

"He should listen to her though. To her ideas. Well, some of them. She is a smart one."

He looked away, shifting his weight.

Ona didn't like where this was going. She could already see

Seren beaten and bloodied at Adem's feet. "We also nabbed the king, don't forget."

He wouldn't look at her. "You must keep this from the other mercenary."

Could he tell that Lucca had feelings for Seren?

"You will not tell him anything or I'll have your head. I'll know who told and I'll have you surrounded and beaten before you can utter a word."

"I get it. I get it. I won't tell him." It was as if someone else had said the words. How could she so easily throw off Lucca? But Adem was right. He wouldn't see the situation clearly.

Ona offered her forearm in agreement. Adem wrapped his wiry fingers around her sleeve and squeezed, a copy of her own movement.

"It is agreed." He cast a glance over his shoulder at the door.

Ona studied his face. Was he hiding the fact that he'd go right now to Seren and order her death? It wouldn't be impossible. Ona swallowed, her head pounding suddenly. Ona cared about Seren, even if she didn't agree with her. She didn't want the woman killed.

"I love her too, mercenary," he said softly and Ona moved away, shocked that he'd been able to tell what she was thinking, that her own emotions were so plainly written on her face. "I didn't care for her family, but...Varol is simply the proper ruler. He has the royal blood. And I truly hope she stops lying about the Holy Fire and these..." His gaze sharpened. "Are you certain you know nothing about the kyros's death?"

Ona's skin prickled like lightning was about to strike. "He was sick. Now he's dead. Not much to that story." She cleared her face of the lie. Wiped her fear and deceit away like she had so many times while training under Dom. One couldn't survive that man without some well-told lies. When Lucca wasn't watching, he stripped weaklings clean of silver and dignity both.

Adem stared, weighing her words.

"Listen, this isn't my world here," Ona said. "It's yours. Don't ask me to untangle the mess you and yours have made. I'll play my part."

With one last look, Sweet Bean turned. "Fine. Just so you know, you're a gifted liar. And Kyros Meric's brother is a gifted leader. You'll see." He began pacing. "As for your part, talk to those with only desert blood and feed their fear that Pearl and those with her blood might wrest the Empire from the royal family. As for the rest, with mixed blood like mine and hers, we'll rely on their training. High General Varol outranks Pearl." He crossed his arms over his chest. "Kyros Varol will make all of this worth the trouble. You'll see. He is a force unto himself. A born ruler."

A quiet shiver spread under Ona's skin.

Adem raised an eyebrow. "That smile alone tells me you're equal to this delicate mission."

"I live to destroy the Invader pigs and do whatever I must to make that happen. Never doubt that fact."

22

SEREN

That night, Seren slept—and the city with her—
everyone lost in sheer exhaustion. Lying on the bed
in Meekra's section of the chamber, Seren pushed the
thought of Meric and Adem and blood and lies out of her mind
and savored the memory of Lucca smelling like pine and
leather, his large hands on her waist. She forced herself to
dream about what she'd accomplished. She'd driven off the
Invaders—they even held their king—and she'd done it without
Meric, and without Adem finding out about Meric. She had
success, but it didn't...it didn't feel like she'd thought it would.

She woke before dawn, thinking about the engineer, a man
who'd been her enemy, but who was currently working toward
bringing her idea to life. A square of the rubberized silk he'd
given her before she met with the scouts sat on the side table.

"Meekra, I'm alert enough for a report on anything else
you've heard."

Meekra stretched and yawned, her eyes tired. "I haven't

gathered any information that will really help I don't think. I walked past them in a crowd of merchants and heard something about the rumors of catapults in the siege."

It was nothing Seren didn't already know.

"There was one thing that seemed odd. My father said Adem and an ore master were talking as he walked through the injured troops. It doesn't make sense. The ore master said something about putting the jewel in its box."

Jewel? The city? It was the jewel of the Empire. Or maybe something about the ransom chests they still held? Seren's mind churned with images, snippets of conversation, voices. But nothing materialized into an explanation.

Meekra shrugged and brushed out Seren's hair. "I'm sorry I wasn't more help to you, my kyros."

"Just having you at my side is a great help." Seren touched Meekra's hand. "Sometimes I feel like all I have around me are vultures waiting to pick my bones clean."

"But everything is going well. Considering."

Seren rubbed her head, feeling less like she'd slept and more like she'd gone into battle again. "Considering, yes."

"What is that, Kyros Seren?" The one lamp they'd kept lit danced in what was left of the night's darkness and made the square of rubberized silk glow.

"It's a treated fabric we're going to try to use in a special weapon."

Meekra smiled, her white teeth bright in the dim tent. "The Holy Fire gave you this idea."

"Yes. Please keep it to yourself though. I don't want General Adem to know what I'm up to. Not yet."

Meekra nodded and scooped a cup of water from an enameled bowl. She handed it to Seren. "I worry about him, my lady."

Seren sipped the cool water, then handed the cup back to Meekra before removing the shift she'd slept in. "I do too, Meekra. I do too."

Meekra handed Seren a fresh mourning kaftan, pants, and sash, and after they'd dressed, they walked into the main part of the bed chamber.

Seren stared at the bed, where Meric's body had once been.

"Lucca Hand of Ruination to see you, my kyros," Erol said from the door into the main tent.

Blinking, Seren looked away. "Please let him pass, Erol."

Lucca appeared, holding a thick door flap up, and she waved him in.

He smiled sadly and leaned toward her ear. "Your engineer nearly blew his hands off near the mine wall."

Meekra had told Seren as much when she'd sent her for an update last night. "He'll figure it out. Don't look at me like that, Lucca Hand of Ruination. He will figure it out. He is quick as lightning."

"I'd say I'm jealous of the admiration you bestow on this pale hero," Lucca whispered as they walked into the main tent. "But quickness isn't always enviable."

The mischievous tilt to his eyebrow explained the innuendo. Heat seared Seren from chest to forehead. The bell hanging on her forehead was a coal against her skin.

Meekra smiled shyly behind them and pretended to be busy with her sash.

Seren looked back at the mercenary. "Lucca."

He shrugged and walked with her, Erol, Cansu, and Hossam into the purple light. No one but them was awake yet, it seemed.

"You did get some sleep before coming back to my door?" Seren eyed her guards one at a time.

"We did. For four good hours. We are fine, my lady." Hossam grinned.

They headed out of the Kyros Walls and into the sleeping city.

A hand flashed from the dark and grabbed Seren's neck.

Not even thinking, she drove a palm upward to break the hold as Lucca shouted for help. Steel blinked from Cansu's hand as he spun. Meekra put herself between Seren and the attacker—attackers. There were six now. All cloaked in thick headscarves that hid everything but their shining eyes. Hossam engaged two with his yatagan, shifting left so Erol and Lucca could fight the others swarming in the fading night.

One attacker held small daggers in each hand. Tapered fingers fanned out and heat jabbed Seren's thigh. Seren looked down, whirling to get behind a lotus tower. A line of blood streamed down her leg. A tiny knife lay on the ground beside her slipper. She dipped to pick up the weapon, a slight pain curling around her shallow wound. She cursed herself for not carrying a good weapon.

Erol watched Lucca fight. Why wasn't Erol moving? Was he too shocked? But he was a trained warrior. "Erol!" She threw the dagger that had been in her leg at the slim attacker.

Erol rolled a shoulder and drove an elbow into an attacker's face, dropping her to her knees as Hossam stepped back. His attackers were faster than him.

"Scatter!" Seren shouted.

Her guards and Meekra split down the alleys and streets, disappearing into the night. Seren's wound screamed as she pounded down the stony road, heading back toward the Kyros

Walls. If she could get to the enclosure, someone would defend her, hand her a weapon, something. She was a fool for not carrying her own yatagan. All she had was her jeweled dagger, which was near to worthless against a well-armed fighter. Her lungs burned as she pulled in as much air as she could. The road went right in a quick curve and as her foot landed in the turn, the pressure in her cut threw stars into her view of the Kyros Walls gate.

"I am your kyros and I need your protection!"

Guards stepped away from the gate and drew their yatagans, their movements too slow. Were they confused? Or bought? One jolted away from the walls and ran at an attacker following Seren. The man attempted a chant. The two clashed together as Seren passed through the gate. The second guard dashed after her, slowing as she did, alarm written in his features.

"I didn't realize what was happening, my lady. Forgive how slow I am!" His gaze went to the blood on her kaftan.

"It's fine." Her breath wouldn't come. Her heart was trampling through her chest. "Leave. Find Meekra, my handmaiden. You know her?"

"Yes, yes. Of course. Where do you think—"

"Somewhere between here and the physician's tent. Barir. Her family. To the East. Go! Go!"

Nodding, he sped off, his boot scooping out the dusty earth near the edge of the cobblestone pathway and his yatagan drawn and ready.

A crowd was already gathering around Seren in the dawning light. She straightened. Was it Varol or Adem? Or both? The attackers had their faces covered so they didn't want to be seen coming after her. The plot had failed to kill her. So far. She spun and the faces around her blurred. A financial advisor. A clutch of ore masters. Two clan chieftains with hot tea still in their ringed fingers. And Kaptan Rashiel.

"Kaptan."

He bowed deeply.

"Please escort me to my chambers." Her leg hurt, but it wasn't serious. "I need to wrap this cut."

"Of course, Pearl—kyros." The poor man didn't know how to address her.

"I am still your kyros," she said, her declaration sounding too much like a sad little plea.

Rashiel bowed again, holding a fist to his chest. "Of course, my kyros. May I ask what happened to your guard? And are you certain I shouldn't call for your physician? And just so you know, there is talk about Varol. He is planning something," he whispered as he came close, keeping the others at bay.

"I think he was planning this." She gestured to her leg, then to the city beyond the walls where only the Fire knew was happening to Lucca, Erol, Cansu, Meekra, and Hossam.

Then there was a shout and Seren turned to see Hossam, Erol, and Cansu hurry through the gate. Her heart relaxed a little. Erol was bleeding from the eyebrow. Cansu held one arm against his side and Hossam had a large gash down his arm, the fabric of his shirt lying open like dead skin.

If she admitted to being attacked, it might only encourage others to side against her. Since she'd stopped the practice of slaves wearing the tall waist-to-head contraptions, there had been talk against her.

"I arranged a practice attack to prepare my guards for assassins in case the Invaders try to kill me or take me to trade for their king," she said loud enough for all to hear. *Please, Holy Fire, let Meekra be safe. Please let Lucca be safe.*

"Very wise, my kyros," Rashiel said. "And brave."

"My lady!" Hossam's booming voice echoed off the pale stone walls. His eyes were round and worried.

"I'm fine. I trust you did well during our practice attack?"

He looked to Erol, who of course frowned, and then to Cansu whose lips parted. "Ah," Cansu said, realization of what she was doing dawning on his face. "Yes. We drove all of the sparring partners away."

"And Meekra? Did you escort her to my chambers or maybe to her home?"

They exchanged tight glances. "No," Hossam said. "She ran away from the action. Seeing as she isn't trained, that was wise, yes, my lady?"

"Very. And the mercenary?" Seren twisted her wool piece and swallowed the bitter taste at the back of her throat.

"I haven't seen him yet, my lady."

Seren tried to swallow, coughed, and tried again. "You three go tend to your wounds. Kaptan Rashiel will escort me to my chambers."

"You're sure, Kyros Seren?" Cansu's voice was an oud string about to snap.

"Yes." She was far from sure about anything, but cowering beside her wounded guards wasn't going to fix anything.

The older scout from yesterday appeared at Rashiel's side. "My kyros, Varol called a pre-dawn meeting with the kaptans. He did not include Lucca Hand of Ruination."

Everything was falling apart. Seren couldn't help but imagine Meekra and Lucca bleeding to death in the street and the Invaders readying to change the color of their tent and sharpening their blades.

Holy Fire, help me.

23

ONA

Varol stood at the front of the room looking exactly like what Ona wanted in her life. No one whispered while his dark gaze swept through the room like a storm. Every kaptan here straightened sash and weapon and back under his eye, his natural command whipping them into their best. What had he done to them—what kind of reputation did he have—to get this kind of response out of such a varied group? Ona grinned. He was absolutely terrifying. Most of the kaptans were here, or so it seemed. But Lucca was nowhere. Rashiel wasn't here either. Hadn't Lucca heard the horn? Hadn't Adem or Varol sent him a messenger boy? Maybe not. Maybe they knew Lucca was too infatuated with Seren to get any real work done.

"Kaptans." Every head turned to watch Varol. "We come up against the beast we hoped never to see again. The beast is vicious. Unwavering. But we have made it bleed already." He grinned and Ona was pretty sure it matched her own smile. "We insulted it with our victory. We made it whimper and run."

Murmurs floated up. Some might've been questioning— maybe Seren's supporters—but Varol was what was important here and now. He was the solution. He was the key to revenge.

"We have a plan to deal with this little siege." Varol cocked his head and glanced at Adem, who stood silent in the tent's shadowed corner.

Little siege? Well, that wasn't Varol's best comment. Although Ona hadn't seen a siege herself, there didn't seem like there was anything little about it. But he was just being delight- fully arrogant, right?

"Yes we do, Kyros Varol." Adem stomped his feet, and with a look, encouraged the rest of the room to join in. Some did. Some didn't. Varol didn't seem to notice either way as he spread a map on the table and began to talk strategy.

A man next with a thin beard leaned closer, interrupting Ona's conversation with herself. "What do you think of this, Kaptan Onaratta Paints with Blood?"

"Varol is the one to follow."

"You truly believe that?"

"You don't?"

The man cast a look at Adem, then the door. "I know what Kyros Seren says about him. That he is ruthless. As spoiled and rash as his brother was. More cruel and selfish."

"When did she say this?"

The man cleared his throat and coughed. "Um, well, I over- heard her at Kyros Meric's Age Day feast."

Ona painted Varol in her mind. Dark slashes of that strong, hawk nose. The slant of his cunning eyes. She unwound the scarf from her neck and tied it to her belt, suddenly really warm. "He's a take-charge kind of person and that's what we need. Seren shows too much mercy when it comes to prisoners."

The kaptan grinned. "You'd kill them all."

"Wouldn't you?"

"Probably."

"Then we're agreed."

BACK AT THE GUEST TENT, Lucca paced a line in front of the brazier. Fresh blood marred the shoulder of his brigantine.

"What happened to you? Why weren't you at the kaptans' meeting?"

"Because I was busy being attacked by Adem and Varol's fighters."

"What?"

"They tried to kill Seren."

"How do you know it was Adem and Varol?"

Lucca stopped, lifted his chin. "Ona. Really."

"I bet there are a bunch of people who want to take her down. She keeps the Invader king like a pet, frees slaves—which I'm fine with of course but still it'll anger the people who used to benefit from it—and now she's taking an Invader's advice on weapons to fight his own siege! She's being an idiot!"

"They cut her leg up, Ona. They tried to kill me. And Meekra. They were this close to slicing Seren's throat open."

Ona's stomach turned. She knew what that looked like and didn't want to imagine it on a person like Seren, a good person like her aunt had been. Suddenly, a weight sat on Ona's shoulders. "She doesn't deserve that. I, I'm sorry."

"Well you didn't do it. Don't apologize."

Ona rubbed her stomach and stretched her neck. "Maybe they weren't going to kill her. Maybe they were just going to lock her up or something."

Lucca's knuckle pressed into his mouth and his eyes shut in thought.

Ona grabbed a skin of water and drank down the contents. The liquid cooled her throat, but it didn't taste like water should. She missed Silvania.

"You aren't going to like what I have to say." She threw the empty skin on her bedding.

Lucca turned, his big brown eyes looking right into her. She pushed on.

"Seren should be restrained. For her own good."

Lucca's eyes flashed, quick and mean as lightning. "Ona."

Ona fought the discomfort of disagreeing openly with Lucca for the millionth time lately. She didn't want them to be at odds. But... "She is at risk. You said it yourself. Varol could decide her actions with this foreign engineer constitute treason or—"

"What are you really worried about?"

"I'm worried about Seren."

"And?"

"She wants to undermine Varol's authority. She said she wanted to get Adem alone and talk to him. If she disrupts what Varol is trying to do, if she asserts her claim as kyros—there are a lot of those with the same blood as her, and they'll support her—we'll be mired in an internal fight while we lose the real war."

A ragged sigh slipped out of Lucca. His fingers tore into his thick head of hair. He had to know Ona was right. "She

deserves to rule," he said. "Just because she isn't of royal blood...
I can't believe I have to argue this with you."

"It's not an argument."

"It's feels like one."

"Well, it's not. I don't even think she wants to rule. She
should. But she doesn't. She's too fearful. Stop shaking your
head. I'm right, and you need to shut your mouth and listen.
Varol has the steel to finish the Invaders—you've seen how he
commands—and he has the right to rule. We don't have time to
let Seren get in the way. This war is only beginning and you
know it."

She knew full well he was picturing exactly the same thing
as her.

The tent the Invaders had probably already put up today.
The red tent. Even if Akhayma surrendered now, they would
cut down every man in the city. Tomorrow would see the
black...No city survived an Invader siege. If Akhayma did
surrender, which they never would if Ona had any breath left in
her body, the city's population would be turned into slaves,
beaten, tortured. They'd be lower than the Invaders' underfed
camp dogs.

Ona grabbed Lucca's arm. "Our only advantage is that we
have their king. And Seren wants to risk losing him and use this
new weapon she developed with one of the enemy!"

"You supported her—"

"Before she began trusting an Invader. How can you not see
this is madness? Stupidity. The division she could cause, it will
cost us the win!"

His face hardened. "I am loyal to Kyros Seren. I pledged my
sword to her. As you did."

On her toes, Ona leaned into his face, heart shuddering, fingers pulsing against the hilt of her blade. "No. You pledged your prick and it's ruined us."

Spinning, she blasted out of the tent, ignoring Lucca's calls and half-hearted attempt to catch up.

ONA WAS BACK IN THE KAPTANS' tent before anyone could stop her.

Two guards she didn't know leaped inside after her, their big hands grasping her shoulders and a hunk of her hair.

She glared at Varol, who stood over a table, a map laid out before him. The lantern hanging from the ceiling nearly touched his head. He met her gaze with his amber, snake-sharp eyes. Fire lashed through her body, and she swallowed, fingers twitching, longing to draw the lines of him. For a second, she thought maybe he'd order her cut into pieces and hung from the walls. But by all the sand in the Empire, she wasn't about to tremble.

"I need to speak to you." It probably would've been better if she'd waited to talk.

He did nothing more than give the guards a glance, but they scurried out, leaving them alone.

His breath was steady, quiet. He straightened, graceful and lean, walked around the table, and stood not a hand's width away, his chest moving slowly, surely. His cheeks, above his trim beard, had to be soft as the finest sand. Charcoal could sweep across the surface, easy and smooth. She could draw his kingdom there beneath those flickering eyes. The dramatic rise and flats of the hammadas. The long stretches of peaked dunes beyond the city. Hawks circling. And the bodies of his enemies like wheat broken by the scythe. Varol was more than a man. He was a Place, the Power of that Place, and the Strength to beat back those who'd ruined Ona's life.

"The Pearl of the Desert means well," Ona said in the trade tongue. Her voice was quieter than normal, but she didn't hate it as she would've guessed. "But she plans to undermine your authority." She stumbled a little over the words, hoping he wasn't behind the attack on Seren. "You need to restrain her or some of your warriors will rise up. We'll lose the siege before it's begun."

"You know a great deal, mercenary," he said.

"Yes, I do."

"There is a steep punishment for barging into my presence uninvited."

Ona grinned, sparks punching under the skin of her neck, back, and thighs. "Try it."

He had his emerald-heavy dagger unsheathed before she finished her whispered chant, but she still drove him back and onto the ground. Her knee pinned his wrist before he could draw blood.

"You are fast," he breathed, his throat moving, his eyes like death. His gaze touched on her chin, on her palm raised to strike, on her eyelashes. "Why do you look at me like you do?"

This was the strangest, most exciting conversation she'd ever had. No pleasantries. No polite talk easing into an understanding. It cut to the quick.

"Because I wish I could draw you."

"You are an artist?"

"I used to be." Ona spat the words, wanting them out of her

mouth before they could soften her. "Before the Invaders ripped my life apart."

"Why do you want to draw me?"

"I like powerful people. Especially handsome ones."

His smile was the strongest sword, a storm in the desert. So even though she seriously enjoyed the feel of his body under her, she let him up.

"Does that mean you'll tell me everything you know, mercenary?" He brushed himself off and sheathed his curved dagger. "Do you know anything about what happened to my brother?"

A chill brushed over Ona's skin.

A guard pushed into the tent, his freckled face pinched as he passed his hands quickly over the Holy Fire bowl. "Kyros," he said, bowing. "The Invaders replaced the white tent with the red."

Varol rolled up his map and tucked it into his sash. "How many now? Any more troops?"

"We don't have an updated count yet, my kyros."

"Get the others." Varol downed a cup of something and slammed it back onto the table. "Meet me at the parapet. Send for Adem."

The guard dipped his head and hurried out of the tent.

Ona's hands curled into fists. "Are you going to hang their king from the walls?"

A shadow flitted over Varol's eyes. "What is your name, mercenary?"

"Onaratta Paints with Blood."

He smiled again. A shiver flashed through her body, all the way to her toes.

"I'd bet that is a fitting name for you, little falcon."

Ona bristled. "Little?"

He lifted a finger and traced his lower lip, thinking. "All the better to surprise and cut deeply."

"I'll take it." Ona owned the night, owned her life a bit more, as he swept out of the tent to begin the destruction of her enemies. She'd never felt so satisfied.

24

SEREN

Hossam, Erol, Cansu, and Meekra flanked Seren as she sat in Meric's chair and listened. A line of supplicants, all in mourning brown, waited to speak to her inside the main tent's shade. Varol and Adem had turned them away. She understood reducing supplicants' pleas during this war, but pushing them all away with no explanation? That wasn't the way to keep the city calm and cared for.

A wooler with a respected name told Seren how he'd been urged to raise his prices. Meekra quickly scrawled down amounts and other information into her report.

"I don't think anyone will be able to pay that much. I'm afraid my...contributors," he said, meaning the noble family who'd invested in his wool trade, "will find a way to show their displeasure."

It was Qadira's clan, Seren just knew it. Meekra traded a look with her that only solidified her thought. "But you haven't been forced to alter contracts you already established?"

"No, Pearl of the Desert—ah!—I mean, Kyros Seren." He winced. The people didn't know whom to call what and she didn't blame them. The power struggle wasn't their doing. She was simply grateful Varol hadn't contradicted her title in the open since the funeral. It was coming though. Like pressure in the air, it pressed against her skin and spoke of high winds and rough skies.

"Let it be known," she looked to Meekra to make certain this decree made it to the scribe for official recording, "no prices will be raised during a time of war. We do not profit from problems we experience together. We must remain united."

She needed to organize a system. The people had to share necessary goods to survive. She had to take the noble families out of the equation. She could already imagine Qadira's sneer at her judgment call here.

"Nidal." His eyes widened as she said his name. She knew many of their names. She and Meekra used to sit up at night and recall names, something Meric scoffed at and Varol would too, if he knew of it. "I'll announce a city-wide gathering of basic goods and I myself will pay those who contribute."

She removed all the rings from her fingers and tucked the emeralds, pearls, and rubies into Hossam's large hand.

"We can collect food stuffs, milk, blankets, bandages, and medicines at the economic advisory tent beside the back gates. That way, if the customers can't pay, your family will still eat."

She motioned for Hossam to hand the rings over to Nidal.

"I place you in charge of this endeavor and you may employ anyone else willing to help."

Hope smoothed Nidal's wrinkles. "Thank you, Chosen One."

Erol arrived wearing the mean-eyed look that meant he had

a message. Seren waved him forward as he fussed with his mourning kaftan.

"I have a message from the engineer. He hasn't been able to make the weapon work yet, but he is hopeful that a new arrangement on the fuse line will help. And, Kyros Seren? I want you to know, we, all of us, your guard, want you to know that if you challenge Varol openly, we're with you."

A sunny light filled her and she pressed a hand over her heart. She hadn't asked them, not wanting them to risk their lives for her. It'd been silly really because they'd risk it anyway, had already risked it. It was all too much to bear but she had to bear it. She'd let the Flames burn through her and find courage for this moment, to make it to the next.

"Thank you," she said.

Erol nodded, meeting her eyes. Beside him, Hossam and Cansu inclined their heads too.

AT THE ARCHERY RANGE, clouds interrupted the moonlight and turned it into strands like spider webs. The ends of Seren's hair lifted lightly in the breeze. The engineer waved as she walked to where he stood alongside the training field, bare except for three archery targets. Leaping from foot to foot like a boy, he gestured to ten contraptions. They were lined up opposite the leather and sand-stuffed targets.

He rambled until the harried interpreter grabbed his arm. "Slow down!"

Each of the contraptions included a shiny, silk pocket and a two-sectioned clay pot attached to the silk by way of thin wires. Seren squatted by the closest one to examine the contraption.

"Lahabshjara Fires." The engineer pointed to the top section. It looked like a deep bowl.

"And here is where the powder sits, yes?" She tapped the head-sized ball at the base. One wire, attached to one that ran up to the silk pocket, hung near the ball's side. "This will take the static—built up by the pocket going through the air—and bring it down through this." She touched a tiny hole in the ball's wall, through which the wire would eventually be threaded. "And it will spark the powder blend."

He frowned until the interpreter finished his work. After a little backtracking, the engineer nodded, giving her the rest of the conversation through the interpreter.

"So," she said, "the wire isn't quite ready." She pointed to where it would go. "But you have an idea on how to fix that."

Nodding, the engineer grinned and pressed his palms together. "Never seen woman with," he made a flourishing kind of motion with his hands, "these…type ideas."

"It's the Holy Fire that gives me these ideas. And perhaps if you asked more women about their thoughts, you'd hear more good ideas."

He bowed in that awkward way the Invaders had. "Should we get to work now?"

"Yes."

With careful fingers, they inserted the magnesium fuse wires into the small holes in the sides of the clay pots. The containers held rust, saltpeter, and another ingredient with a name as difficult as the engineer's, which she didn't bother trying to say. The complicatedly named ingredient provided oxidation to improve the weapon's performance. She understood that much.

"What about the wind?" she asked, using the interpreter's services.

The engineer glanced at her, then the sky. The interpreter gave her his words. "No wind, Kyros."

"There is a little," she said. "The winds are unpredictable here, engineer. Tell me the weight will be enough to keep the pockets of hot air from drifting too far."

"I'm certain. We aim for the targets. Just there. Fuses should spark by then and..."

She imagined the puffs and sparks she'd seen in her vision. "Inferno."

"Yes."

"The warriors and stable hands have been warned?" Fig's stall window was open, but Seren was too far away to see her.

"Yes," the interpreter answered for the engineer.

"All right then. But only try the three first." She stood, dusting her kaftan and going to stand behind Erol, Hossam, and Cansu.

Cansu smiled, approving her choice of safe vantage point. But honestly, if the wind blew wrong, it wouldn't matter how many big men or women she stood behind.

The wind had died and there weren't any reports of sandstorms or otherwise. It wasn't the rainy season, so they had no fronts of cold wet to worry about. Seren's hands shook anyway.

Holding the pockets of rubberized silk up, the engineer and two other warriors lit the small exterior fire bowls. One man dropped his flint and had to be replaced with someone less nervous around this new technology.

Seren leaned around Erol to see better. It was taking an eternity. If they couldn't get the fire going properly, the silk pockets would never fill and rise. The whole thing could catch fire. She twisted her green wool around her fingers, pulled, and released it, the soft fabric, the memory of them, helping her breathe.

Please don't let the flames get too near the fuse strips.

Slowly, the heat from the small flames filled the silk bladders with hot air. The first lifted into the sky. Then another. She clapped her hands together. The Holy Fire's idea had come to fruition. Adem may not have witnessed its success, but he'd hear of it. From more than her. He'd present the idea to Varol. It would work out. This weapon, set off next time from the parapet to descend and ignite the Invaders, would end the war.

Two of the weapons—one refused to light—floated toward the archery targets like silent ships on invisible water.

She pushed past Cansu and found the engineer's side. "When will the static be enough to ignite the magnesium strip?"

He crossed his arms and tapped a lip. "I do not know."

"If they don't explode within the training field walls, the Invaders might see them. They would know…"

"Many variable in this experiment."

"Yes." Sweat pooled at the base of her neck, between her collar and skin. Her heart strained to keep beating regularly.

A flash of white and orange blinded her.

She rubbed at her eyes and looked again. Two weapons blazed with flame and ate the targets in great washes of light. A cheer went up from the fighters behind them.

"Somehow, I'll make you safe here in the city," she said to the engineer. "Or anywhere you chose to go in the Empire."

"How?"

"I don't know. But I will do it. I promise you."

"Thank you, Kyros."

Another of the flying weapons sizzled, but a sudden rush of

air lifted it. Seren's hair blew against her cheek and pressed her toward the gate to the city.

"No." Cansu was at her side then, his mouth open.

The weapon danced and twirled in the sudden wind like a demon. It reached the top of the wall that divided the training fields from the market, the shops, and everyone's homes.

She had to shoot it down. Her bow was in the stables.

Horses snorted and stamped, smelling the black powder. Seren grabbed her quiver and bow and ran back outside. In the center of the fields, she spied the swollen silk and fire heading over the wall. She loosed an arrow. Her shot pushed the weapon over the wall. It dropped out of sight.

No.

Everyone was running now. Calling for water. For people to back away. Shouting for the gate guards to clear the area nearest the wall. The residential area.

A sudden shift threw another weapon at the stable roof. A flash of light and the hay outside the main entrance went up in flames.

Seren called out to the men staring. "Don't just stand there, my warriors! Go to the city and help the people. Stop the fire from spreading! And you, you, and you, come help me put out the one there." She ran for the stables.

Hands shaking, Seren tried to slide the bolt on Fig's stall door open as others worked to smother the spreading fire surrounding the entrance and inching up the wooden walls. Panicked whinnies sounded beyond the thick wood slats of Fig's stall. Sweat slicked Seren's palms. The bolt didn't want to move. Ironically, rust—the same thing as what was currently causing the thatch and mud roof to smoke into angry arms of fire—blocked the latch's mechanism.

Screams tore out of the city, beyond the wall, and Seren's heart lurched, tears pooling in her eyes.

Lucca ran into the stables, his face marked with ash and his mouth pinched. "Step back." With one boot, he smashed the stall's bolt loose.

Seren leaned past him and slid the bolt free. Fig shot from the stall, not that Seren could see her. Smoke clouded the world and clawed at her lungs.

"Free the other horses," she coughed.

"They're already—" He pointed to the small herd galloping and stomping around the fields, indistinguishable in the dark and chaos.

In the city, smoke rose into the night sky. No one was left in the training field except them. And Seren knew she should've been the one to rush into the city. A warrior rushed down the hill from the back gates and toward the stable, Lucca shouting at him. This was entirely Seren's fault. Turning from Lucca and the other man, she threw herself further into the stables, rushing, stumbling in the smoke and dodging frightening snorting horses, to reach one more latched stall.

"One more!" she called back to Lucca.

His head turned. His hair whipped against his face. "Seren! No! Get out of there!"

She ran into a wall of gray. Acrid smoke burned her throat and eyes as the fire ate at the stables. A thud rocked a closed stall door. A hoof hitting the wood.

"I'm coming!" She worked the bolt. Three tries. Four. Finally, it came free. The stall was full of smoke. But no horse. She clicked her tongue. "Where are you?"

Eyes watering, she looked down. One white sock showed near a hoof, like Fig's foreleg, but this wasn't Fig's stall. Thank the Holy Fire this wasn't her stall. It was a horrible, selfish thought, but at that second, she didn't care.

Her heart in her burning throat, she tugged at the animal's leg to try and wake it.

"Wake!" She clapped her hands, coughing and spitting ash. Heat roared above her head and there was a crack. A beam crashed through the roof and into the stall. Smoke blocked the view of where it landed. "Wake up!"

She clambered over the animal's body. To its muzzle. The horse's lips were still and soft. Every curve and dip of the animal's mouth was as familiar as her own and her heart stopped beating, hanging in her chest as her mind screamed the truth. It was Fig.

She sucked a breath, choking, and a shout crawled out of her throat somewhere between a cry and a scream. Lucca split the clouds of smoke and grabbed her arm. He dragged her from the stables as the roof caved in.

Fig was lost in the monster of smoke and fire and broken beams.

Not caring about the possible consequences, Seren let him hold her tight against his chest. She couldn't breathe. Grief and guilt joined the smoke in clogging her lungs and squeezing her heart. Lucca covered her mouth and nose with a wet cloth. Finally, she could take one breath, two.

The smoke cleared and let the moonlight coat the awful scene. Coughs tore from Seren's chest, horribly reminding her of the night Meric died.

"They controlled the fire in the city," he said. "None are dead."

Thank the Fire. Her stomach twisted. Fig. Her poor, poor Fig. "Injuries?"

"A few," he whispered into her hair.

Tears ripped down her face. Her eyes felt like coals and her heart sank and sank. The ground under her feet threatened to break, or maybe it was her legs that didn't want to hold her anymore.

"If the wind hadn't turned, if we'd had more weight..." Her tongue grew too dry. Words failed her.

Lucca took the wet cloth as she pulled away and started toward the city gate.

"What are you going to do?" he asked.

"I'm not sure," she said. "But I can't hide from this."

Four fighters brought out a cart filled with smoking debris. Ruined tent sections. Charred stools, shields, and baskets. She gritted her teeth, and they walked around the cart, to the gate, meeting Erol, Hossam, and Cansu, as well as a group of fighters she didn't know as well—a grim welcome party.

Cansu came forward. Gray ringed his normally perky eyes and he stammered as he greeted her formally. His throat moved in a slow swallow and he looked at the ground.

"Pearl of the Desert, Kyros Varol ordered we take you to him for questioning. Do you...do you want us to..." He threw a look at the fighters behind him.

She was numb. They had to be Varol and Adem's men. Not loyal to her. Should she ask her loyal fighters to call her kyros? Was this the time to make a stand? Cansu's eyes moved like a bird's. No. She couldn't order them to their death. Not if she wasn't certain this meant the end of her and the beginning of Varol. She had to be sure.

Lucca was asking Hossam and Erol something, but she couldn't hear what he said. Her feet were somehow already moving past the damage her weapon had done, the smoking shops that lined the wall between the city and the training fields.

She whirled to see Lucca and her guard on her heels. "Lucca Hand of Ruination, I command you to reinstate order at the training fields and secure temporary lodging for the warriors who lost their tents."

"Are you—"

"Go." Her demand came out like a plea. *Please, go, Lucca. Go and hide among the fighters, find some way to disappear.*

"But I can come with you," he said quietly.

"No. Do as I order." Seren fought her desperate need to get him to safety and burned her words with an authority she didn't feel.

His lips parted. He searched her face, then nodded curtly and spun on his heel. Seren memorized his broad, round shoulders, the blood-red belt at his trim waist, and the lilt to his walk. Lucca. He knew she was trying to protect him, didn't he? She scratched at her hot skin and pressed fingers against the pounding pulse in her neck.

She had no sun now to think of the fever of love.

Her world was crumbling.

25

ONA

The moon began to show through the last of the daylight. Seren was off seeing supplicants right now. Just more proof she couldn't run this war. She should've been here, plotting. Well, nothing was stopping Ona from forcing her way into the planning now that the red tent was up and the black was close on its heels. She'd see Varol and she'd be a part of this strategy if it killed her. Varol's guards—both could've been the dead kyros's twin brothers—stopped her at the door to Varol's tent on the western side of the Kyros Walls courtyard.

"Kyros Varol requested my attendance." She had to get in. She couldn't live with herself if she ended up having to go along with some stupid plan against the Invaders. But surely Varol's plan was magnificent. If anything, she just wanted to know about it.

"You have a message you can show us?" the first asked.

"No."

"Then you may not enter."

"I'm Kaptan Onaratta Paints with Blood."

"We know, Kaptan Onaratta. And please forgive us. But we're not permitted to allow anyone entry unless there is a proper reason."

Mentioning Seren might work. But what title to use? These were obviously Varol supporters if they were guarding his meeting.

"Pearl of the Desert sent me with a message." The guards straightened. "It's urgent." They shifted their weight foot to foot and Ona could hear Varol's distinctive voice calling a meeting to order. "If you don't let me in, I'll put one of my favorite chants to work and your best parts will drop right off your worthless bodies."

The guards practically jumped away from the door. "Please, yes. Kyros Varol will want to hear your message."

"You bet he will." As she passed, she glanced over her shoulder and waved a feigned farewell to their groins. They winced in unison and Ona barked a laugh, sauntering into the meeting.

Varol's men barely looked at her as she walked the plush rug path to their table. None made a move, only shifting their gaze back to their leader.

"This meeting is short one Silvanian mercenary," she said.

Varol's mouth lifted a fraction at one side. He stood and his men copied the gesture. "Indeed?"

"I'm sure you want to hear how the chanting units are evolving. Adem told you about this, yes? Also, you especially need info from someone who traveled through the Empire, listening to tales of past sieges like the one that is about to start up at our front door."

He ran a finger over a dirtied sword that looked familiar with its twisted hilt. "You served a fine helping of information already."

"That was only about what I could do. It wasn't the sum of what I know." The back of her neck prickled. She was pushing her luck. Varol could order these men to kill her with one word —a word she might not even understand. If she chanted, she could most likely best six men, but getting out of the city, that would be a feat. And if she did, an ocean of Invaders could be waiting outside the pale stone walls.

"So tell me what you know." Varol's words were quiet as a well-sharpened blade slicing through skin.

His men's eyes were cool, appraising. They were nothing compared to their leader though. Mere stars beside the sun. Every one of them would've already had her taken away. They had closed little minds. No new ideas. Their Holy Fire probably did nothing more than warm their hands when they passed their palms over its flame.

"My unit is coming along. There are five men who can chant and improve their speed on foot. It won't be long until they'll be better in battle."

"I already know all of this," Varol said. "Anything else?"

She cleared her throat. "The Invaders are blind with arrogance. If you slay their king as you plan to, then attack from the opening to the mines behind them, they'll be confused twice over. They won't believe their king could die or that we could surprise them. We'll come at them from the back on horses, with those small bows you all have, the ones shaped like a calligrapher's stroke."

"We don't have enough horses."

"You don't need too many. Just enough to appear serious

about the attack. They will rage at us with their proud chins high and we'll pretend to retreat. Instead, the warriors will shoot backward and cut them down. I've seen what your fighters can do with the bow. It'll be easy for them and it'll muddle the Invaders' minds. We'll paint the plains red as a field of poppies."

Varol rubbed his hands together. "So we split our forces. Fighters on foot at the gates and on the parapet. Horseback archers at the back in a false retreat. I like it." His gaze went to her mouth. "I like you."

Smiling a little, he dismissed his men with a flick of a hand.

They were alone. She was alone with the man who was going to humiliate, then annihilate the ones who'd ruined her life.

He walked toward her. "Tell me your story. Why are you like you are?" He raised one sharp, black eyebrow.

Stars burst under her flesh, waking her up. She was so alive with this man. His amber eyes glowed, invited her to lay her soul in his hands.

And so she did.

When she'd told him about her aunt and the palette knife, she stepped closer. Light from the tent's ornate ceiling spun a web over Varol's swept-back hair, his wide shoulders.

"For the first time, I truly believe the Invaders have enjoyed their last victory. You, Varol." His gaze cut her for using his name. "You will restore my ruined life. Not the innocence, but the beauty. Seren can't do it. She is too weak. Right now, she's developing a weapon with an Invader engineer. No one who thinks *they* can be trusted is good for our cause. You, Kyros Varol, are our savior."

"You don't know me."

"I know enough."

"I doubt that."

"Then tell me your story," Ona said.

"I shouldn't waste my time."

She shrugged. "Your choice." He could whistle the tune of *Old Goat, New Hen* for all she cared. Just being this close to a person so powerful was heaven itself.

His gaze went to the door. She couldn't let this talk end now. She'd go back to the guest tent and Lucca would be gone, going after Seren. She wanted something of her own. Not just something. She wanted Varol.

She took another step. Varol's breath touched her cheek and neck. Her heart kicked like a spirited horse. "Tell me about the worst moment of your life."

"Aside from my brother's funeral."

"That wasn't the worst. I saw your face. You're angry it was out of your control, but you don't miss him."

"You really don't care if I kill you, do you?" Varol smiled. He untied and retied a second sash at his waist. Odd he wore one creased with dirt over the fine brown he already had on. Must've been part of the mourning.

"You won't."

"You're a bit of a fool."

Ona shrugged. "Or courageous. It's a fine line."

"I think you crossed that line long ago."

"I'm here, aren't I? Talking alone with the most powerful person in the Empire?"

"You should work on the art of conversation."

"My own style has gotten me pretty far," Ona snapped.

He laughed. It was a pointed sound that would always be aimed at someone. She had to lean her head back to look him in the eye, but she was all right with it. After all, she could gut him if he became a problem.

"I was a second son," he said, "in a family who only had need of one. I was more cunning than my brother. Smarter. But none of it mattered. My brother's smallest feat was echoed through the world. My greatest accomplishments were lost in the noise of my father ordering me around."

"That's what gives you your will though. Your strong will."

He smirked. "A blade sharpened in the fire, hm?" His tone bit the air.

"Trite, but true."

"You're so young."

"I've seen more than most old women. And you're only twenty? Twenty-one?"

He nodded. "How would you draw me?" He took her hand and put it against his cheek. A shiver rolled down her back and stomach.

She traced the fine bones around his snake eyes, the hook of his proud nose. "I'd concentrate here and here and here. This is the center of your power."

"It's where I feel the Holy Fire's ideas when they come." A sheen of sarcasm pooled around his words. Ona didn't think he held too tightly to the almighty fire.

He closed his eyes as her palm slid over his cheek, to his trim beard, and down his sinuous neck. He was so warm.

"I'd show the world the lines of you," she said. "How your Will holds the Empire up toward the heavens."

His hands gripped hers and heat flooded her body. He cupped her skull and dragged his thumbs over her shivering lips. His mouth found hers, and she dissolved into a wash of red, black, blue, and green, the world a buzz around them. His lips forged a path down her neck, and she blinked, catching a glimpse of an elegant jawline, a peek of tendons wrapped around a strong shoulder under the edge of his fine, harvest-brown kaftan. Head moving down, Varol found her collarbone. She tried to say something saucy, but gasped instead.

If he thought she'd tell him to stop, he was wrong. Minutes or hours passed, Ona wasn't sure about the time. All she knew was Varol's power and the way it made her mouth feel, her body feel, her heart feel. This was how it was supposed to be. A man powerful enough to challenge her, to frighten her a little. In his strong arms, his cobra eyes on her, she was the person she'd longed to be for what felt like forever. She was steel and he was flint, and together they burned the hurt out of her soul.

A VOICE SHOUTED beyond the tent walls. Whoever it was called out in the desert tongue, then finally in the trade language.

"Fire! In the city! The training fields! Fire!"

They pushed away from one another, and Varol tucked his kaftan into place. He pulled the door open to trade words with his guard in his quick native tongue.

He turned to her, eyes still hot, and Ona said, "Go."

In the quiet of the tent, Ona's mind returned to the sword on the table.

26

SEREN

Throwing worried glances over his shoulder, Cansu led Seren to the sacred bowl. Varol and Adem waited. They stood beside a row of Adem's loyal followers, three lines of warriors behind them. The moon bleached their faces into the white of picked bones.

Seren's heart fell into her stomach.

Adem's eyes, ringed in purple, held defeat instead of triumph. Maybe he agreed that the planned flaying of the king was the wrong move. Maybe he'd support her.

Cansu, Hossam, Erol, and Seren stopped at the edge of the pool. Water lapped against the sides, a drop splashing Seren's sandal, cooling her heated skin. Before Varol could say a word, she bent, dipped both sets of fingers, and stood to draw the water over her forehead and down her cheeks. A blessing from her city, her water, her people.

"Pearl of the Desert," Varol said, his voice like a heavy bell. "You're charged with the murder of Kyros Meric."

Varol held out the water bowl that they'd used to dig Meric's shallow grave. Varol tipped it over. Sandy dirt and a tassel from Meric's favorite sash ghosted into the air.

Seren's body turned to water. She stumbled, Hossam and Erol catching her. She was no longer kyros, or the kyros's wife, no longer untouchable.

They must've left the bowl and tassel under the bed, with the extra dirt. That—along with the information Varol had probably gained from Adem and whoever else supported him—would be plenty to sentence her for murder.

This was it. This was her end. *I'm sorry, sisters, Father.*

Ona walked out from behind Varol, her face washed of any emotion. She stopped for a breath, eyes on Seren, and started toward her. To speak up for Seren? To further crush her? To stand by her side? But before Ona could move away, Varol put a hand to Ona's waist, keeping her there, by his side. Her body almost seemed to melt into his.

Seren gripped her guards' arms, heart hammering. Every conversation with Ona—since Varol's arrival—unraveled, then wove itself into a new pattern. The people gasped at the break in tradition, at the touching between Kyros Varol and a woman who wasn't his wife.

This was Ona's secret. She and Varol had been lovers.

A crack cut through Seren's heart and a shudder ripped through her limbs.

Her friend had lied. She cared for her enemy, taken into her arms the man who would take Seren's people from her and endanger their lives. When Adem had sent for Varol, Seren had felt a sting, but he'd done it because tradition was in his bones. He'd done it because that was what was expected of him. Ona had sided with Varol because she believed he was the better ruler. She believed he could save them from the Invaders, not Seren.

It was a bleeding, burning rendering of Seren's heart.

True betrayal.

Varol raised his hands. "As your kyros, I'm here to comfort and protect you in this trying time. I promise today will see our victory against the Invaders. I'll kill their king before their very eyes. And to avenge your former kyros and my brother's death, I condemn Seren, Pearl of the Desert to death."

Seren couldn't breathe, let alone beg Varol to listen to reason. Or ask for help.

He turned to her. "Take her to her cell. She, along with that Invader pig, hangs from the walls at dawn."

The moon bled silver into her eyes, blinding her as strong arms dragged her away from her people. "You can't hang their king from the walls. It'll only anger them and make them fight harder!"

But Varol wasn't listening. Adem glanced her way, face unreadable.

ONA

"Y ou aren't going to kill her, are you? She didn't kill your brother." Ona followed Varol into Adem's tent. The walls were darker than Varol's quarters or Seren's. The place was like a cave and Ona swallowed, suddenly feeling like she was being buried alive.

Varol spun. His eyes blazed. "She hid my brother's death from General Adem. From me. She never sent word. Adem did. After the fire that she started, the general told me the whole story. I believe it because, although he never approved of Seren, he didn't want to see her dead."

But Adem couldn't have told him everything. If he had, Lucca would already be dead.

Varol stormed toward Ona, step by thunderous step, and she backed up, a little bit enjoying his venom.

"Adem told me she hired some unknown person to pose as Meric in my brother's own bed," he spat. "Seren is a devil." Varol's hips pinned hers to the lotus pillar that supported the tent's heavy fabric walls. The stone chilled Ona's bones. "I will not permit her to live on after making a mockery of my family and our line of rule. She will die and she will die in pain."

She shivered, and this time it had nothing to do with attraction. She decided she only liked his venom aimed at her enemies. Seren wasn't quite an enemy. She didn't want to see her die either. She only wanted her...out of the way. Out of the way of revenge. If she proved to be a barrier again, well, that'd be her fault. Nothing mattered more than making the Invaders bleed.

"Fine. All right. I understand." Ona ran a hand up Varol's chest. "But kill their king first. Not at the same time. He doesn't deserve to die beside one of yours."

"She is not one of mine."

"The people don't see it that way. Neither would the Invaders. They'll see one of ours dying and think it's chaos within our ranks."

Adem walked through the door. "It's time, my kyros."

"What do you think of Seren dying beside the Invader king?" Varol kept to the trade tongue.

Adem's lip curled for a second. It was so quick, Ona thought she might've imagined it. "You meant to say *Pearl of the Desert*, my kyros," he said, giving Seren his version of a proper title. "And your will is ours, my lord."

"Onaratta Paints with Blood says if I kill her beside him, the Invaders will think there is chaos within our ranks."

Adem shrugged, but his eyes didn't match the carefree statement of his body language. "So what if they do? They'll only become more arrogant, or more confused. Either way, it won't be true. You are the kyros and no one will speak against you."

"They won't speak against me, but will they act against me, General Adem? Have you heard rumors?"

He swallowed. "Those born in the Green Mountains like... her, they may wish she was given more honors."

"You are of her blood."

"But I never lived there. I was born to middle-caste soldiers who raised me to fight for the Empire, not for one of its tiny borderlands."

"I've seen your loyalty. Don't fear me."

Adem gave a small bow. "As you wish, my kyros."

"We'll take Onaratta's advice. Now, let's go kill a king."

His words thrilled Ona's blood. She flexed her hand on her sword hilt, ready to see her enemy die.

～

VAROL, Adem, and two fighters had the Invaders' king on the parapet right above the main city gates. The heavy wood doors were shut tight against the enemy army. It was something of a risk for Varol to be up there. If an Invader could slip past their archers, he could let an arrow loose and bring their kyros down. But she guessed risk was part of the show. They wanted to confuse, enrage, stir up the pigs.

Men, women, and children jostled around the ranks, bumping the lines into disarray with their pointing and shouting, their kabobs of peppered, green-herbed goat, and their caste bells jingling everywhere. The atmosphere was celebration with a bright stripe of fear.

Ona had bought Seren some time with the whole *not proper to die beside the king* thing. Ona wanted to get her out and persuade her to flee. The plan for success was in place—trick the Invaders and outmaneuver them. They didn't need Seren's unpredictable weapons. Her instability. And Ona needed Lucca focused too.

Speak of the devil. Some ridiculous half cloak and hood shadowed Lucca's face. Nuh walked beside him, eyes on the parapet.

"What are we doing about Seren?" Lucca said into her ear.

"What is this?" Ona picked at the half cloak's ratty edges.

"Who cares? Focus, Ona. No one knows where they took Seren. He hid her somewhere. By sundown, she'll be dead."

"He'll wait until we destroy the Invaders." He was the one who needed to focus.

"What if he doesn't?" Lucca's eyes were wild. "Or what if we lose and she is trapped?"

"I don't know where her cell is," she said. "How can we get her out if we don't even know where to look?"

Lucca growled and leaned left and right, like he might burst right out of his skin.

"It can't be that hard to find," she said, giving Nuh a look. "Try the farming district. It's the only area that isn't stuffed with people. I'd hide someone there and set a guard. You can ask around. Someone will talk. A wife who likes your eyes. A child you can bribe…"

"Well then, let's get to it," Lucca said.

"I'm watching the king die."

"Ona. Please." He pushed fists against the front of his brigantine like he was trying to keep his heart in his chest.

But Ona's empathy only glowed so bright. Inside her, revenge blazed like a beacon fire. "Absolutely not."

A woman with green eye cosmetics like Seren wore bumped

into Lucca and Ona. The lady craned her neck to see Adem's men fitting the king with a noose.

"This is the meaning of my life," Ona said. "To watch Invaders suffer and die. I wouldn't miss this for her, for me, for you. You must understand that. You're the one who introduced me to the idea."

She didn't know when Lucca had backed away a step, but he had, and his lips had paled. "I shouldn't have," he said. "You don't even know what you're so upset about losing anymore."

"I lost my life." Heads turned. Ona lowered her voice. "Now I'm going to watch him lose his."

Varol spat words into the king's face, words in the desert race's tongue, lovely, complicated, hate-filled words. Ona loved the shape of them on Varol's deadly mouth.

When she turned back, Lucca was gone.

Varol faced the Invaders and shouted something at them in the Invaders' beast-like language. He grabbed the king by the back of the collar and showed him to his army. The king barked out words and the kyros slammed him against the parapet. Adem lashed the king to the stone and Varol began his bloody work.

Everyone went silent.

Each time the whip's metal tips flashed in the sun, Ona smiled.

The steel had to be some of the best. They didn't make anything less in this iron ore city. Despite the amazing cut of the weapon currently ripping him to shreds, the king had been impressively stoic, holding fairly still and not crying out. At the fifth stroke, he lurched and shouted.

Ona cupped a hand to her mouth to help her words fly. "Is it strange to see your own blood pooled at your feet?" she shouted in the trade tongue, and laughed, loud, though none near her joined in. She stared at the warriors and merchants and wives and brothers. "What's wrong with you? He is our enemy. He has taken our loved ones and poured their blood on the ground. Why don't you enjoy his suffering? It's cleansing." She laughed again. "I love it."

The whip cracked again. Snapped. Whooshed through the silence.

Varol stopped, handed the whip to Adem, then took a long dagger from his sash. He said something in the king's ear, pulled the man up by the hair and sliced the golden locks away, dropping them outside the walls.

The crowd did shout then, and the fighters banged fists on chests and shields.

Ona rubbed her hands together. It was time for the pig king to die.

The warriors near Adem and Varol lifted the king and his arms reached out. They pushed him over the wall, and the rope was the only thing left to see from inside the capitol city.

Varol looked down. His gaze latched onto Ona. She raised her sword, hilt first, and touched it to her forehead, swearing fealty the way Silvanian mercenaries did. She lowered her weapon to see him smiling, and he was the most vicious, gorgeous thing in the world. Heat flooded her stomach and tingled in her thighs and the tips of her fingers. She'd never wanted a man so much.

A rumbling rose from the Invaders, but she didn't wait around to see what would happen next. She still loved Lucca, and he needed Seren to live through this. Ona didn't want Seren to die either, so she had to find the woman and free her before the battle began.

~

WHEN SHE FINALLY FOUND LUCCA, he and Nuh were questioning a reed-thin man in the farming district. Lucca grabbed the man by the arms, shook him. From this distance, Lucca looked like a crazy person.

"Tell him, Nuh," Lucca shouted. "Tell him his kyros has been tricked and needs him to tell us every single detail." A curl dropped over Lucca's face and a dot of spittle appeared on his lower lip. "We don't have time for this. We have no time!"

The man let out a string of foreign words, and Nuh released him. Nuh rubbed a hand over the back of his neck and explained. "He doesn't know anything. No one here has seen her. Or any of the high general—the kyros's—guards."

Lucca let out a loud, gritty breath toward the sun. He pulled out his sword and slashed through a sapling with a shout.

Ona came up behind him. Carefully. He was her friend. But he was a dangerous man. Especially when he was like this.

Once, right after Ona was promoted to condotierri, Dom had enjoyed enough wine for four people and had jumped onto Lucca's horse bareback.

"Let's race, Ona!" Dom's words had slurred together like a smeared painting. "I want to see how Lucca's two ripe fillies perform." He'd smacked the horse's side hard and taken off into the black night of the forest.

Lucca had moved fast, not needing a chant. Mounting the nearest horse, he'd taken off, then returned later with a laughing Dom. Foam ringed the horses' mouths. Lucca tied them up and spun to face Dom.

Lucca struck Dom twice with a fist across the jaw, dropping

the taller man. His foot on Dom's throat, Lucca took Dom's sword and threw it to Ona.

"Do what you want to him for speaking to you like that. Just don't kill him. You know what he's worth in a fight."

Ona had cut her initials into Dom's thigh, a permanent reminder that she'd get her vengeance no matter who wronged her.

Now, Ona put an easy hand on Lucca's back.

"Let's look somewhere else," she said, wondering what he'd do if he'd seen her with Varol during Seren's arrest. "We have time. We aren't attacking until nightfall, when the moon will show the Invaders' stupid, overly shiny breastplates, but won't give them the light to see exactly what we're up to."

He nodded too quickly. His color was high.

She glanced at his sword and he seemed surprised to see it unsheathed. He tucked it away and followed her and Nuh away from the farm district.

"I'll find out where they're keeping her," she said. "From Varol."

"Why would he tell you?"

"Even in the middle of a siege a man is a man." Ona raised her eyebrows. "Bet on it."

Lucca's grin lacked any sort of good humor. "I'd never bet against you."

28

ONA

"When do we send the first wave through the front gates?" In Adem's tent, Ona paced a line in front of Varol and his men. Adem ran a hand over his chin, glancing up every now and then from his war map. Nuh and Haris stood beside Ona like her own retinue. "We should wait until we have the group who'll perform the false retreat at the mouth of the mine."

Varol nodded. His finger drew a line down Adem's map. "Agreed. How many should make up the front division, General Adem?"

Sweet Bean's eyes narrowed like he could see the warriors moving along the parchment's markers. "Three units, I think. I'll lead them."

Nuh made a noise that almost sounded like "No."

Ona knew why. Adem was basically offering himself as a sacrifice for the city. The front force would take the heaviest hit as the false retreat unit performed their little act.

Varol glided past the table and came up close to Ona. The men around them stiffened at the second breach in tradition with regard to him and her and their glaringly obvious physical attraction.

Sweet Bean looked ready to pop out of his hard shell. "Kyros Varol, please. This is not proper behavior from one such as illustrious as you. The royal line must uphold our—"

Varol's fingers started at Ona's temples, ran down the two sides of her face, and came together at her chin. Ona was clay for him to mold. She sighed. He was cruel, but just. Finally, at long, long last, she'd found a leader worthy of her purpose. She allowed him to tilt her mouth to his where he paused.

"General Adem, are you my father?" he asked.

"No, Kyros, of course not."

"Then why—"

"Your father is dead," Adem said.

"Exactly so. And so is my brother. You know all the secrets about that."

Adem breathed out through his nose. Ona's stomach tightened. Varol's mouth touched her ear, made her shiver. Neither man knew everything.

"Would you agree then, General, that I am the embodiment of our Empire?" Varol asked. "That I am the pinnacle of what it means to be of the Holy Fire's home?"

"That's why you must act with reserve until you are wed to a woman who equals your beauty and who shows patience and calm."

"*Must act.* Hm. That doesn't sound like something you should say to a kyros, does it, mercenary?"

His eyes made Ona dizzy with want. He could order anyone he wanted to fall on their sword.

"No, it doesn't," she whispered.

"See? Even this lowly, foreign mercenary knows. She'd lead the charge at the front gates if I asked it."

"I would," Ona said, "but I'll fight beside you, my kyros."

"Beside me? I don't think so."

"I thought—"

"That we were equals?"

"We..." The room's heat closed in. Ona searched for the right word. He understood her, didn't he? "We connected."

"We certainly did."

"I thought up this plan. You can't throw me into the fray as a distraction. My unit will be more useful in the second wave, after the false retreat depletes their numbers."

"I *can't*?" Varol's voice raised the hairs on the back of her neck. "Kneel, mercenary."

She swallowed. "Varol."

Adem stepped closer. "You will address him properly, Silvanian."

Ona gave in. A rock under the rugs jabbed her knee. She wiped her palms on her brigantine as Varol looked down, his cobra eyes were trained on her, instead of aimed at her enemy. Where had she gone wrong?

"You will lead the distraction attack," he said. "At the front. With that unit you and the other mercenary supposedly trained."

She would die. She might cut through twenty, thirty Invaders, but there'd be a thousand more and she'd be a sacrifice for this city. Her unit couldn't chant well enough. Only a few showed true promise. They'd all die.

"And if I refuse?" she asked, almost whispering.

A light in his eyes struck out. "Then you'll lose your pretty hands. Or your head, depending on my mood."

"I betrayed my friend for you," she said, thinking of Lucca's wild eyes. "And Seren. I kept her under control while you plotted." Ona thought of the look on Seren's face when she stood beside Varol.

Adem pressed two fingers into the bridge of his nose.

Varol glanced at him, then back at Ona. "Yes, but you didn't tell me their secrets. General Adem did. And you…" He moved a hand over her head, pressing harder and harder until her neck cramped. "You were a part of their deceit."

"Kyros Meric died of a cough and a fever."

"You, a filthy, low mercenary posed as my own royal brother in his very bed. You attempted to fool my general."

Icy fingers tore at her confidence. She gritted her teeth against the chill. "I was good enough for you and your wandering hands. And I *did* fool him."

His hand struck her cheek hard. Blood heated her lip and dripped off her chin. "Or perhaps my general was biding his time," he said.

Adem studied the ground. He'd been tricked by Seren, Lucca, and Ona. But she'd been fooled, too. By Varol.

Her veins shouted, but her words refused to rise. She stood, pushing against Varol's hand, rebelling against her own weakness, her mistake, those icy fingers. "I'll lead the first strike, the distraction. And I'll slay more Invaders than anyone in history." For the first time in her life, her voice shook and her words thinned.

"Of course you will. Because I have ordered it so," he said. She was choking, suffocating, his words—instead of hers—held all the strength of a chant as they smothered her. "It is truly sad the Invader king told me one truth that none of you could," Varol continued. "That pig told me a story about a rodent and a lioness."

Ona grabbed the front of her vest. Choking. Smothering. She remembered the slur the king had spat at Seren. She hadn't understood it then, but now...

"Ah, I see you know what I'm talking about. Are you ever telling the whole truth, mercenary? Forget it. I don't care. Lucca Hand of Ruination has designed his own ruin." Varol snapped at two of his personal guards. "Find the male mercenary. Don't wait to run him through. Do it fast and let it be done. I have better things to worry me."

Before Ona could fall to her knees, defeated, Nuh and Haris dragged her from the spinning tent and away from the man she'd thought was the answer to everything.

29

SEREN

Varol's men moved Seren quickly through the streets, presumably so no one could follow without being noticed. She'd seen Cansu's face when Varol announced her arrest. He would try to free her. Erol and Hossam, maybe not. They'd merely looked at the ground like they were afraid to meet her eyes.

And Ona.

Her friend. Or she'd thought she was.

Varol's men walked Seren into the main tent, tugged a hooded cloak over her, and steered her out the servants' door. The only sound this far from the gathered crowd was the water trickling through the shallow canals as it slipped from tent shadow to tent shadow, hiding from the sun.

"Where are you taking me?"

The men stared ahead, their silence as loud as any shout. They passed out of the Kyros Walls, through the back gates, and into the training field. The clay pot weapons made a border between the archery range and the stables. What a waste. Where was the engineer now? Had he escaped? He was probably dead. Another waste.

Seren could hardly put one foot in front of the other. The sun bleached the sky and scorched her head, turning her high-caste bell into a branding iron. She may've been the highest ranked woman in the Empire, but now she was nothing more than a prisoner.

There wasn't a soul in the training fields. If the Invaders managed to scale the walls here, they'd enter without a yatagan drawn or an Invader's sword unsheathed. The idea of steel brought Ona punching into her thoughts.

Had she been lying this whole time? Had she told Adem Seren had hidden Meric's death? But why had Ona helped her only to turn on her?

Varol couldn't know she was the one who'd posed as Meric. He'd never stomach kissing a woman who'd been involved in that. Not that he'd loved Meric. Well, perhaps he had a little. But his jealousy had been the main player in that drama. The foremost affront to Varol was what he'd see as a humiliation, the dragging down of his royal family. He could verbally attack Meric, but Holy Fire help anyone else who did so.

How deeply was Ona involved? When had Ona given up on Seren?

One of the men looked back toward the city as they entered the scorched stables. Seren's throat closed and she forced a sob down. Her Fig. Someone had dragged the bodies of the horses that had been lost past the stables and covered them in sackcloth. They'd be burned soon. Seren would never run a thumb over Fig's scarred ear again. Fig wouldn't nuzzle against her shoulder and make her feel like no matter what problems she had, mistakes she made, that she was enough. At least Fig's half-brother, the young colt, had survived. She strained to hear his high whinny, but there was only the wind and the men beside her.

Gray-green scrub grew in tight fists on the hill behind the stables.

"There is nothing here. You've made some mistake," Seren said.

They urged her on with the butt of their yatagans, closer to the hill and the empty, dry space stretching to the outer walls. They stopped at the incline's base and one guard shifted dusty earth from a spot in the ground below a lone tree that had stubbornly sprouted and boasted a handful of leaves. As the guard cleared more sandy dirt, a line appeared, then two.

Someone had set a wooden frame into the dirt. No. It was a door. A secret door lying against the slight rise in the ground.

The guards lifted the door and led her down a set of sunken steps. Lamps hung from posts that jutted out of the rough, wooden walls. It was like a mine but without the noise, carts, and tools. Newer slats ran along an opening to the right. This had been a mine a very long time ago. At the end of the passage, they veered left. Bars extended from ceiling to floor, broken by a latched door of shorter cylinders of iron.

This was to be her prison.

The cell shrank and she was miles away. Only habit kept her from grabbing the guards to stay standing. She fisted her hands and her nails branded her palms. Clearing her throat, she ignored the sweat pooling on her lip and along her back.

"This will be satisfactory." She lifted the cell door herself and climbed inside before they could force her. "I'll be very safe here." A bed of grasses lay against the wall. "Maybe the Holy

Fire—oh!—there isn't a Fire bowl." If she couldn't pray, she'd never last an hour. She needed something to focus on.

The guards traded a look. One nodded. "I'll bring you one, Pearl of the Desert. It'd be wrong for you to go without in your position."

Her position. Was that as a person who'd ruled the Empire for a matter of hours, or as a person who was about to die?

The lock on the latch door clicked as the guard turned the key. They walked away and left her in the cell. Alone.

The lamps burned steadily. Silence weighted her ears. Her heart beat, urging her to panic, scream, shout out for help that would never, could never hear. A shush-shush sounded all around and reverberated off the walls like drums. It wasn't someone coming for her. It wasn't the pound of hooves or boots. It was only her pulse.

No one was coming.

Would the horses—those still alive—startle if she screamed? Would they hear her at all?

Lucca would've searched for her, but she'd sent him away. She pictured his easy smile, his confident gait, and the way his eyes widened as he listened, really listened. *Lucca.* She pressed her palms together, remembering the feel of his hand, the promise of support. Had he understood why she ordered him to go? The hurt in his eyes had looked so real. He had to know he wasn't below her, no matter their respective ranks. She'd only wanted to protect him.

She hoped he was long gone, escaping before the Invaders grew comfortable in their siege and had time to watch for single riders. She imagined him galloping away, his mount kicking up the dust as he drove toward his home full of dark green trees.

But that was optimistic. More likely, the Invaders would catch and question him.

Her stomach dropped.

Their questioning involved fists, blades. He wouldn't tell them a thing. Her heart knew that. At least there, if he survived, he had a chance at a life. If he'd stayed here, Varol would've had him put to death alongside her. It was only a matter of time.

Cansu would look for her. She knew it. But Adem would know it, too. He'd assign Cansu to a position where he'd have no opportunity to attempt freeing her. Could Cansu break away and gather people loyal to her? What then? She didn't want a war within a war.

If she stayed here, kept quiet and accepted her punishment —part of which she surely deserved—her warriors would be led by a pompous, self-serving kyros. He was no good for them. Adem would advise him well, but Varol wouldn't listen. He never had. Not when Meric and Varol's father gave him direction during the first trade attempts with Silvania and the negotiations with Jakobden's amir. It was why they'd had to send another group to Silvania. He'd insulted their reigning families so much that they'd refused to meet with representatives for three years. Why did Adem have such faith in him?

Seren pressed her fingers against her temples. Her head pounded. She could reach through the bars, but even if she had something she could work into the locking mechanism, she'd never have the angle to dislodge the spring.

Footsteps sounded. Seren leaned into the iron rods. Before whoever it was came around the corner, she straightened and smoothed her hair.

One of the guards who'd brought her there held out a Fire bowl. "For you, Pearl of the Desert."

She bit her lip, hiding the hope she shouldn't even have. It was *good* Lucca was gone, that he wasn't here to try in vain to save her, that he was far, far away from Varol.

The guard set the bowl of lahabshjara leaves and little flames on a collapsible pedestal beyond the door. He lit it, and with a nod, turned to leave. It was a poor setup for the Holy Fire, the bowl precariously perched on the wobbly pedestal.

Working her arms through the bars, she stretched hands over the flame. "Holy Fire, I..."

No prayer came to her. No visions or comforting ideas. It was over.

Varol held her people in his cruel hands. The red tent would be gone by sundown and that meant no one would survive this siege. Tonight they would raise the black tent and all would be cut down when the Invaders won.

She fisted her hands, the Fire licking her knuckles. Why wouldn't Varol at least try her weapon? It would decrease their numbers. There were probably more ideas, too. From their fighters, from Lucca and Ona. She'd ruined everything. She pulled her hands back and accidentally knocked the Fire. The bowl tipped and slid to the ground. The Fire thinned, then went dark, its potential snuffed as surely as her own.

30

ONA

The noise stirred and lifted the dust as Ona's unit gathered behind the towering doors to Akhayma. The doors' carved and molded flames reflected the moonlight and formed eyes that watched them assemble for a battle people were probably going to make wild tales about for eons. Ona was sick to her stomach. The tales were probably going to be true. And not good. Not good at all. Warriors of all sizes, ages, breathed the same desert air as her. They held their weapons ready, hers straight and familiar—theirs slightly curved, thin, more wicked. How did she end up here? It felt so very wrong to be away from Lucca and going into a fight. Like she was missing a leg or something.

Archers fired from the walls far above. There was no way to tell if they were having an effect on the Invaders' massive army beyond the layers of stone and wood. Her ears couldn't pick out the sound of arrow tips hitting metal or flesh. It was only the noise like a storm of shouting, pleading, feet on the ground, hooves against the earth, steel, and her own heart's fierce thrust to win, win, win.

And then she had no room left in her to worry about Lucca, Seren, or herself.

The men on the opposite side of these walls had shaped her into a creature who only saw beauty in shattered bones and ripe blood. She had no room for friendship. Certainly not for love. Seren was a fool for not focusing on her purpose. Lucca, a fool with her.

Varol might've tricked Ona, but she'd win. She'd survive this and her revenge would shine bright all over his city, so bright he couldn't ignore or blame her. She'd be the instrument of victory. Nothing could push her off course.

Her body thrummed as Varol's warriors began to pull the doors open. The archers let thousands of arrows fly into the dusty air. She dragged her flint across her blade, sparks flying around her unit as they began chanting and striking their own flints. Power sang through her muscle and bone, buzzing, howling, shrieking. Sound blasted through the open doors, so many voices and shields and swords, and Ona ran straight into her enemy.

"Wake iron! Wake!
Take my enemy's breath
Steal from him
As he has stolen from me!"

Her sword clanged against another. The man spit at her and shouted in his ugly language. She swung their linked weapons down and jerked back.

"Wake iron!"

She drove her sword under his plated chest. He fell forward. Spinning, the steel and horses a blur, she met another. Dragged her sword across his throat. Varol's fighters cut and hit around her, a river of movement and death. Nuh flipped his yatagan and drove the tip into a shorter man's eye. Ona ended three more Invaders, her hands so much faster than theirs, wrapping them in death like an invisible shroud.

Stepping onto bodies, she drove toward a man wearing a finer surcoat over his armor. He shouldn't have been here. This was a place for grunts. Ona's rage shrieked from her mouth and she ran her blade straight through his neck before he could raise a hand. Beyond his shoulder, the Invaders were grains of sand. So many. So, so many. Gooseflesh rippled over her arms.

A shape up on the city walls jerked her out of the moment.

He still wore his hood, but she knew the set of those shoulders, the lift of that chin.

"Lucca."

He waved for her to retreat, a quick movement, singular and loaded with panic.

"No!" As if he could hear her.

He gripped the parapet.

A force knocked against Ona's spine. Cold and heat both fizzed up her skin. She whispered a chant and kicked the attacker away before spinning to bring her sword down on the exposed flesh at the back of his neck.

Her body sagged. Lucca was still there, but now he fired his bow along with the others, the dark arms of his sleeves moving in rhythm with the warriors around him.

Ona brought her aunt's face to mind as she leaped over a pair of Invaders. She pulled out her dagger, and in one move, drove steel into the base of their necks and through their worthless spines. Her aunt's face flickered. Changed. Ona's stomach lurched.

She cut down another enemy, and three more, chanting as she painted the ground red.

The familiar horror in her aunt's face shifted to sadness. Her imagined eyes met Ona's. Her lips turned down at the edges, a smear of blue paint marring her olive skin.

Pushing the image away, Ona sheathed her dagger, drew her flint again. Atop an overturned cart, she tore the flint across the steel. Light flashed in the dark. This was her path.

"Wake! Wake! Wake!"

Something burned down her cheeks as she twisted and struck, severing an Invader's arm. Her sword ate into an enemy's leg. Blood's metal scent swallowed everything except the image of her aunt, the haunting exactness of every pore and wrinkle and color.

Ona blinked as Nuh tripped, crashed against a dead man, and was stabbed.

Her aunt looked at her from her memory. Looked. At. Her.

Shoving her thoughts back into the fray, she saw Varol's men—her unit—surrounded by silver, red, and white. The enemy coiled around them and her, and opened its mouth to swallow. Beyond them, there were so many more, an endless nightmare made of sword fangs, moon-washed faces, and shining carapaces of armor.

In Ona's head, her aunt stared. She mouthed one word. It rushed through Ona like a cold wind. *Wake.*

"No!" she shouted at her memory, refusing her.

Blind with the need to paint the world with blood, Ona ran directly into the tip of a sword.

The world blurred, stilled.

The Invader smiled.

Ona looked up to find Lucca, but he was gone.

Pain launched itself from the wound and screamed its way into her heart. Her aunt—the memory of her aunt—lowered her chin, looked at her clean hands, lifted them for Ona to see.

"Your wishes are my wishes," Ona whispered to Lucca, to wherever he was. "As long as yours don't war with mine."

Enemies faded to gray, her revenge bled out of her, and she knew no more.

31

SEREN

A noise from the tunnel, beyond the bars, had Seren on
her feet.

"Guard?" Her hands shook, so she clasped them
behind her back.

But it wasn't the guard.

A figure with dark brown curls and parted lips came around
the corner, bow and arrow at the ready.

"Lucca." Her shoulders fell away from her ears where they'd
been strung up tight. A warmth slid over her bones. Her trembling hands slid through the bars.

Two vicious, foreign words broke from his mouth. He threw
his weapon to the ground and rushed to her, banging one palm
against the iron. "How do I get you out?" His hair stuck to his
sweating face as he turned right and left.

"I don't know." She hated how defeated she sounded, but she
couldn't pretend with Lucca. He'd see through it.

"How did you find me?"

"Erol. He saw them take you into the stables. Cansu guessed there was a place here. Some rumor the men heard."

Her soul swelled. "They're loyal after all." But dark circles had formed under Lucca's eyes and an invisible weight pulled on him.

He dropped to the ground, the bars a wall between them. "She's gone, Seren."

She grabbed his hand. "What? Who?"

He coughed and pulled away, covering his face with his fingers. "Ona...he killed her."

She gripped the bars to stay standing. "Varol?"

"Yes."

She knew he'd turn on Ona. Seren should've warned her about his ability to manipulate and the black place where his soul should've been. "How?"

"He put her at the front. Her whole unit. She was the distraction for the false retreat unit going out through the mines now."

"Did you...did you watch her fall?" The trade language didn't translate this the way Seren wanted it to. She wanted to ask if he experienced her end—a respect for doomed loved ones —but she didn't know the words.

Finding her hand, Lucca's fingers curled around hers. His words were ghosts. "I couldn't. I walked away. I left her."

He kept glancing over his shoulder as if Ona would appear. Like a fighter who'd lost a limb, Seren could tell he felt her phantom presence.

"She betrayed you," Lucca said. "Us. I'm sorry. I should've known he'd be too tempting for her."

"What turned her?" Seren asked quietly.

"It wasn't anything you did. At least, I don't think so. She saw Varol as more powerful. Capable of bringing down the Invaders. It's all she cared about. Revenge. And his presence had to tempt her physically. She loved beauty. In her strange way, she still loved beauty."

His tears wet her fingertips as she pushed his hair out of his eyes. "Lucca. We will honor her."

"You have to hate her."

"I don't. I think I understand why she did what she did. We will honor her. After all of this…"

But she knew it was impossible. He had to flee. Seren had to die. Varol wouldn't honor a Silvanian.

"I should've warned her about him," Seren said. "How he flips easy as a coin. How he hates anyone not of the desert race." She squeezed Lucca's fingers.

He shrugged, but it was a stiff movement, a show, an act. "I suppose someone had to lead the unit. She dropped more than most before her end." He breathed in through his nose. "She looked up at me before…she saw me on the walls in my hood."

"You shouldn't have been there. What if Varol saw you?"

It was as if he didn't hear her. His mind was there, with Ona in the battle. Seren ran a finger over his thumb and a scar on the back of his hand.

"There was no injustice in her being chosen," he said. "Not really. I know Varol did it to get rid of her, but someone had to go. Nuh fell beside her. I should've been there."

Seren swallowed and tasted salt. No one should have to die. But this was war. "But it wasn't her war," she said.

Lucca's eyes flashed. "It was her war. Every battle with the Invaders would always have been *her war*. That's why she's dead. She wouldn't let go of the blood. She clutched at her past like a talisman. A foul token. It didn't protect her. It didn't move her to greatness. It…it killed her."

He shuddered, and his words shone a flickering light into Seren's mind, though she couldn't see what they illuminated. She touched the green wool tucked into her sash as he straightened himself and stood.

Such power in his face. Would it be enough to survive grief and a kyros who wanted him dead?

"You need to escape the city, Lucca. Before Varol or Adem finds you. They won't hesitate to kill you now. Please. I can't lose someone else." The shape of him had become such a comfort. So quickly, he'd soaked into her doomed heart.

"I'm not leaving without you," he said.

She hit the bars with a palm, surprising him with the force of it. "There's nothing I can do. I deceived everyone. I pushed myself into things I shouldn't have. I wasn't careful."

"You are the kyros."

"No. I'm not."

"You are. I've seen you lead. This is your fate. This is your purpose. Why are you letting it fall between your fingers?"

"I'm in a cell, Lucca. You don't have the key. Varol and Adem have an army behind them. Another army lies beyond the walls. This is impossible. It's over."

"Capturing the Invaders' king seemed impossible, but you did it. Leading a city that's never seen a woman at its helm seemed impossible. You did it." He gripped the bars and stared into her face. His tears had left lines on his strong cheekbones, in the stubble on his jawline. "What is holding you back from at least trying to get out of here?"

She touched his face, then stepped back, her fingers lighting on the scrap of her wool skirt.

"I just don't know what to do. It's not like I've been here before! What do you expect from me? I'm only a girl from a little village with grief I can't lay down and—"

He didn't say a word. He didn't have to. Her words echoed in her mind, spinning into an image of Ona's rage and need for revenge. Heat reared up behind her eyes. She wasn't letting the past go and moving forward. Ona hadn't either, and she'd died because of it.

For a second, Seren could almost see her sisters' small fingers bunched in her green, woolen skirts. She remembered her father's black boot, the sound of his heel against the wood floor as he stepped between them and the small band of Invaders who'd kicked their way into their home in the mountains.

"Ona wouldn't let go of what happened to her," Seren said, mostly to herself. "She was a slave to revenge. And where has it thrown her? Varol didn't repay her betrayal of us. Revenge isn't a just master. She wouldn't release her past, and now she is gone. Dead on the field."

Her throat closed on the words. They both fought tears, their breath mingling in the dank cell. Seren gripped Lucca's fingers around the bars.

"Our Ona died at the hands of the ones she hated," she said.

The ones she hated. Seren's chest collapsed as she relived the sound of her family dying. Her heart stuttered. The feel of foreign fingers on her arm as she was dragged into the sun. The shout of Meric and his father as they fought off the Invaders.

Her soul quaked with the sensations of the past.

She remembered riding in a cart, jostling away from the Green Mountains.

The first sight of Akhayma.

Her new life.

Then it was as if the Holy Fire itself burned inside Seren. She could see everything inside her soul. And she hid from what she saw.

"No." She pushed away from the bars and crossed her arms over herself, the muscles in her throat strangling her. "But what if I fail and die? My sisters, they didn't even have the chance to live. They should be here. My sisters. My sweet sisters. Their soft cheeks. Their sharp, little minds. They could've been so much, lived so much."

She wasn't making sense. The room spun around her, and she ripped the wool from her sash and pressed it into her skin, remembering every laugh, touch of a hand, joke by the fire, their little wishes and hopes and wild dreams.

"It isn't fair. It isn't right that I'm here. I'm nothing to them. They were so colorful, Lucca. You should've seen them. If you could only see them."

She ended up slumped against the bars with Lucca's body warming one arm, one leg, both hands. She pressed her wet face into his sleeve, into the bars, until she only saw black and the stars behind her eyes.

Lucca's finger lifted her chin—an awkward angle through the iron—and he took her green wool, tucked it back into her sash.

"Keep the sour-sweet memories. I'll do the same." His gaze drifted over his belt where a shape had been scratched into the leather—a remnant from some memory with Ona, probably. He met Seren's eyes. "But don't let the tragedy hold you back. Let it move you forward."

Seren set her palm against her sash and the hidden spot of green inside.

Squeezing her eyes shut, she tried to ignore Lucca's words and the Holy Fire's clarity, the light of them. But they wouldn't let her shift them away.

Lucca was right. The Fire was right.

Ona died holding on to her pain. If Seren clutched at her own horror and held it and acted with it always judging her every word, not only would she die too, but her people would bleed under Invaders' swords. That couldn't be the path the Holy Fire wanted for her. Not after thrusting her to the highest position in the Empire.

She breathed once, slow and shaking, and let the light wash over her. They sat there for long time. Breathing. Grieving.

Then Seren opened her blurry eyes.

Blinking, she settled her past into her heart to keep it, to use it.

Ona's mistake may've betrayed Seren, but it had also saved Seren. Seren would not make Ona's mistake.

When Seren's vision cleared, she was someone different.

Lucca's lips made a line and he nodded once. "Time to move forward?"

She wiped her face and rose. "Too bad there is a wall of iron in my way."

He did a little half laugh, half smile, and her heart tripped even though she was stuck in a cell with only a handful of hours left to her on this earth and death all around them both.

"What's so funny?" she asked.

"They didn't think a chanter would find you," he said.

Stepping back, he pulled out his sword and flint. He slashed the flint across the steel and a spark danced into the air. He chanted in Silvanian, then grinned again and switched to the trade tongue.

"Don't change it so I can understand," she said. "Just do what you need to do."

"I think it'll help if your will is behind it too."

"I wish I had a Fire bowl."

The lines around his intense eyes smoothed. "Can you use the spark I create?"

Seren stepped back, thrown by the idea. "Maybe. The improbable sometimes happens. After all, I never would've predicted I'd fall for a Silvanian mercenary."

His eyes burned. "Seren."

Her insides melted, and she wanted out of this cell for yet another reason altogether.

He began to chant, his trade tongue strong and direct.

"Wake iron!

Be stronger than your kin here,

Force your will through your lessers!

Part what has been joined!

Join what has been parted!"

The fire leaped from his sword. Seren opened her hands to aim her palms at the tumultuous light.

"Holy Fire," she whispered under his chanting. "Tell me what to do. Lead us. Help us."

He struck the flint. Two arms of orange unfurled into the near dark. She kept praying.

"Shout it, Seren!"

"I can't...I don't know if this is right. I don't want to say something wrong..."

"Feel it, Seren. You are the kyros. This is your Holy Fire. I give it to you. I submit to you. Own your place, Seren. Shout! Shout! Shout!"

The sparks dove out his sword and flint, jumping, twisting,

striving, as he chanted his power into the room. Her bones, warmed by his presence, now burned like she was the spark, the flame, the power he was calling forward. She was shaking. Gasping. Her words grew and grew and grew.

"Holy Fire." Her voice reverberated off the ceiling, the walls. "Please give me the spark of ideas. I am the sultana and I will aid my people." The words echoed in her ears.

Lucca slashed at the bars. His sword caught against the iron. He'd bent the bars, not broken them. "Don't hold anything back!" he shouted above his flint-striking.

She splayed her fingers and Lucca's sparks danced toward her flesh. "Holy Fire, I am Kyros Seren and I ask for your guidance, your help. Free me to protect the innocents from the errors of a wayward man."

Her palms lit up like bright candles, and the Fire appeared between her eyebrows, falling to a jagged spot on the door. A flaw in the iron, an opportunity.

A smile like a blade sliced over Lucca's face. *"Wake iron, wake!"*

He drew his sword back and slammed its edge into the Fire's chosen place.

32

SEREN

Outside the cell, Seren crashed into Lucca. His hands drove up her neck and into her hair. Her mouth found his and she could never get enough. The taste of him, the scent of Silvanian pines in his skin, the feel of his jaw under her fingertips, the beat of his heart against hers.

She pulled away. "We need cloaks."

Lucca was panting. "Wh-what?"

"Ore master cloaks. They wear better hoods than this." As he picked up his sword and sheathed it, she held up the end of the hooded clothing he'd found.

She grabbed his hand and started to run.

The tunnel gave way to the moonlit night and the distant sound of battle. The stables had been emptied and the archery field was an ocean of stillness.

"Oh, I've seen the cloaks," he said. "Those long, black ones."

"Yes. I need Meekra. She'll know where to find some. The royal household has a few for guests Meric didn't want others to know about. I sent Meekra to help with some things near the western side of the city. But do you know if Meekra was imprisoned or..."

Seren clutched at her stomach. She hadn't thought of her until now, thinking Meekra was safe because she hadn't been around during the arrest. Seren and Lucca scanned the cells at the far end of the training field but only saw prisoners in homespun, filthy wools, darker clothing too, but none of Meekra's finer clothing. The moon was a blank-eyed skull, a reflection of the death suffocating her city.

"I don't think so," Lucca said of Meekra. "I haven't seen her. Not since you ordered me away."

"You know why I did." Seren pulled him through the inner gates and toward Barir's home. Surely she'd go there when she learned Seren had been arrested. "If you die too, if I lose you too..."

Lucca's mouth found Seren's disheveled hair and he breathed, "Shhh. We'll come through this. Somehow. Now, where are you taking me?"

"To the physician's. He is Meekra's father."

Thankfully, people were either hiding with their children in their tents or the adults were out there, in the fighting. No faces appeared at windows. No curious families manned the tables in the market. All the merchandise had been locked away and only a bat swooped over the oasis pool. Something small rummaged through a dropped sack of grain.

Meekra herself opened the door when we arrived. "Come in, Kyros. Thank the Holy Fire you're alive."

Seren crushed Meekra in a hug. "I'm so glad you're all right," Seren said, looking at Barir's whole family. "I'm so glad all of you are all right."

Meekra smiled gravely as Seren moved to the Holy Fire bowl. Seren passed hands over the bowl, and her eyes shuttered closed as she murmured a prayer from childhood, a blend of old beliefs and new. She wasn't going to ignore any parts of herself anymore. She was from the Green Mountains. But she was in love with the desert. She was a woman and a leader. She was kind, but she was fierce. She needed new ways to pray, and the combination suited her soul.

Lucca's large fingers uncurled over the Holy Fire after hers. He spoke in his language, his lips puckering and his tongue dancing.

She gave him a sad smile. He'd have to learn new ways to live too. Ona had been his family and she was gone. His smile answered hers, he nodded once to leave that conversation until later. She agreed. It wouldn't be a good thing for both of them to end up on the floor crying. They had to hold the rest of their grief until they either won this or lost it.

Barir and the rest of his family stared at Seren's torn kaftan sleeve, her smudged cosmetics, and swollen eyes. Coming close, Meekra's little brother lifted a woven blanket worn to thread-bare spots along one side. They didn't have time for this, but she *had* to make time for this.

Seren kneeled and reached out a hand to touch the blanket. It was soft as a spring lamb and obviously well-loved. It was probably his mother's coming-of-age ceremonial blanket, given to her youngest and last child to mark the end of her child-bearing years.

"I can't take this from you, good man," she said to him.

His big eyes shone. "Oh no, Kyros." His S slipped through the place where two front teeth should've been. "I only mean you can borrow it. 'Til you're happy again."

Meekra gasped and took his shoulders, but Seren smiled, tears threatening her, and brushed a hand over the faded fabric.

"Of course." Seren pressed the blanket once against her heart, then handed it back. "I feel happier already."

The boy grinned and hid his head in his mother's kaftan. She patted his jet hair, and Seren's chest ached for a mother and father she'd lost too soon.

Standing, she spread her hands. "I hope I don't endanger you further with my visit," she said, then explained what she needed with as few details as possible.

With a solemn nod, Barir left to find the ore master cloaks while his wife served mint tea, her younger children heading to the sleeping mat to shut their tired eyes.

"What happens next?" Meekra asked quietly.

"I have to see what's happening beyond the walls," Seren said. "I can't make any decisions until I know how many warriors both sides have left. Have you been to look? Have you heard anything?"

"No. The front gate unit assembled, then I left." Her face told me she knew no one in that force would live past tonight.

Lucca's eyes fluttered shut and his fist pressed into his stomach.

"Though I have, I see, um, Onaratta Paints with Blood in… error," she said to him in broken trade tongue, "I honor her courage."

He must've understood enough of it. His sad eyes flicked to her face and he bowed his head.

"I need to speak plainly, Kyros," Meekra said.

"Of course." Did she worry they weren't friends? "We've been through enough to shed this formality."

A small smile tried to bend Meekra's mouth. "But we need

you to keep some of it. We need you to be a leader, not merely another person. Will you finally stand up to General Adem and High General Varol?" Seren loved that she refused to call Varol anything but his original rank. "We need you," Meekra said. "We need you to be strong. Not only smart or kind. Akhayma must have your power."

Lucca's hand warmed Seren's back, not touching, but hovering just above. She could feel the Holy Fire inside her too, driving her to embrace her calling. "I swear by the Fire I'll do everything in my power to save this city."

"If you don't," Meekra said, "we won't be the only ones to fall under the Invaders' yatagans. The entire Empire will be open to attack." Moisture gathered on her thick lashes and she made a noise like a sob.

Seren squeezed her hands. "I'll do my best. That's all I can promise."

Meekra nodded and wiped her eyes.

"Will you find Cansu, another fighter named Haris, and maybe Hossam and Erol?" Seren asked. "Be careful, but will you see if they'll help us? It's very risky. But…"

"But we're all going to die if we don't all take some risks."

"Well said."

Barir came to the door, arms were heavy with black cloth. "I have three ore master cloaks. Here." He handed them out.

"Where should we meet you?" Meekra asked as she pulled one over her head.

Seren slipped hers on. Lucca did the same. They'd be nearly invisible in the night and beyond question in the day. Hopefully. At least until Varol realized Seren wasn't waiting for her death in that awful hole in the ground anymore.

"Meet us at the archery range," Seren whispered to Meekra,

watching the younger siblings huddle together in bed. "If the men know where any of the clay pot explosives are, tell them to bring them."

"What if they're afraid to join you?" Barir asked.

Meekra raised her chin and tilted her head. Seren knew she was waiting for her to rise up like she'd promised she would.

Lucca pursed his lips and gave Seren an encouraging nod.

"Tell them their kyros asks them only to do as much as they would for their own families. That is to say, I am their mother. Their sister. Daughter. Aunt. They have to join me now or die in shame tomorrow."

Meekra smiled and everyone raised a palm and bent at the waist.

"May the Holy Fire bless our kyros," everyone said in unison.

And with one last prayer over the Fire, Seren, Lucca, and Meekra bid the family farewell and launched into the deep night.

WARRIORS RUSHED past Seren and Lucca to mount a group of stomping horses held by low-castes. Fig's soft nose moved in Seren's memory and she shook it away to focus. The group gathered at the ring road that led to the old mine exit. Most never knew the dusty path had been smoothed and kept free of tents originally for that purpose. Now, it was only a way to move more quickly to the part of the city where people gambled at all hours and if you didn't watch yourself, skilled fingers would pluck you clean of every coin, ring, and bit of treasure.

Behind a group of archers—newly stocked quivers boasting arrows with fletching in the Empire's blue and black—Lucca and Seren climbed the stairs to the top of the walls.

"We'll need more tips soon, master," one fighter said, seeing Seren's ore master cloak. He nocked an arrow and let it fly into the teeming mass below.

The moon exposed the Invaders' glinting armor and brushed lightly over our warriors' peaked helmets. The clash of steel on steel punctuated the rough, lower sounds of human effort.

The white tent was gone. In its place, a red tent commanded the plains and the army swarming in its dust and around our walls.

"No mercy for any man. Isn't that what it means?" Seren asked Lucca quietly.

His hands clutched the parapet as he scanned the horizon. He held on like he was afraid he might lose his mind and jump off. Seren shivered. This was probably where he watched Ona die.

"The red tent." Pain tied his voice in knots. "Yes, if they take us, they'll kill every man in the city."

A shiver quaked through Seren's chest. She pulled her cloak more tightly around herself. "You should've tried to escape."

"I made my choice."

Seren thrilled to hear it, but his decision also gutted her. Gutted her as well as any yatagan's edge.

At the front, near the gates, the Invaders set ladders against the city walls. When one fell from our warriors' arrows, another took his place. Seren's eyes couldn't help but search for Ona's body. But it was so dark. Even in that green brigantine, so different from all the other soldiers' blood red jerkins and the

Invaders's white, silver, and red, Seren still couldn't spot her. She didn't want to ask Lucca. He wore his grief on his shoulders, the weight unhinging his usual grace.

"Look. Here they come," Lucca whispered at her ear. He pointed to the old mine, on a hill a half hour's ride away when the plains were clear.

A dark river of shapes—horses and their riders—poured from the spot where the flat land gave way to a ridge surrounded by the thick-leaved lahabshjara trees.

"I can hardly see them. Are they firing now?" She tugged Lucca close. "Wait. They must be. The Invaders there are turning to face them. Do you see?"

The enemies moved like the sand stirred by a wind, swirling back, then around. The Invaders had no archers that far back, so the Empire warriors shot arrows into them and advanced quickly. But the Invaders were no cowards. They rushed to close the distance, their numbers far exceeding the mounted unit. Two went down under the western swords, then a handful more. A shape at the back waved a hand three times and the movement was echoed through the unit, and they turned their horses back the way they'd come. A swathe of fifty or so Invaders pursued them on foot. Seren was sure Adem had wanted more to chase them, so the unit could circle a good hundred or two and take them out with the false retreat.

"It's not enough," she said.

An enemy's arrow sliced the air beside Lucca. Both of them dropped to a crouch, the archers nearby firing shot after shot.

Lucca's face was shadowed by his hood. "You're right. That's not going to win us this battle. What do we do?"

The wind tugged at Seren's hood and she grabbed the edge to keep hidden. She looked past the parapet, the night air tangy with the scent of blood. The mounted unit fell one by one to the dark, to the wide swords of the Invaders.

They were all going to die.

"We have to get the clay weapons released," Seren said. "Now."

~

THEY RACED to the prison cells.

The first row of cells held Invaders captured during the battle. Most were bandaged from being forcefully questioned. All wore a unique blend of fear and defiance in their light eyes. The engineer was nowhere.

"He has to be here. If not, he's gone and we're finished."

"There!" Lucca pointed at a small cell, too short to hold a man really, at the end of the row.

Cold bars held her engineer with the unpronounceable name. Fists curled into his lap, he sat at the very back. Sweat rolled down his pale face.

"Broken," he said in terrible trade tongue. He held up a shaking mess of what used to be his hands.

Seren's stomach lurched, and Lucca butted his head against the framing with a shout of disgust.

"We're going to free you. I'll get medicine for you. For the pain. We need to make more weapons and release them now. Lucca, should we try our magic on these bars, too?" She had to smile and laugh and cry at the same time. Life was full, bursting, pushing the real Seren out of the fertile soil of horror and joy.

Lucca dipped his chin respectfully and drew flint and sword. As quickly as they could, they chanted together, the Holy Fire from his spark leaping at her palms. Heat twinged at her forehead, and in her hands, and a column of orange and blue twisted from the air in front of her eyes before trailing onto a bar near the base of the cell door.

In two strokes, Lucca had the engineer free.

The man couldn't seem to stop talking, but they had no idea what he was saying. The other Invaders answered him, their talk awed, afraid. The engineer only seemed excited as he gave Seren a quick bow.

Meekra's voice came out of the dark behind us. "I know you said not to bow and give you away, but what you did...that wasn't exactly discreet."

Seren turned to a group of warriors, five or so untrained men and women from the city, and Izzet, Qadira, as well as two of the older male cousins from Clan Azjorr. Everyone carried a bag or sack—hopefully supplies to make more weapons—and some held the ready pots uncovered.

Izzet giggled a little hysterically. "Thank you for trusting us to support you, Kyros Seren."

Seren smiled. "Thank you for agreeing to come. And Qadira...I have to say I'm pretty surprised."

The girl huffed. "It's not like I have much of a choice," she replied, sticking with the desert tongue. Seren knew the girl couldn't resist any chance to be exclusive. "My entire clan is behind you. Even if they can't all show their faces here right now."

Cansu's long face wore a grim smile. Hossam walked beside him, his bushy hair like a storm around his wide face. Erol glided through the moonlight, frowning as ever, as he brought up the rear with nine other warriors. Meekra had brought Barir too.

Meekra held out the leather vest she'd ordered for Seren. A phoenix spread silver and copper wings over the black leather. Bronze studs flickered in the moonlight. With reverent movements, careful and solemn, Seren accepted the vest. She temporarily removed her ore master cloak and slid the vest over her head. She tied the side laces up herself, adjusted her sash, and put the cloak on again, keeping the front open for the time being so she could see the phoenix. She looked up and Meekra nodded approvingly.

The vest felt right even though it covered most of her kaftan's fine embroidery. This was her. Kyros and General. A true leader as Meric had never been. A lover of the people as Varol never would be. This was who her people needed and this was who she would be. An image of the Holy Fire blazed in her mind's eye. Warmth flowed through her veins as she smiled gravely at Meekra, Lucca, and the rest. She refused to disappoint them. She would prevail. They would win. The Invaders would be destroyed and Varol would be brought to his knees, thankful for what the Holy Fire had shown her.

Wind tossed her hair around her as she stood tall and held her arms open wide. "The Fire in me burns to see you. We have to keep this secret as long as we can."

Meekra covered her lips to hide a nervous laugh. "Well, perhaps you should stop making such bright sparks with this handsome Silvanian."

"Hush, you." Seren gestured toward the engineer. "Please, Barir, will you look after his hands? We need him at his best. Alert. He is the brains of this operation."

Meekra urged a man in a pale brown kaftan to the front. The interpreter. Seren took a breath, and her engineer smiled despite the pain he was surely in.

Lucca leaned left to see the whole of our small band. "Meekra, did you speak with Haris? I hadn't seen him with Kaptan Ona's unit, so I wondered if he...if he escaped that...duty."

Her face bunched as she translated the trade tongue. "No. In market maybe. But not." She faced me and switched to the desert tongue. "I thought I saw the soldier he is talking about. But when I looked again, he was gone."

Lucca rubbed a hand over his face. Seren wished she could hold his head in her lap and wash his fear away with her fingertips and lips.

"I think he went with Nuh," Lucca said. "To the front. With Ona. He didn't have much of a choice. Like Nuh. They had him and would've killed him."

"No time to worry about it now," Seren said. "The red tent's been raised. There'll be no mercy for any man if they win. And at the end of this awful night, the black will go up." Her throat tightened, and she pushed her grief for Ona off her mind.

Meekra's hands fisted in her kaftan. "What does the black mean?"

"Death to all. Every man, woman, and child, if the Invaders take the city. There's no use in worrying. We have to create more of these terrible weapons and do our best to thwart the enemy. We will not go down so easily."

Cansu clapped a hand on Lucca's back and they set themselves to the dangerous plan.

33

VAROL

The men, slaves and warriors alike, scattered like mice as Varol hurled his helmet through the tent flap and stormed to the bowl of Holy Fire. The distraction of five full units and the false retreat had failed. They'd fought through the night. Only pulled back at sunrise. As Varol waved hands over the Holy Flame, words flashed out of his mouth, almost painful.

"Holy Fire. I need you now. I need ideas. I need more men. What can you do for me? I am your kyros, leader of the only people in the world who properly honor your Flame."

He wiped a hand, two hands, over the licking heat, his heart hammering his bones. It sounded too much like the Invaders' ladders bracing against the walls his forefathers built. But no ideas came, no flame curled from his hands, heart, or mind.

The Invaders would take this city. They'd kill Varol in the worst possible way. Cut limb from limb. Dragged by horses in opposite directions. Crucified upside down. Only their imaginations would limit them.

Why had he even come here? Foolish. This city was a lost cause. He should've regrouped in Jakobden or farther north. Now these pigs would grind their way through his family's lands, foul the earth, and muddle his people's blood even further.

This was all because of that woman.

Seren, Pearl of the Desert. Ha. She was no pearl. Yes, she had lovely eyes and a body that would make any man's blood rise, but she was no woman of the desert. Her soul lacked the passion of the desert's heat, the voice of the wind across the plains. She was weak. She should've kept to the high-caste women's gossip and made children. She'd done nothing but harm the Empire. She claimed she loved the people, but what did her actions show?

She'd taken that Silvanian, Lucca Hand of Ruination, as a lover. She'd thrown off Varol's own brother, a virile man with royal blood for a green-tinged mercenary. Varol spat onto the rugs and fisted his hands over the Holy Fire. He'd enjoyed the female mercenary's company, but he never, ever would've chosen her over a woman of his own land, his own desert blood.

The Fire wasn't giving him anything. Why? He was worthy. More worthy than anyone alive. The orange tongues flickered and went out. He kicked the pedestal. The holy bowl rolled and crashed to the ground.

"Kyros!" Adem stopped at the entrance to the tent, his mouth dropping open. He held a roll of parchment.

Varol jerked it from his grip. "What's this? More foul news? Can't you give me some strategy? What good are you?"

Adem raised a palm and bowed.

Varol snorted. "A bit late, don't you think? Stick with shocked shouts of my title. It's more in tune with my mood, General."

"My kyros, the missive shows our numbers and theirs. And the last count on arrowheads we have in the city as well as our food supply, which is quickly dwindling."

A red heat rose inside Varol. He launched himself at the General, dagger going to the old man's throat. Varol held it there against his pale, wrinkled skin, Varol's mouth at the general's ear. "I hear the judgment in your tone. Your people always have that sneering edge to their words, even when you speak the proper tongue." Varol moved the blade to Adem's mouth. "Maybe I should cut the sickly attitude from your mouth."

"As you wish, my kyros."

To his credit, the man didn't shake. Not at all.

Varol released him and sheathed his steel. "Good answer. And you are in luck, my friend. I have an idea."

Varol glanced at the Fire bowl, askew at the corner of the red and blue rug. He motioned to a slave, who hurried to pick up the copper basin, refill it with lahabshjara leaves, and relight the Fire.

Pacing helped Varol think. "We'll send out another force with axes. Their aim will be to cut down those ladders, to destroy them beyond repair. A ring of our most skilled warriors will surround them with shields and—"

His guards and two others burst into the tent, panting and sweating. A river of blood poured from the younger man's brow. Dark circles ringed the older warrior's eyes. They both raised palms and bent.

Varol waved a hand, impatient. "Speak. Speak."

Adem jerked his head at the Fire bowl and they each headed over to pay their respects and say a prayer.

"We have no time for that!" Varol motioned to a slave to bring the older one to him. "Tell me what I need to know." The slave grabbed the man by the sleeve and pulled him to the table.

The warrior rubbed one of his puffed, dark eyes with a rough hand. "The Pearl of the Desert has escaped."

"From her cell? Who reported this? Where are Badi and Hanif?" They'd sworn they locked her in the secret cell. No one knew where that was.

The younger fighter stepped forward. "This is more important, my kyros. There is a breach. In the south wall. The Invaders, they're driving through the break we repaired last season!"

Varol's heart burned black. "Send the blue and gold units to the breach. The general and I are right behind you." The older of the reporting warriors started out of the tent. "You. Find Seren. If she is still in the city, find her and report back to me. Do not act. Do you understand?"

"Of course, my kyros."

"What is your name?"

"Haris, my kyros."

With a nod, Varol left his new spy and headed into the new day to mount his steed and see how long he had to live.

THE CITY WAS EERILY quiet as Varol and his guard wove through the tents and over the canals to the south wall. The sun soared, already clearing the walls. That damned black tent was out there. Sitting in Varol's plains like a blight about to spread plague. He could not let them win. If he did, he'd forever be the kyros who lost the Empire. For all the ages, he'd be the beaten snake, the husk of what used to be a proud line of rulers.

Digging heels into his horse's sides, he spurred them faster toward the first Invaders ever to force their way into Akhayma's walls.

Varol reined in as the group approached the break in the striped stone. Already, twenty or more Invaders had climbed through the formerly plastered crack and were engaged with Empire warriors. They were big men. So much taller, broader than Varol remembered. What had their kind been like before drought took their green lands and turned them to dust? They must've been grotesque. Like giant, pale beasts.

"Larger only means a louder sound when they fall," Varol said to himself, recalling his father's words. "General Adem! You and yours move to the area there by the smaller canal. I'll cut off their leading head."

But Adem wasn't beside him. He didn't ride up next to the warriors to Varol's back either.

"Where is the General?"

A shout spewed from outside the wall's crack and another clutch of enemies broached the barrier, foreign swords flashing in the sun.

Varol leaped from his saddle and drew his steel. Spinning and cutting, they were no match for him and his royal blood. The only reason the Empire was losing to these people was because there were so many of the beasts.

Varol and his men slashed throats and Onaratta would've

said, *painted the ground with their blood.* Varol ducked another blow and slid his sword clean through a shin, meat and bone nothing to Akhayma steel. Warmth rushed over him. What a power he had in his hands. The steel born of his blood and his land.

Two more dead. Another. Another. The Empire warriors were beating them back. Only six Invaders still stood on this side of the wall.

Hanif galloped around Varol and ordered a group of men and women to block up the crack. Good man that he was, he set an additional archer on the walls above to keep the enemies at bay while they stuffed the crack with plaster and rock and whatever else they could get their hands on, whatever would make it difficult for the Invaders.

"Yes, Hanif! Very good!" Varol swung his weapon over his left shoulder and arced the metal down, separating a man from his head. "Is Badi at the cell?" he shouted above the din.

"No, my kyros." Hanif took an arrow to the arm, a wayward shot from over the parapet. He grunted, broke the end off, and cut down a man heading for his repair crew.

"Where is he?"

"At the front, my kyros. The Invaders are gaining ground. Our archers are slowing. Fatigue, my kyros."

"The ladders!" one of Varol's shouted from behind. "They've cleared the top of the walls, my kyros!"

"Holy Fire save us!"

With a push kick to the man he fought, Varol freed himself from the fight. His mount stomped beside the nearest canal, smart eyes on Varol. He whistled and the horse flew to his side. Varol was mounted and galloping before he could look again for Adem. Maybe the general heard the report as he rode in the back of the group. Maybe he knew about the ladders.

Varol rose up in his saddle, the tassels whipping his thighs and the wind tearing at his hair. Varol had to get to him, formulate some strategy. If they didn't pull this nightmare together, in hours, they'd all be dead, no matter who supported who as leader.

34

SEREN

S eren didn't want to sleep. If she did, she might wake up to Lucca in chains. Or everyone in Akhayma dead. But her body was still only a body and it hadn't rested in what felt like years. The scrape of sandals and boots on grit and the muttering of her loyal group working together to create more clay pot explosives filled her ears as she settled onto the straw in Fig's old stall. The black of the scorched roof beams and the sun through the partially burned out wall pressed on her eyes like pointing fingers.

"Just for an hour," Lucca said, throwing a horse blanket over her. It was hot, but she was shivering anyway.

"Wake me if anything..."

WHEN SHE OPENED HER EYES, Lucca was curled up beside her and the sky had gone a vicious red. She scooted closer and made her shape fit Lucca's, pushing wakefulness away, denying what tonight would be. The black tent was up. Had been all day. Death was close enough to hear, taste, smell. Seren breathed against Lucca's back, driving fear away, enjoying the press of his body on her chest. His voice rumbled through them both.

"I wish Death wasn't slithering up our trail," he whispered, his voice raspy. "I'd be doing more than sleeping."

Hot shivers rose along her neck and fell over her shoulders and down her legs. She pressed her cheek against his shirt. "So would I."

He spun. "Ah. Forget Death. We have plenty of time to die." His hands slid around the back of her neck, soft and certain.

"I'm not entirely sure that makes sense," she said.

Lucca's lips moved along her neck. If she stayed here, it'd be a lovely way to die. "I'm very sure I don't care," he whispered, the moisture of his lips warm on her skin.

A little moan escaped her mouth. She pulled away before they forgot things they couldn't forget. With a reluctant nod, Lucca joined her in standing up and brushing the straw away.

Cansu walked in, his face grim. "The black tent, Kyros. I saw it."

Seren touched the wool at her sash. "It's nothing we didn't already know." The rest of the group gathered in the ruined stables. She fought to keep her voice loud enough for them to hear. She wanted to go back to the straw and Lucca and be ignorant of all this, but of course she could never—would never —do such a thing.

"We knew if we lost this war, we'd all be killed. Don't let scare tactics throw your focus. We have our plan. Launch the weapons over the walls. Bring their numbers down so we can strike and have a chance to come out victorious."

"What about wind?" the engineer said through the interpreter. Both men's faces were streaked with dirt and sweat.

"We can't worry about it," Seren said. "We don't have the time to wait for a perfect moment." The loss of Fig tugged at her like the little mare was still here, nuzzling and giving Seren strength. She wished she could feel something of Ona, despite what she'd done. "Are the weapons prepared?"

"Kyros Seren." Her chest seized at the sound of Adem's voice.

Hossam had him by the arm in a flash. Lucca slipped to come up behind him, faster than Seren thought a man could move. Adem's color was high, but he didn't fight Lucca or Hossam's hold on him. He had blood all down the front of his jerkin, black smears on red leather. A blade had sheared a spot so deeply that Seren could see his brown mourning shirt underneath. Blood crusted one long earlobe, but his earth-hued headtie, another tribute to Meric, remained firmly in place across his forehead.

Seren stepped past Cansu, Meekra, Barir, and the engineer. The clay pots lined up like soldiers along the stables. Their silk inflatables lay like long cloaks behind them. They couldn't hide this. Adem would know exactly what they were doing. But he didn't have any warriors with him, none of his usual retinue.

"General." Seren kept her face clear. It was better to let him give some information before he took anything more from her.

He raised a palm and bent low, so low that his knee rasped the ground before he stood again. "Please forgive me. Take me into your confidence. And even if you won't, know that I will no longer support the high general. I accept your decision either way."

"What changed your mind? You were ready to watch me die."

"I must speak bluntly if this is to work," Adem said.

Lucca unsheathed his sword an inch, but Seren held up a hand to hold him back.

"Please do." She clasped her hands and tried to be calm, still, confident.

"I still believe you're a criminal. What you did, hiding Kyros Meric's death, giving orders and telling me, telling us all, they were from him..." His lip curled. "It disgusts me. You dishonored the true kyros, the true royal blood."

"I did what needed to be done."

He opened his mouth to add something, his gaze going to the burned stables behind her, but she cut him off.

"I made mistakes," she said. "I'll make more. That doesn't mean I can't lead my people."

Meekra smiled so brightly Seren could practically hear it. Lucca's fiery eyes made her feel like she could take on the entire world.

"I mourn my husband in my own way." Seren put two fingers on her chest, above her heart. "I didn't love Meric. But he was my husband, and I appreciate the fact that because of him I found my purpose, my people. He is why I have a chance to help our people survive this war."

"I don't doubt your passion for the Empire, Kyros Seren. That, I've never doubted. We can come together on that point. Varol is a fool. He throws our people, and himself, into the fight without a calm head. He is a bright fire that will burn itself out and scorch the rest of us with its heat."

"Sounds like Ona," Lucca whispered.

"Very much so, from what I saw," Adem agreed. "I was

wrong to choose Varol over you because of tradition. I don't know how this will turn out, but I'd rather die on the right side. But know this, we will most likely die. Varol has an army loyal to him. The Invaders, well, I don't see how we can win this. My best guess is they will sleep tonight—they don't have much to fear from us and they know it—and after dawn, they'll overcome our walls and lay waste to the city. We won't be able to hold back another concerted effort with the ladders and their numbers."

"We have a plan," Seren said.

"A good one," Lucca said, releasing Adem. "Just as brave as our kyros."

Adem kneeled beside one of the pots. "How exactly are these meant to work?"

Seren rubbed her hands together and joined him as the rest went back to work. "The leaves will burn and fill the silk with hot air. This," she held up the fuse line, "will charge as it lifts into the sky. The charge will ignite the chemicals we have inside the pot." She showed him the tiny hole where the fuse would be set at take off.

"And then?"

Lucca stood over them, arms crossed. "Boom."

Adem stood and dusted his hands. "I hope *they* experience the boom and not us."

"That is the risk." Seren eyed the walls leading into the city. Stars shone like one thousand eyes. "It's time."

WITH THE WEAPONS in wooden crates, they started toward the city.

"We'll have to move quickly," Adem said, "or the high general will hear about what we're doing."

Seren shook her head. "No. Walk strong and calm. Act as though this is our duty and there is no need for secrecy. If the people believe this is all a part of the kyros's plan, they won't think to report anything. They'll talk, yes. But not report. Besides, no one will notice me in this cloak in the night."

"And this is why I should've supported you, ore master," Adem said slyly.

"It's never too late to start a new friendship. One of mutual respect."

"Your mercy is commendable, my kyros."

Seren couldn't help but smile.

~

NEAR THE MAIN GATES, lines of warriors held shields above their heads to hold off enemy arrows raining over the walls. Their blood flowed into the canal that curved beside the first row of tents, and all had bandaged limbs or heads. Most held their yatagans low, their arms shaking with fatigue.

Varol was there, on his prancing, black steed. He shouted orders and lifted his fist to the stars. The moon was a mere sliver, the edge of a silver blade above the chaos.

"Lucca, take your group past Varol, to the top of the walls. Meekra, show him the best way to go. General Adem, come with me. We'll start this to the right, in the direction of the black tent. If we can get that to go up, the fire may spread more easily."

"It is the mercenary!" A man pointed at Lucca and pulled the hood from his head.

Hossam jerked the man away. "Haris! No!"

Varol swung around and charged up to Lucca.

Seren's stomach dropped and she ripped her hood down. "High General Varol, if you have something to say, you may say it to me."

Something between a laugh and a shout pealed from Varol's mouth. "Good of you all to arrive together. Makes it much easier to dispatch you in the middle of this mess."

"Mess indeed. Let's put away our rivalry for now and focus on protecting our people."

"Rivalry? There is no rivalry." He waved a hand and his army took hold of her much smaller one. A man grabbed Seren and laughed close to her face, his breath foul and hot. "There is only you a criminal and me a kyros," Varol said. He smiled at Haris. "Bring me a very long, very sturdy rope."

Varol unsheathed his yatagan, nearing Lucca.

"Lucca!"

Lucca couldn't move. He was surrounded.

Without a word, like Lucca wasn't worth a moment of his time, Varol sliced his steel along Lucca's leg. He fell hard.

Seren's world went white for a breath.

Varol eyed her, riding closer, stepping through the army and raising a shield one fighter handed him. "I hope all that foreign food hasn't made you too heavy for what I have in mind. Bring her to the top of the walls. And the former general, too."

Fewer and fewer of the enemies' arrows fell over the walls. The Invaders were headed to their tents to sleep. All the better to kill everyone at sunrise.

The warriors holding Seren took the clay pots, then dragged her up the stairs to the parapet, Varol like a shadow behind her.

Haris appeared, a heavy rope circling his body like an enormous snake.

"Tie her hands," Varol ordered the archers, who were wet with sweat. The battlefield beyond them showed campfires flickering to life and that horrible black tent at the heart of the swarming Invaders.

"I don't have..." an archer started, holding out his bow and arrow.

Varol tore the black cloak off Seren, exposing her brown, silken kaftan and the face everyone recognized. Below, warriors whispered her name. They traded her varied titles like coins.

Varol grunted and tugged the sash from her middle. "This will do."

She leaned onto one foot and twisted to see Lucca as Varol bound her hands behind her back. It was dark, she could make out Lucca's shape—a seated man in the middle of a standing army. He reached a hand up. He had to be bleeding heavily. Varol knew how to make a cut that would kill slowly but surely. She squinted, willing her eyes to work like some night creature. Was he telling her something?

Varol's hands were rough as he finished the knot at her wrists. She kept twisting to try and see everything, to see Varol. The whites of his eyes showed too much, like a panicked horse. He knew as well as her that Death was close, very, very close. It was a stench in the air, a finger running along the neck, an ache in the bones.

Freed from her sash, Seren's green wool fluttered from the folds of her clothing, to the ground. It was only a dark spot near her feet. It was her world.

Varol picked it up. His gaze snapped to her mouth. "And this will keep you quiet until I have you where I want you."

Adem ripped his arm away from the soldier who held him. His gray hair fell over one eye. "What will you do?"

Death's nearness had stripped them of titles and rituals.

The warriors at the foot of the walls stared up, faces pale in the night's uneven light. Seren's fingers twitched, longing to wipe their hot cheeks with cool water. They needed comfort, support.

"Pray over the Holy Fire. Don't give up hope!" Some of her words threaded through the horses' hooves shuffling, the sound of thousands moving, coughing, moaning, dying, but most were lost to the night.

Varol gagged her with the green wool. "Keep quiet, Pearl." Disdain oozed off the name.

Then a change washed over his features. His jaw set. His eyes narrowed.

"My brother, my royal blood," he said, "deserved full mourning. *The soul is tired, You slept through the night, Give your sleep to the Dead.*" He quoted the mourning folk song. "You never mourned. You. Rebelled." He flicked his kaftan back and stepped away, lifting a hand toward the battlefield. "Lower her down. Over the walls. You'll spend one night awake, criminal, staring at Death for a true kyros's passing, for mourning. It isn't enough, but it's all you can offer. And offer it, you will."

The men tied the rope to the parapet and pushed Seren over the side.

She didn't fall far.

The rope caught abruptly, and she thought her shoulders would pop out of her skin. Her stomach and ribs screamed as the rope cut into her and her descent continued. The body-strewn ground, the stomped out campfires' ghostly smoke, and the sleeping Invaders crept closer and closer as Varol's men slowly lowered her.

Varol's voice dripped from the walls and into her ears, his words a hissing whisper. "When the sun rises, they will end you in what I would imagine will be a spectacular fashion. But for now, stay awake and bear a portion of what you should've when my brother first left this world."

The descent halted. Her slippered toes dragged along the gritty earth and her stomach lurched with the pain of the rope and the smell of war.

Directly in front of her, close enough to hear a shout if she uttered one, the black tent hulked like a sleeping beast.

The rope had slid up her body. Her sleeves bunched above her elbows. She pushed one arm down, twisted—bumping the wall painfully—and worked her way out of the binding. It moved up and over her head, and she hit the ground on one side, jaw smacking the earth. She sat up and shook her head. Her sash remained tight on her wrists.

Varol had to be watching still, but she couldn't see him. A bank of clouds choked the stars' light and a gentle wind teased the ends of her hair. One thousand thoughts flew through her mind, but one shone clear.

If she was going to die, she wanted to see Ona one more time.

As if the wind read her thoughts, it increased and pushed the strip of clouds into the horizon. The stars once again illuminated the plains and hammadas, the desert to the Southwest, hills and lahabshjara trees to the North and East.

And then she saw the sword.

The broad, steel surface of Ona's weapon reflected a swathe of silver in the middle of three fallen yatagans and more bodies than Seren could count. Her stomach heaved. She vomited into the muck at her feet.

But could she find her?

She squinted into the dark, looking for the bright points of brass on the back of Ona's brigantine. The white streak in her brown hair. It was impossible.

Stumbling over bodies, she kneeled beside the sword. It'd fallen along a smooth boulder where it shone like melted starlight. Seren wanted to touch the hilt and imagine Ona's strong, pale hand, but her own hands were still bound. Blood and dirt caked the sword's edges. But it was sharp enough to work.

Between the bodies of two Invaders Ona had most likely killed, Seren leaned against the propped sword and pressed the sash that held her wrists into the metal.

There was movement on the parapet. *Varol.* She could see his shape, the way he moved.

The blade divided the sash and Seren's hands fell to her sides. The flesh burned, not only because she'd nicked herself, but also because the blood had been inhibited too long by the knot. Feeling pricked its way back into her hands as she took the wool from her mouth. The wool had nearly gagged her. A cough built in her throat. The Invaders would hear her, realize how close she was if she made any noise. But maybe they'd only think it was one of their own? The cough echoed from her mouth. She couldn't stop it.

A pop sounded to the right.

Her pulse jumped. She couldn't see what had made the noise. The smell of the field and the fear in her heart blinded her as much as the dark.

There wasn't a Fire here, but Seren sat by Ona's sword and

prayed. Prayed for Ona's soul. Prayed that her dearest friend, her Lucca, was still alive. Prayed Adem had kept the clay pot weapons close by and undamaged.

Even if Seren had to die, maybe they could persuade Varol to use the weapons and they could live. Some of her people could live through this. Tears came then, hot and fast and untamable.

"I understand," she whispered to Ona's sword, Death's perfume overpowering. "You gave me so much. I don't know if it matters, but I...I forgive you. I miss you already. Varol did seem like the strongest voice for our side, but—"

Voice.

Seren had the strongest voice now. She'd used it in the cell, when Lucca helped her escape. She only needed to wield her words now.

A plan formed in her head. She wouldn't know for certain if it worked, the walls blocked her view of her loyal warriors and the fuses, but...the truth of what she might accomplish sang through her like a song. The notes had always lived inside her, but she'd never known the words. Until now.

She looked at Ona's steel, the filthy ground, the dead warriors and their open eyes and swollen limbs. Just beyond the sword's hilt lay Ona's flint. Seren gathered the piece of cool stone and took up the familiar weapon. A sound built in her chest.

With one last silent prayer to bless her defeated friend, Seren marched to the front gate, speared her green wool on the tip of Ona's sword, and struck the flint to raise a spark like a falling star.

"*Wake iron!*" she called out.

Varol appeared on the parapet, his face in darkness.

"Wake soul and Holy Fire!" She switched to the desert tongue, then repeated the words in the trade language. She wanted all to understand. All who would listen. The flint drew out another spear of blinding light. The Invaders would hear. She didn't care. "Light the fuses of our weapons. Beg our people to show the Invaders Death!"

"You do not rule here, Seren!" Varol called out, his words erratic and pitching up and down.

"I am your kyros!" She shouted. She raised the sword as the sun rose over the hills and lit the green of her talisman. "This ends on my word!" Striking the flint, power tugged at her heart and burned between her eyebrows.

Shouts erupted behind Akhayma's gates.

New, strange clouds filled the morning sky.

The creations the Holy Fire had shown her soared through the gentle wind on silk. In the glowing light of dawn, they fluttered, their metal fuses like silver tails.

Seren spun to see Invaders emerging from tents and bedrolls to stare at the lone madwoman on the battlefield in her silken slippers.

One of the clay pots sparked. The silk incinerated. There was a bang.

The weapon blasted into a thousand pieces.

Seren's ears rang. An Invader gripped his leg, his mouth open to yell as blood poured between his fingers. Another weapon exploded in a flash of light. Shards tore through a small tent. A third broke apart and fell onto a group of pikemen. They covered their faces, shouting, as the bits of clay embedded into their exposed arms and scalps. They screamed and fell, never to raise a sword against her people again. Two weapons exploded, not far away. A chip of clay hurled through the air and snapped at her back. Heat seared through her skin.

She ran for the walls.

Archers fought with Hossam on the parapet, with Cansu, too. Their hands flew at one another. Cansu called out.

Ona's sword thudded to the ground as Seren grabbed the rope they'd lowered her down on. She put her feet on the wall to begin a climb. Something knocked the pale rock beside her head. She looked down to see an arrow with bright red fletching. The Invaders were firing at her. Hand over hand, foot by foot, she ascended. Her arms shook and another arrow landed above her head.

Booms and crashes sounded in the Invaders' camp. Orders. Gasps. Shouted commands.

Sudden screams eroded her focus. Gasping, she slipped to the earth. She covered her ears. More explosions. More. More.

She spun and shouted, "It's only because you wouldn't stop! You left me no choice! I have to protect my people!"

Only because of the men running from the last of the weapons drifting down and the skull-splitting shrieks was she still alive.

She looked up and took the rope again.

Varol appeared on the parapet. His hair stuck out at all angles and his kaftan lay in shreds over his chest as if he'd torn it with his own hands. "Go ahead, try to climb, little kyros!"

This was the end. She was bleeding. Trapped, an enemy before and behind.

An arm and a yatagan snaked around Varol's throat. Adem.

She cupped her hands at her mouth. "Kill him!"

Adem's blade slid like a minnow, flashing and quick, and

Varol tipped over the wall and fell. He was a blur of silk as he passed Seren and slammed into the ground.

Victory poured strength into Seren's limbs. She tried to climb again. Slid down. Arrows were coming fast and she was cut again, on the arm, then along her calf. Quickly, she tied a knot in the rope and shoved her foot inside.

Adem leaned over the wall.

"Pull me up!" she shouted. The howls of pain behind her squeezed her chest. She could hardly breathe.

At the top, strong hands helped her over and she fell into a familiar chest.

Dirt and blood lined Lucca's strong-boned face. Two lengths of cloth wrapped around his injured leg and he'd slung his bow over a shoulder.

"How did it happen?" she asked. "How did you light and release the explosives?" She wanted to think it was her, but that was impossible, wasn't it?

He smiled and pressed his mouth to hers. She tasted salt and him and knew if he hadn't been here, she'd have been at Adem's feet weeping. Lucca's power gave her power.

"When you called up the Holy Fire," he said, "the fuses...a spark bloomed over each one. The loyal soldiers, and some high-castes hiding in the crowd, grabbed the devices and lifted them into the air before Varol's men could shake off their surprise."

Seren closed her eyes and whispered gratitude into Lucca's arms. The terrible sounds of the final victory clambered over the walls and shot into her ears.

It wasn't beautiful. It was war. But her voice had proved strong enough to protect the city that had become her home, and for that, she'd never stop being grateful.

Meekra draped a deep purple kaftan over Seren's shoulders and looked toward the door, smile widening. "I'd tell you that you shouldn't be here, but I believe I'd be outvoted."

Seren turned to see who she was talking to. Lucca ducked inside.

Sadness hung on his shoulders like a thick, unwanted cloak he couldn't seem to shed. She still saw Ona every time she looked at him. She was sure he still saw his friend everywhere. In his sword. The scars he'd made when they fought side by side. Under the trees, though the ones here were nothing like the green giants they'd lived under back in Silvania.

"Ah, my noble mercenary," Seren said, working to raise the corners of his frown.

His gaze drifted to the ground and he sighed, pulling himself up as best he could these days. Then humor lit his eyes and he smiled, setting his grief aside for a little while.

With his chin tilted down like that she could almost see what he'd rather be doing than letting her have time to prepare for the Fire Ceremony.

Meekra left through the back. "I know when I'm not wanted." A laugh hid in her words.

Lucca took Seren's fingertips in his but glanced Meekra's way. "If your mistress is late for her appointment, rest assured it'll be for a good reason. A great reason."

"Stop bragging, Silvanian," Meekra muttered, her voice fading beyond the tent walls.

Seren kissed him. "You've been into the spicy tabouli I ordered for the feast."

"I thought it might improve my chances. Increase your attraction to me."

"Like you need help with that."

A sly grin pulled at his mouth. "Now that you have undisputed control of half the globe, I wondered…" He shrugged.

She grabbed his face and enjoyed the widening of his eyes. "Slave or kyros, I am yours and you are mine. Besides, you're the reason I have the role I do. You and Ona."

She pressed lips to his palms. Though it'd been months, losing Ona still burned. It was so much worse for Lucca. He looked to the floor, studying the blue star shapes and black calligraphy woven into the rug. She wished she could take a measure of his hurt and help him carry the weight of it.

He shook a little, then blinked. "Don't frown for too long. There will always be losses." His silver ring caught the firelight as he put a finger to her chin. "Life is a battle."

"If that's true, I think all in all, we are winning." She set her forehead against his and the next half hour was pleasure and healing, breath and hearts beating, the joy of being alive.

~

THE STRIPED TENTS of the city sat in rolled bundles along the lotus towers. The canals glittered and showed all the constellations of the plains. The Basket, the Stallion's Neck, the Old Man's Hand. Women holding family Fire bowls and smiling men wearing their darkest black gathered with children around the oasis pool.

And there was Fig's half-brother, the colt she'd named Flame, held gently by Meekra's sisters. He danced a little sideways as they braided pink blossoms into his mane and tail. He'd never, ever replace Fig, but he would ease the hurt in Seren's heart as he grew and became her primary mount, a new friend.

Volunteers from every merchant group had scrubbed the mosaic tiles holding the water and the pieces shone like rings. The moon was a pearl in the sky and again in the water. Everything was rich, beautiful, and so very dear to Seren.

Akhayma was not her birthplace, but it was home.

Nobles and successful merchants filled the silver basin with more lahabshjara leaves, then lit the emerald heap. The Holy Fire danced into the night and painted children's cheeks yellow. The workers pulled the ladders clear of the basin, and stepped aside for Adem, who was walking tall and straight around the pool. His reflection moved across the silver bowl as he approached.

In his shining helmet, he bowed deeply and came close. "My kyros, I would like to again offer my apologies for—"

"Stop."

He looked up.

She came closer, waited for him to rise. "We've been through this. You only did what you thought was best for the Empire, for our people. For that, I can't fault you. I consider you my most valued general and advisor. As long as you stay in line anyway."

He sighed and bowed again. He'd changed in good ways so far. Reducing punishments for lesser crimes. He himself had put forward the idea to reduce the silver required for lower castes to move into higher castes. General Adem was becoming a veritable leader on the trail into the future.

"I will forever be your old steed, stubborn and true, Kyros," he said.

"May the Fire hear your will." Seren couldn't seem to stop smiling as he maneuvered the blue steps into place below the Holy Fire's bowl.

With Lucca standing beside Adem, and the city gathered and kneeling, she climbed the three steps to come face-to-face with the holiest of Flames. Her hand found Ona's sword at her sash, the metal cool and sure.

I wish you were here, Seren whispered to Ona, wherever she was. They'd never found her body. Lucca had led a Silvanian funeral for her anyway.

Seren lifted her palms and raised her voice. "Holy Fire, grant us the Flame of your strength and invention. May we see ideas flicker from dreams and into reality."

A red glow illuminated the center of her outstretched hands and turned her fingers to sunlight. Heat touched her forehead, gathered in front of her eyes, then drew power from her palms and spun into a visible flame, floating. The small curl of Fire turned inward at the top and bottom, rose up, then cascaded into the roaring Holy Fire. The sacred Flames reached toward the moon and her people sighed, her name on their lips.

"Kyros Seren, our Pearl."

EPILOGUE

Cold seeped into Ona's pores and came out through her shaking teeth. She clamped her mouth shut and hoped that might make it easier to see where she was. A big white striped something loomed in the distance, bouncing as she flew away.

Flew? No. She tried to move her hands. Only her left responded. Splintered wood supported her cold, cold, cold body. She was in a cart. But she still had no idea what that big white striped something was.

She'd been hit hard over the head before. During a raid on the ocean-facing villas near Holy Iacopo's Piazza when she first began her mercenary work.

She thought maybe she'd been hit hard again.

But she'd never been this frozen. That was new. She closed her eyes and began to thaw a little. The shaking in her teeth moved as she warmed. The trembling faded into a larger feeling she hadn't been warm enough to notice until now. A heat, aching and wrong, pulsed out of her chest, right above her heart.

A face appeared above her. Though he had brown hair laced with a copper hue, his chest was covered in the blood red and ghostly white uniform of the enemy.

Invader.

She tried to sit up, and both the cold and the heat swallowed her whole. Before the black took her again, words—first in the Invaders' tongue, intelligible, then in Silvanian—crept over her ears.

"You're alive." The Invader's gray eyes flickered with something that might've been hope, but Ona was too dizzy to know for sure. "You might soon wish you aren't. Don't tell the others I speak this tongue. It's not difficult to kill someone who is already mostly dead."

If you'd like a free prequel and to sign up for updates, visit
Alisha at her website
http://www.alishaklapheke.com

The next Uncommon World book, *Forest of Silver and Secrets,*
releases in August 2018!

ABOUT THE AUTHOR

USA Today bestselling author Alisha Klapheke is the author of the Uncommon World series and The Edinburgh Seer Trilogy. When she isn't crafting new worlds, she can be found teaching kids, teens, and adults Muay Thai kickboxing, Krav Maga, and Brazilian Jiu Jitsu with her husband at their school. Much of Alisha's inspiration comes from traveling to far off museums, ruins, and markets across the globe.

Please consider leaving a review for Plains of Sand and Steel. Reviews are important for everyone!

Find me on Instagram @alishaKlapheke
Join the Uncommon Crew on Facebook for giveaways, chats, and behind the scenes fun.
https://www.facebook.com/groups/1325484257474943/

ALSO BY ALISHA KLAPHEKE

The Uncommon World Series

Waters of Salt and Sin

Fever

Plains of Sand and Steel

Forest of Silver and Secrets (August 2018)

The Edinburgh Seer Trilogy

The Edinburgh Seer

The Edinburgh Heir

The Edinburgh Fate

www.ingramcontent.com/pod-product-compliance
Lightning Source LLC
Chambersburg PA
CBHW031026120726
47905CB00007B/2061